Fine print:
It will cost you starlight.

EARTHQUAKES

CANDY
LAND

IN

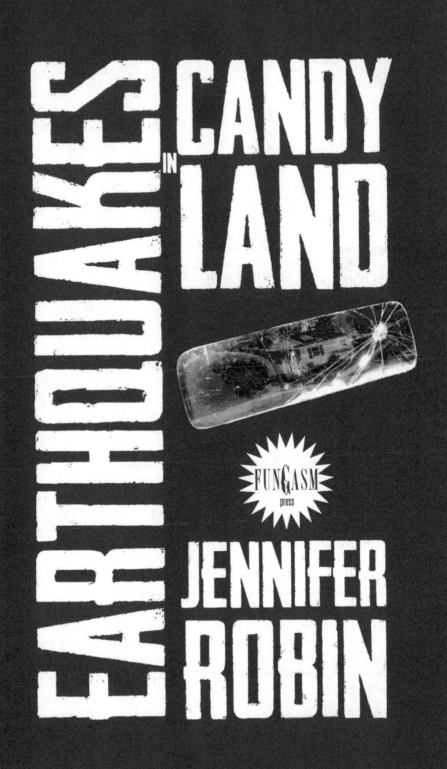

FUNGASM
press

JENNIFER
ROBIN

FUNGASM PRESS
an imprint of Eraserhead Press
PO Box 10065
Portland, OR 97296

www.fungasmpress.com
facebook/fungasmpress

ISBN: 978-1-62105-297-5
Copyright © 2019 by Jennifer Robin
Cover art copyright © 2019 Matthew Revert
Title page photo copyright © 2019 Kurt Eisenlohr
Back cover photo copyright © 2019 Jennifer Robin
Edited by John Skipp

*An American Soap Opera In Four Parts, As Seen From Inside The Portland
Bubble* Originally published in Clash Media, November 2016

CONTENTS

Orphans

Your Tax Dollars at Work

The Great Divide

The Eyes That Bear Witness to the Soul of the Whole

(As the American Dream Awakens, in a Cold Sweat, to Itself)

An Awe-struck Introduction by John Skipp

It's hard to talk about America without fighting anymore. Not that it's ever been easy. It's a nation founded on wildly disparate ideals and mythic origin stories, just for starters. All of them birthed in blood.

On the one hand, it's a game-changing experiment in democracy and freedom, offering hope to the downtrodden of the long-suffering world that they, too, might at last find a voice and a chance at life, liberty, and the pursuit of happiness, free of the entrenched monarchies and religious/military tyrannies of the Old World they fled. An Old World that exists to this day.

On the other hand, it's a New World built entirely on kleptocracy, starting with the slaughter of nearly every single person who previously inhabited this prime slab of real estate. A vast plenitude to plunder, which it has not stopped doing ever since.

So, yeah, there's a lot to fight about. If you stand for freedom and equality, you're probably fighting for your stake on the claim: America as the shining city on the hill, the gleaming beacon that draws and inspires you. Lady Liberty, in the New York harbor, saying, "Welcome. You can do this! Time to take your best shot."

All that said, the tragic truth of the matter is that almost NOBODY is more attracted to this experiment in freedom than the kleptomaniacs, who swiftly and ruthlessly seize every asset they see and claim it for their own. Because theft is the ultimate freedom. The freedom to say, "Fuck you. IT'S MINE NOW!"

When pretty much everyone is getting robbed blind, you'd think people would come together and put a stop to it. But that's when the sneakiest, most time-dishonored trick in the book comes in. Which is, *divide and conquer*. Pit us against each other. Subdivide us on issues of difference. Tribal identity. Sex. Race. Income. Taste. You name it, and we are fighting about it. While the kleptocrats rob us blind.

And the ultimate casualty—if the possible end of a sustainable Earth isn't ultimate enough—is our inability to simply listen to each other.

Enter Jennifer Robin: street poet, performance artist, and scrupulous chronicler of our shared lives and times. We may not be listening, but she sure as hell is. Like a psychedelicized 21st century Studs Terkel, she bears witness, then writes it all down with stunningly elegant and eloquent language that retains all the rough, unvarnished edges of real life, then makes them gleam like polished gold.

Past the jaw-dropping precision of her prose, though—and, in fact, its central motivating force—is a wide-open willingness to not just listen but *truly hear* the voices that most feel themselves unheard. To understand the misunderstood. To give them an ear, and absorb like a sin-eater as they honestly and unflinchingly unspool their truths to her, the way you talk to a friend you love and trust. And not recoiling from a speck of it, in judgment or repulsion. Whether she agrees with it or not.

In the process, revealing herself just as unflinchingly as she peels back the world itself, so that all of our flaws and deepest dreams intermingle equally, in every moment recorded.

This is—at this time, in this world—a staggeringly rare and wondrous quality. The true essence of democracy, distilled. And it drips from Jennifer Robin's every word, like the juice of a fruit called the human race which is meant to be tasted by everyone. To remind us that we're really just one species, no matter how tribally divided. Living on this one Earth. Every one of us, going through our shit. Hurting in our own ways. Fighting our own battles. But, like it or not, in this world together.

What I love most about the book you're about to read is that I feel *each and every one of us* in it. Feel every speck of EVERYBODY's American dream. The 99% waking up in a cold sweat now, and the strategies of the 1%, who are probably waking up and sweating just as hard.

We may, in fact, be at the end of the road, shuffling deck chairs on the Titanic's sixth and last extinction event. (And along the way,

Jennifer meticulously tracks the evidence trail that might suggest this sorry fate.) Or we may be at a pivotal turning point in the maturation of the species. Growing up. Taking stock of who we are, and what we're doing. Recognizing that we are, in fact, responsible. Then pushing astoundingly forward and free. Together. Forever. Into what we were meant to be, as a civilization made of truly human beings on a beautiful planet we are lucky to share.

Personally, I'm not holding my breath. But I ain't giving up, neither. This shit could go either way. And I know which side I'm rooting for.

The everyone side.

With *Earthquakes in Candyland*, Jennifer Robin has gloriously, savagely, lovingly, hilariously, tragically, empathically, and encouragingly nailed who we are, where we are, and the truth that confronts us so hard that every American dreamer has all the evidence they need to wake up and choose wisely. From the soul of the whole.

From here, it's all up to you, Hope you listen. And not just listen, but hear.

Yer pal in the trenches,
Skipp
9/17/2018

It is America, like The Man. The man as he always was, ever was; the violent birth, the slow corrosion; cupidity, pistons, horsemeat. Land of prayer and industry where birdsong is memory and rust is the backbone, the lynching, the scapegoat stabbed once, forty, forever times. Heads dragged through the market, intestines strewn like taffy, twine, this is our alphabet mashed. The Man, the nation, the life of crime. You cannot pronounce America phonetically without the wind's intrusion. It whispers its secret song: War-blood. War-dolls glisten like butterfat, smell like dollar soap, stiff with tax-tripe; prisons of false minstrels, war-dance with war crystals. War-veils. Blood-veils. Vale of veils is factory-made: toenails, constitution, mother, ice, inception. Cough after a decimal point! Can we fix you? If your death doesn't leave a debt, what is the point of you?

SNAPSHOTS
OF
CANDYLAND

Then You Run

I used to take the Amtrak cross-country to visit my mother every year. I grew up in New York and my mother lives in the house I grew up in, the house in which she may one day die. The train took four days each way, and it was a radical transformation to see the forest and wetlands of the city in which I live give way to flat Montana ghost towns inhabited by zombies in puffer jackets, lone rangers on meth-fueled midnight bike rides, sons of farmers who raged all year to AC/DC, fathered five hundred kids, drank diet beer and shed tears talkin' bout the alpine clarity of the night sky away from city lights. I boozed with bad boyz from Louisiana lookin' to get high or walk the talk of an errant blow job in Amtrak toilets, antiquated piss booths smelling of vomit and fuel that reminded me of astronaut suits and dry-cleaning bags.

I would see dirt-poor farm elders creak on the train with cardboard boxes to their names, no luggage. We're talking American Gothic with garbage bags full of socks and picture frames. And the middle-class people, all elderly, all adherents to the train being "scenic" guzzled coffee in their polyester daywear from 5 AM to 9 PM. Forget T-cells, forget hemoglobin. Their bodily liquids hold miniature DNA strands that spell out the name of Juan Valdez. (Okay, I know not many of you remember the fictional coffee guy Juan Valdez and his sad Columbian donkey!)

I remember the shy smiles of every heavy metal farm boy. I remember the orphans of this nation, guys saying they had "something lined up" in city x y and z, guys who stopped washing, guys who were not going to inherit the family business. I remember sneaker feet and oversized white t-shirts that leaked the scent of unrinsed detergent.

I remember the microwave pizza, the hair gel, the simple sacs of hormones who hoped with a smile, a cigarette, that they would win the jackpot. Tell me your life story; tell me about your mother and the home you will never see again. I can close my eyes and see the shredded mattress leaning against the side of a house, I can see your child foot kick, kick kick it. I know about gypsies and the boxcar full of smoke, I know about the waiting…waiting in long rooms for the one to show up, the one who has what you need. And then you run.

The Tarot Reader of Troy, New York

There is a certain point on every long-distance journey when the traveler finds herself lulled by the repetition of trees and hills and shacks viewed through the window of a train cabin at 4 AM, or in a car crossing the thatch-colored stretches of Nebraska where every valley is full of upended cars, metal carapaces turned by snow and the beady eye of sun to colors like dried blood and pumice and calamine; and when the telephone poles and electrical transformers and basketball hoops began to mount in the tens of thousands, one starts to view these structures not as rewards or destinations but as the erections of an alien culture, viral in nature, unchecked by the elements, unopposed by animals covered in feathers and fur which scurry at the edges of each tar-embalmed driveway. What are these mailboxes for? What happens behind these walls? When the sun sets and blue light flashes against huddled shapes, lives comprehensively hoarded in the World's Ultimate Collect-Them-All Cargo Cult? Do the beasts who reside within these walls sit on thrones reading bibles as their breath grows thin, or are they crawling on their haunches to locate crack rocks in the weave of a polypropylene rug? Are they plotting for the hour when the water quits? When locusts cease to fly, and the groceries and drugs and K-Y love lotion are all gone? What quiet stretches of pain do the old ones enact, as they have enacted for the past fifty years, from the dank lockdown mindset of no exit—no levers to pull for divorce, no voice to sing rather than shush, slow rivulets of vengeance sapping the vitality from jerky-tough limbs until an old one dies and the toilet is baptized yet by months of urine turned brown?

The year is 1995, and I don't wear underwear, a choice that one of my friends tells me is scandalous, especially when I'm hitching. Instead of scandalous, I find my wardrobe choices liberating. In a small backpack I carry a makeup bag, a Crowley Thoth tarot deck, a set of silverware, a facecloth, a sweatshirt, a sheaf of paper stolen from Kinko's Copies, on which I intend to make sketches of people in each town. I have one pair of leggings, one t-shirt. I hand-wash them when I can. Through the leggings the shape of my labial folds is visible from twenty yards down a road, but my combat boots, and the dyed white hair say I am not what you expect. I am a sore of awareness; the busted bloom of a planet's DNA.

I hitch with Fabio. He is in his uniform of green corduroy pants, Converse sneakers, button-down shirts covered in flowers which barely hug his muscular chest. His shirts are filled with holes from climbing fences, heaving his wine-sotted meat headfirst into mausoleums and across highway overpasses with the lupine gait of a soul who cannot imagine reaching thirty.

His hair is long and brown, like his gaze. His fingers are stained yellow from hand-rolled Drum cigarettes. He is feral but knows how to shift his brow, purse his lips, fold his arms behind his back in an attentive posture that changes his tall bones from menace to obedience when necessary.

We start in Rochester, make a jagged line south to the Pennsylvania border, my mind salivating at the sight of plywood shacks in mist-covered gullies where people live free and surrounded by humming things.

Our destination is Baltimore. Three years before this road and setting sun I gave birth to a daughter and found a family to adopt her. I have gone on paths, many, not looking back, wanting to clarify what I'm living for before sewing others to my skin. This is the first time I'll be facing her since she pressed from my depths.

"You like a good time, don't you? You like to party, huh? I kin tell. You're the kind of girl who likes to stay out all night, gettin' up to no good. I had some beer in here but I run out by now. Man, I wish I could offer you guys somethin', wish I had more time, but I gotta make time. I'm five hours behind and my boss'll have my ass unless I catch up."

The trucker has a cast on his leg and a shrine of cocker spaniel photographs. He presses buttons on a radio dial to find a station with music for party people. We sing with him to Teenage Wasteland, Highway to Hell, Bad Bad LeRoy Brown. He offers a personal testimonial about International Delights flavored creamers. He fills his pockets with them. "Night and day, night and day," he repeats, about the transformation of his coffee. He's been driving forty-six hours, takes us a hundred-fifty miles before pulling into a Jubitz truck stop.

"I'm hittin' the sack," he says. I visualize him falling on a cot like a hamburger patty slapped on a grill.

Climbing down from his cabin we find ourselves in a nursery of metal monsters, pumps and pulleys attached to rigs as if they are living things. A dry heat radiates from beneath their hoods and heavy undercarriages. They carry clothing from China, tangerines from Texas, diapers from Louisiana, guns, liquid soap, leaf blowers, cans of aerosol cheese, vacuum-sealed palliatives and corrective devices whispering of eternal dreamtime: You are going somewhere, even when you're not.

Industrial arc-lights loom above us, blot sky.

The Jubitz fortress lies before us.

Coffee and running water are available for a price. We pass through a video arcade, blue phantoms with pig-snouts, bodies weary without running, seeking a zenlike inner focus in dry-humping boxes that beep, each console coated, like glory holes, with the combined effluvium of thousands of men's sweat. We inspect a selection of commemorative Operation Desert Storm t-shirts and keychains, twelve-packs of underwear, and hermetically-sealed Reba McIntyre cassettes in a shopping stall where the neon burns surgery-bright.

The objects look so pretty. The people look like expired food.

We walk. The sounds of crickets rise on all sides. They outnumber us here. They could suffocate us. The country is deep, no electric lights, plowed fields and loose dust on the road from a week without rain.

Forty minutes outside of Jubitz, the sky is filled with spools of light—the Perseid meteor shower. We crane our heads upwards until our necks threaten to snap; it is imperative we mainline messages from Sky-Mind. The sky feels close enough to chew, a teat made of velvet and orgasm.

In the afternoon we are dropped off in the town where Fabio's mother lives. She is a small blonde with scarlet cheeks and the hands of a rag doll. I sense that she was once as tall as a water tower, could leap over oceans, but has shrunken from what she once was.

We meet Fabio's boyhood friend, a twenty-one year old named Cody who has been diagnosed with schizophrenia. The three of us eat in a train caboose that has been converted to a diner. Cody frequently turns his head behind his back, insisting that people are trying to lock him up. I am overcome with the sense that I have dreamed about Cody before arriving here: his child-star face and auburn hair, the way he speaks about everyone trying to trap in him a maze, the way he slams his fist on the table and says the dimension he is in is an illusion, and he has to escape.

"You can escape. You can come with us," I say.
"Really?"
Fabio and I nod yes.

To the relief of the elderly Italians trying to pace their ingestion of lasagna and sirloin steak, we leave the caboose.

"Then I won't need these anymore," Cody says, tossing a bottle of anti-psychotic pills in a ravine overgrown by weeds. The three of us walk up a highway onramp and present our thumbs.

Fabio prefers to sing rather than speak. We tap our thighs and pivot on our heels like clockwork dancers as the sun goes down.

"Do you hear that? The insects!"

The cicadas are hatching out of their waxy nests and surrounding us with their drone.

"They live seventeen years and this is their mating call," I tell the men. "Imagine incubating for seventeen years so that you can live three months, a span of time in which you must find a mate or your juice-line will be at an end."

"Ci-cayyyyydahhhhhh! Orrrrr-yach!" Fabio sings, and when I look for Cody to join in, his smile is nervous, his head turning behind him, as if he can see the tether that connects him to his hometown growing very thin, a pearl-color string snaking through the vines and ether, tied firmly around his leg.

The carpenters pick us up. They are young and their sandy hair and freckled brown faces speak of idle summer afternoons drinking Miller High Life, Boone's Farm at the ready for a series of string-bikinied ladyfriends who have no hips and jump into freshwater streams, just like in a breath mint commercial. The carpenters are headed to Newberg to deliver these special tables. The smells of wood and fresh varnish fill the vehicle. There is enough room in the covered truck bed for us to get into fetal positions, our knobby knees and backs flush with the tables as if we are having a dress rehearsal for starring roles in a coffin. We try to have idle conversation with the carpenters along the way, but their engine is loud and the windows are open so we are relieved of the duty of being charming.

Over the course of an hour undercurrents of trouble flick through the truck bed like the tail of a crocodile. Cody is moaning.

"I will NOT be fruitful and multiply! I decided it would be a hamburger…Centuries-old factories are turning to the herd god."

"It's okay, Cody, you're with us."

"Yes, you're with us. You're safe."

"Doctors are letting doctors die. They were supposed to save us. She says her car burned, but she's lying. It's a hologram…"

Fabio puts his hand on Cody's shoulder, "It's okay. We will get out soon. You're safe, my man."

"The walls are rotting flesh. Can't you see it?"

Cody is pointing to the roof of the truck bed.

"I believe you see it, but I can't see it, my friend," Fabio says in his smoky baritone.

"This is it…" Cody's expression grows more anguished, "You spend your life doing this and now it's the end…slaves in wooden cages. She has a butterfly tattoo on her back…"

"Let's be with peace," Fabio says.

"Missus Robinson is burned in the fire…" Cody points at me, "she's laughing, back from the hospital. They're driving us to hell!"

"No, we're right here with you." The words tumble out of my mouth, but I see the h-bomb look in Cody's eyes, a siege of pure terror, and I realize that my 'being here' for him holds no currency. Who the hell do I think I am that my simple presence can calm anyone faced with walls of rotten meat?

Cody crawls back and forth in the truck bed, pawing at a toolbox.

"They're starting a new civilization…they're going to kill me…

they make themselves invisible, sneak in with your breath…"

He slams his arms hard against one of the tables.

"Is everything okay back there? Can you get your friend to chill out?" the guy in the passenger seat says.

"We're trying, we're trying," Fabio says. He tries to hug Cody, and Cody shoves him back, pounds the table with the force of a gorilla. "YOU'RE NOT LISTENING!"

The driver swerves to the side of the road, says, "Out! You have to get out!"

How still the road feels after getting used to the rumble of a truck. How *very* still we are, as if we have been glued to the edge of the road.

Cody has grown calm. He is relieved to be out of the truck. The sun has set, leaving us with the swamp-damp that rises from New York ground on late August nights.

The three of us amble into New Paltz, shellacked in cold sweat and spilled coffee. It is a quaint berg on the Thruway's floodplain, one of dozens which absorb the dollars of tourists as they begin their drive north from Manhattan—they make it through the Catskills, push further north, to towns which like tired vaudevillians twist their petticoats for the glint of laughing teeth: See firehouses! Old churches! Inns of cobblestone gone smooth in the rain! Homes of exiled Huguenots, their interiors baptized with soot!

See Main Street—it is *named* Main Street, and like a million Main Streets across the nation it features brick apartments that date from the eighteen-hundreds. Built to hold the bounty of industry, left behind in a receding tide. Their high and narrow windows remind me of eyes.

I do what I do in every small town—peer longingly at lamps illuminating second- and third-story rooms. I index lace curtains and crooked venetian blinds. I index flowerpots, Zulu masks, lineups of empty Cuervo bottles, objects which serve as touchstones long after the tenants of each room yielded to the epiphanies which brought them to collect masks and tequila in the first place. I place myself in their beds, wash in their sinks; hear box fans, drunken brawls, radiator hiss; weather patterns moving like heavy breasts over the grooves of shelter, grinding against sidewalks cracked with cold and sealed by tar which bubbles in summer with a prehistoric stench. I live twenty lifetimes and turn my back on each—before reaching the end of the block.

"Would you rather go home?" Fabio asks Cody.

He speaks as if he is remembering how to form words: "N-n-no! Not back there. Never…"

Traffic fills the streets. An Adirondack chill enters our bones. Fabio and I speak in dulcet tones, extolling the virtues of nourishment after a journey on the road. Cody turns in circles at the doorstep of a bar called McGillicuddy's, and agrees to go in.

The room is crowded with yesterday's beauty queens in soccer stripes tapping Pall Malls against the bar, acid-wash jeans three years too old, men with peppermint squints. Students puffed with hormones float through the air like pink balloons ready to pop.

The smells of bleach and melted cheese move over us like tendrils. The air-conditioning is at full blast.

We seat ourselves in a wooden booth. Fabio orders beer and fries.

The table lamp acts as a spotlight on Cody's acne, a mole on his left cheek. A golf shirt sits on his chest like something selected by a grandmother, far too long for him, in too conservative a shade of blue. The glass of chilled water placed beside him holds no interest. It is as if the glass is in another dimension.

Cody gazes out the window as if he expects the arrival of something grave and life-changing very soon.

"The letters P…L…and C," he says. He says it again.

"P…L…C…what are they?" we ask, wracking our brains for a greater psychic or cultural significance to these ciphers. Perhaps if we can solve the puzzle of P-L-C, Cody can be deposited there and find inner peace.

In truth, we are growing exhausted. Fabio rises from the table and I follow him to a darkened corner by a pay phone.

Fabio's eyes are bloodshot, his lips stained with ketchup. A blue-black stubble forms on his chin. He rubs the back of his neck as if he can prod his mind into clarity.

"We're fucked." Fabio pauses, then adds, "No; *he's* fucked."

"Can we call someone? Should he go home again?"

"He's not the Cody I remember."

"He acts like his family are monsters, but who else can take care of him?"

"Other than blood...blood..." Fabio groans, placing his hand in his mouth to bite at his pinky fingernail. This powerful hand, which looks like the hand of a god or a saint—like it was rendered by DaVinci—can do nothing to ease a friend's pain.

I picture the woods, now seventy or eighty miles away where a bottle of Haldol sits, beetles and snails crawling over the dosage that goes with Cody's name.

"P..." Fabio wracks his brain, "Pandora...prana meditation... panacea...the mathematical Pi..."

"What is a name," I ask, "that has p, l, and c?"

"Paracelsus...place...PLACE!"

"Pluck! Planck!"

Fabio shakes his head 'no,' but the ghost of a smile crosses his lips.

"Maybe it's out of order. Could he be indicating an idea or location with the sequence L-C-P...?"

At this moment a waitress approaches us. She puts her hand on my shoulder.

"Ma'am, sir, your companion has become agitated and he's just run out the door."

We dig for balled-up bills in our bags and toss them on the table, rush into the street. Cody is at the end of the block, wringing his hands, staring at a space above an old-fashioned streetlamp, looking like he wants to cross the street, yet there is something we cannot see blocking his passage.

"Cody! We were afraid we lost you, friend," Fabio says. "What would you like to do?"

"You are not my friend," Cody says, shaking, "These are lies! The see-through one passed through you. I saw. The cream-color one... the darker ones...I know what controls the hand."

"It's *Fabio*, remember when we built forts together? And Jen.

You remember Jen…"

"I am *not* going with you!" Cody yells. He runs toward a street sign and kicks it until it bends, crippled metal; a scarecrow's leg. He sprints down an alley behind the bar. Further back we see an undeveloped block, a lot overgrown with weeds, the steep rise of forest.

We walk in circles calling his name. One hour turns into two. We call for our missing companion behind dumpsters. We call in raspberry bushes, under piles of scrap metal. We call over fences and ice machines. We stand in lobbies of restaurants, giving his description to greeters who say, "Aw, we're sorry han. We're sure he'll turn up!"

"It was his choice. He needed to leave," Fabio says, trying to make both of us feel better. I can tell neither of us do.

We are on Main Street again. The sidewalk is full of life—block after block of chatting, laughing college kids. They sip mystery beverages from plastic cups and smoke cigarettes.

Some are dressed like hippies with flowing scarves, raw cotton peasant shirts. Some are punks. Some wear the plaid flannel and ski caps popularized by musicians they religiously watch on MTV. A woman with a severe jaw and Louise Brooks hair struts by in charcoal overalls. She has stripes painted on her eyes. I feel grimy and underdressed in this crowd, but get distracted by the main attraction—

He is a giant. His forehead is deformed, as big as a football helmet. He is nearing seven feet tall and is clearly the type of tall man who enjoys the amount of eating that his height can afford him.

His body is packed in an oily suit. His hands could bend iron bars. Tied around his mop of black hair is an indigo bandanna. A brass ankh hangs from his neck.

Fabio and I walk up and down Main Street—once, twice, three times—watching the crowds pile in and out of doorways—hoping to catch sight of Cody, yet simultaneously relieved that we don't—and the big man watches. There's a competition between his ankh and his beady black eyes to hypnotize me.

We are about to pass for a fourth time when he speaks. A number of spooks—who I can only call his acolytes—peel off when we approach.

"And who might you be?" he asks. "I have viewed the comings and goings on this block for a good thirteen days and haven't seen spirits like yours before."

His voice is deep. Somewhere in the back of my brain it gels that this man has modeled his voice after the The Wizard of Oz.

"You wouldn't have seen us," I say. "We just got here."

"We are travelers," Fabio adds.

"You are seekers," the man says. "It is obvious that you're missing something."

"You're right," I say. "What is it?"

"I suspect it is a who…"

"Where is he?" Fabio asks.

"Approach me, if you would. I promise it will be painless. I must feel your auras to get a better idea of the situation."

As skeptical as I am, I am under the big man's spell.

"I should introduce myself. I am Mondo Ra. I am a seer and mage."

I watch his hand flutter around my shoulders, my collarbone.

"The neck! You project great strength, but there is weakness in your neck. You strive to protect it."

"Well I did just get over the chicken pox," I say.

Mondo Ra closes his eyes, lifts his hands to his temples, hums for a minute.

"I see your friend. He is a confused soul. He has gone to the place of green. I see green."

"We're in a forest."

"Don't be quick to judge, fiery one. It is an unnaturally green place. It could be…hmmmm…I see a building painted green."

"A house?"

"Bright green, like a traffic light. The only building I can think of like that…is one block over. Go straight one block, take a right. There's a house turned into a restaurant. It's painted green."

"Let's check right now," Fabio says.

"I linger here…until late. I'll be curious to know if you find him."

"You'll just be standing here?" I ask.

"These bars are overpriced shitholes. I feel the energy much *more*…out here. Have you noticed this is a canyon? A basin *absorbs.* "

As Mondo Ra extends his huge arms, I can't help but feel the power of the basin with him.

We follow his directions and reach an Irish pub named Murphy's, which is closed for the night.

"Not very Irish to be closed at ten PM," Fabio says.

We circle the lot, calling a name we have called a hundred times before. We return to Main Street without him.

Mondo is sipping from a flask and talking to a man in a black trenchcoat. The little man has the white hair and red-rimmed eyes of an albino.

Mondo offers us his flask. Fabio accepts.

"You're going to have to sleep somewhere," he says.

We take our chances with the giant.

We walk three blocks with Mondo Ra to the ground floor apartment which he rents in a Victorian house. When he turns his keys in the lock and swings open the door, the scents of urine, Spaghettios, and the high unadulterated tang of vomit race up my nostrils and poke like jagged glass at the base of my brain.

Does Mondo have a sick pet? Does he cast spells with his vomit, the way certain sex magicians wash their hair with sperm?

Mondo turns on the overhead light and fan. Bookshelves line the walls, top-heavy and warping under the weight of yellowed fantasy novels, books about Turkey, Egypt, China—long dead Pharaohs, emperor's tombs, spells. There are hundreds of volumes on meditation, numerology, immortality. Dirty bowls, cups, bottles, and crumpled papers are scattered on every available surface.

I find a wooden stool on which to perch, and start opening his books.

"I was not always this way," he says, once we're settled in a circle near his bed.

We are in a holding pattern of grapefruit and vodka, grooving on Binah and Sephiroth, bubble universes in the shapes of pancakes, the generative urge, the quandary of time existing outside of time, the razor wire between pleasure and pain.

"Several years back, the dark forces had me. I was a bonehead."

"A what?"

"A skinhead."

Mondo rolls up his shirtsleeve to show us tattoos on his mighty bicep.

He shows scars on his chest, where muscles have started to give way to fat.

"I devoted myself to years of violence. I have memories in my head that haunt me. I delighted in causing pain. I fed off other's fear—every part of the equation: Their fear, the chase, the impact of my fists on their flesh. I used my fists, I used ropes, I used chains. Because of my size, very few people would be able to prevail over me…I think of that as another life. I don't share these memories with many."

He gives us a meaningful glance, and swallows.

"I now devote my life to beauty, regeneration. I feel a strong sympathy with the two of you, being fire," he looks at me, "and water…" he aims his eyes with a moist intensity at Fabio.

Mondo lures Fabio to his hash-pipe. I stick with the vodka.

"Everything soft that yields dew is the outflowing of Osiris," he says, holding Fabio's shoulders, staring into Fabio's eyes.

Mondo's breathing grows ragged, filling the room like open heart surgery.

Earlier in the night, our host thoughtfully provided us with a pile of blankets. I wrap a scarf around my head and lean into my nest, which I have arranged at the base of a bookshelf.

I look up once or twice from the pages I read, see Mondo peeling the clothes from Fabio's well-formed body, licking, biting into his thighs. Mondo remains fully clothed, but Fabio is nude, browned by sun, his body taut as a ballet dancer.

They suck each other off, and I can't help but wonder if Fabio is enjoying this, or if he is doing it out of a sense of obligation, offering Mondo payment for our stay.

My mind races. As dawn breaks, I fall asleep.

Mondo's funk is civilized by gashes of noon sun. He bustles in his narrow strip of kitchen, brewing coffee. Every inch of counter space is filled by spice bottles, bowls, and cans. Being touched has changed him. He shimmers, reflecting rainbows, like a soap bubble.

He opens a cabinet obscured by crests of junk, removes a stack of folded towels, and hands them to me.

"For you, madame."

Fabio is splayed across the bed. As the kitchen sounds carry to him, he stretches, cat-like, into waking. He is a film of seduction in reverse, pulling on layers of clothes, tightening the laces on his shoes, rolling a cigarette, back arched forward, filaments of brown hair tipped blue which fall to his chin and punctuate his orphan nature. He peers, hungover, through a mask of freedom.

In the bathroom I repaint my face. Hot water, soap; the drain absolves. I make use of Mondo's towels, so surprising, so fluffy, so white.

On the street I scan each pedestrian for a burst of recognition… Who will be the first to go: Ah! *You* have been to Mondo Ra's, *too!*— but I sense nothing.

Cody's absence blocks our passage. We wonder what's come of him. Front-page news—or a void? Gooseflesh-petals, brain-fever gone blot; simply slipped to another dimension? We search the town for three hours, our feet moving inexorably toward the Thruway onramp, coffee gone tart in our throats. Late-afternoon sun is bone-white, and our muscles cry. We feel old and slightly malignant, and ready for the new.

The trucker's face is a shovel beaten by a shovel, red hair and two-day's stubble white as snow. I'm close enough to kiss him, unzip his fly, unburden him of soul. My eyes return to the hairs which burst through his follicles, an array of miniature swords. His cheeks are too dry, too loose, a photograph to demonstrate g-force. Dandruff covers his flannel shirt like freshly-grated parmesan.

The rig lurches. He forces the semi up a hill so steep it's an optical illusion. The trailer clatters behind us.

After an hour the driver pulls a pill bottle from his pocket, pries open the lid, offers us its contents. A pile of irregular yellow rocks: meth or crack. I say thanks, but not now, hold tight as he tells us he's behind schedule, has to gain time.

He burns rubber on hairpin curves, AM talk radio blaring, sky bleating, metal and breath bearing down, down, through the jungles of Pennsylvania: Swamps capped with green mold, lilypads thick as kitchen sponges, bobbing heads of Queen Anne's lace, sumac trees pregnant with rust-color blooms. On each side of the road, tadpoles have grown to frogs.

"This is your other mommy."

Her hair is frosted blonde and styled in a bubble-shape. Her arms are firm and tan, her breasts in a halter, the musk of Yves Saint Laurent's Opium mixing with her warmth and surrounding me. The bay air presses through the windows, and everything is just so in this house.

This nursery room: drawings on the walls, stuffed animals, streamers, glittery tutus; curtains made of cotton, dyed with patterns of Indian mandalas. The living room is lined with dark-stained wood. The carpets are clouds. Plants proliferate—pendulous leaves, ferns, spikes, flowers with stamens like the cock of Pan. There is a mother and a father and a son who is six, and a daughter—provided by me.

Everything was going so well, until now.

"She's been enjoying this one all week," the woman says, handing me a book of fairy tales.

The sun is setting and our shadows lengthen.

"Oh! I'm so full right now," she says, "of *love*. I will leave you two alone…to explore each other."

I have never met a woman like this. She is beaming at the notion of a child having two mothers. She is beaming because I have entered *all* of their lives.

But I know the truth. I'm too young. While I stand here, I am elsewhere—I, yet to be formed, but already too formed, marching forward in time, to a patchwork of mistakes.

The girl has a pixie face and pixie hair. She wears a striped dress with polka-dot tights. A minute ago she was smiling. Now her face is like a pane of glass hit by a hammer.

"Your *other* mommy is going to read a story to you."

The hammer hits the pane of glass a second time.

The woman squeezes my shoulder and wiggles with delight. There is no doubt in her mind that something remarkable will come of this moment.

"I'll be outside if you need me." She tiptoes out, closes the door.

Shadows climb from the floor, claw at my hip-bones.

"Do you want to hear a story?"

Her head radiates a hot fume of shampoo. Her body is small, but her resistance is great. This small life fashions herself a soldier: Her eyes begin to close. She nods, she quakes.

Once, twice, five times, ten—she wills herself awake, standing on the mattress and gazing at me with an expression of pure horror.

I don't dare get closer. I don't feel comfortable adding to the confusion by pretending to be a Mommy.

At fifteen minutes, her body crumples and she sleeps.

He is an electrical engineer. She is a dreamer. They live on an island and eat organic vegetables and swim at the beach, and their cabinets are filled with tinctures of pau d'arco and echinacea and value-priced tubs of vitamin powder. The man drinks hydrogen water, which he says rejuvenates his blood. They roll out a map of Edward Cayce's ley lines on the kitchen table, tell me the history of Atlantis, of their weekly tantra class. They have met guardian angels—on roadsides and in dreams. Discreet spotlights gleam on granite countertops. I eat several slices of tofu cheesecake, make the mistake of taking out my tarot deck.

"Did you say Aleister Crowley?"

"Y…yes?"

The two of them recoil.

"You mustn't use that! Oh dear! We have to tell you something. He was a black magician."

Lost on a rural route lined with endless cornfields, our saviors appear on the horizon in the shape of an Oldsmobile.

It is ten in the morning. The elderly couple are dressed as if they are on their way to an important event. Their car is a spacious early-eighties four-door sedan, nut brown, preserved in time.

We climb in, man behind man, woman behind woman, not doppelgängers, not cautionary tales, not ghosts.

The car's interior smells of band-aids and soap. The man and his wife—at least that's what I think they are—gaze straight ahead as if they do not want to look upon the creatures who occupy their hard-earned space. Sawdust lungs; Punch and Judy profiles, a thousand fine accordion folds of their flesh as if they have spent a lifetime facing a relentless wind. Have they ever smiled? Have they ever tumbled into soil, kissed earthworms, eaten flowers?

But why did they stop for us, if they won't even say hello? I want to whisper to Fabio, but we decide to straighten our backs, fold our hands in our laps. We shellack ourselves with dignity, like two wedding cakes that have been placed on the sedan's back seat.

It is a quiet ride for forty minutes—so quiet that I start to fantasize a coffin would have more activity than this. I keep wondering why we are here. Are they devout Christians, and despite how *off* their passengers are, their dogma obliges they do a good deed?

After a while I hypothesize that the man behind the wheel has picked us up to drive us across the county line in order to rid his territory of our presence, whatever it entails.

We are dropped at a crossroads overgrown by forest. Young men in overalls with beer bottles in their hands sleepwalk down gravel paths towards a corner store, eye us with suspicion. The more people we see, I wonder if we have traveled through time as well as space.

"I didn't know Pennsylvania was like this. I thought it was all factories and guys who looked like Bruce Springsteen."

"Yeah, *I* always pictured it like a Billy Joel song."

The young man in a baseball hat, sweatpants, and bare feet slinks out of a gas station. He gives a long look at us and spits at our feet.

"What errr you?" he says. "A feeeeg? Sum kinda hukker?"

When he's out of earshot, Fabio whispers to me:

"It's Appalachian here."

We are almost out of money. With great care we pool our change to buy a microscopic bottle of orange juice and a cheese danish.

The earth is eternal. It laughs at our breath. It yearns to pin us to concrete, drink our blood like box-wine; snap our ribs, smash our hands and snort the dust, keep us conscious for the whole thing.

We have been walking for three hours. Why did we walk? Because it was better than standing on the side of the road next to another cornfield, attracting flies like lollipops dropped in mud.

Once an hour, a pickup truck passes, the new kind plated in chrome and metallic paint. These trucks look more expensive than the houses they drive to—rolling jukeboxes displaying an assortment of Jesus-fish and Calvin and Hobbes bumper stickers, and the new kind of tires—toy-tires like on garbage trucks—tires for a dawning age of game-boys, layoffs, and movies starring The Rock. We lift our thumbs, no luck.

Set back from the road, at the end of gravel ribbons, farmhouses rise, Victorian castles with gables and their sisters, decaying barns. Their faces sag yet their eyes are ever-open, wreathed with cobwebs and chipped paint. The passage of years into a new age will not see them resurrected. Many are abandoned, no glass left in their windows, roofs caved in. Not far from these decomposing elders new homes sit, utilitarian and no larger than trailers, surrounded by a consortium of satellite dishes squatting like vultures, their beaks pecking at aluminum siding.

No oxen plow these rows of corn and lettuce and beets. Irrigation rigs, tin silos and mud-covered tractors hold dominion over day.

The sun sets. Lack of food and running water addle our thought. We get a hit of euphoria at signs of commercial life: a shack selling seeds and fertilizer, a roadhouse.

With rubber limbs we enter the parking lot of the Stop-N-Go Mart. It is paved but barely, tall grass rocking over cracks.

Two arc-lights spill powder across the dusty pavement. This is a stage-set: Night's confessional. We arrive in time to see a group of people enter an expensive-looking minivan. They are bopping with party energy.

Through the windows I see a guy with bleached-white hair, long, an inch of black roots. It is 1995 and I feel he is pulling a Cobain—but who is pulling a Cobain out here—in a land where people think a braless woman is a witch, and a boy without a NASCAR cap sucks cock for pocket change?

Cobain is accompanied by a guy in a hoodie with greasy brown hair and pencil-mustache, a white man in a buzzcut who looks like a baseball star, a pregnant blonde cheerleader-type, and a black man who looks old enough to be their father. The ignition turns. A blast of Alice in Chains pulses from their island of light.

The doors slide shut, and the revelers are sealed. The van curls down the road without seeing our thumbs.

"A cast of characters," Fabio says. "I wonder where they're headed."

We share an orange juice, little more than a plastic capsule of corn syrup, trying to convince ourselves that it, combined with a bag of Cheez-its, will give us energy for the road.

We've been walking in the dark for fifteen minutes when the minivan returns and crunches up beside us.

"Hey you guys? Wanna come have dinner with us? Or bunk down for the night? We wouldn't feel right to letcha be stuck out here."

We enter the space-pod, wedge between baseball-boy and the the pregnant blonde. The Red Hot Chili Peppers wrap around our heads.

"We're about to have a barbecue," pencil-mustache adds, "We got ourselves five pounds of ribs and the fixins for tacos. Five twelve-pack-a-Coors, so much weed ya won't see the white of yer eyes 'til next Tuesday. We're set. My buddy and I might cruise up to Syracuse, got a friend comin' in with windowpane and wanna purchase a few sheets."

"Oo—ooo, be careful up there," baseball cap says, "It's the big city. Don't get lost."

"But I like gettin' lost." He winks at us. "You guys know what I'm sayin'?"

The van drives down Route 20, turns onto a maze of access roads, and stops in front of a ranch house.

"Welcome to the compound!" pencil-mustache says.

"Make yourselves at home. My home is your home," the older man says. He wears a utility jacket and a button-down shirt. His hair is clipped in a short fro, and his face reveals the inklings of gray stubble. His eyes light up with an expansive smile. "Stay as long as you need to."

"We're much obliged, man," Fabio says.

As the passengers lift their bags and go in the house, Fabio and I exchange glances. Is this some sort of cult?

The woman is pregnant as if she has been administered a pregnancy drug. The drug is our genes. The drug is our desire. The drug is this haunted chain of things, that life has to be strong, use fists, use chains and lies, compete for bounty before winter comes, instead of being born with a stomach that digests poetry. The order of grits and patties slapped on the grill, air laden with creosote and ganja and expired Quell shampoo, the air that sings we are slaves and we are seeking black ichor, white pills, messiahs and oblivion.

In the distance a siren calls and a chorus of dogs respond as if they sense in their bones that this querulous thing is a greater dog; perhaps a dog-messiah. Do not forget us: we are here.

As the night wears on the people before us move closer to the ground. The living room and one of the bedrooms have dim lighting, and the men and woman are listening to music, playing card games, telling stories.

Geoffrey is the oldest. He refers to the others as his "kids." He invites Fabio and I to a corner of the living room and tells us his reasons:

"They got no where better to be than this. They're...refugees. Turned out by their families, can't find work, or pregnant and starting family...but their own families don't understand. Can't or won't understand, won't let them back in. These are misfits here. This is a world of constant pain. Orphans lookin' for somethin' to hold onto, a single good drop of luck, a single friend, a place to sit without bein' hounded. I came out of the marines, and I was a mess. I saw a lot of stuff that...made me fucked-up for a while. I'm still proud I served my country, but the system leaves you behind when you get back. You come back a shell of what you were. You don't come back the same man. They train you to go over there...and die there. They don't teach you how to fit back in this...groceries and jobs and routine, the lifestyle that you served to protect."

He turns to Fabio. "Have you served, young man?"

"No, sir," Fabio says.

"Things are different, now that the draft's done away with. When I got back, my mind...was like raw hamburger. I was on twenty different drugs, anything to be high, not here. I hit rock bottom, sleepin' in my car. No bank account, no family wanted to take me in, not the way I was. I was always movin' around, coz the cops would see a car parked in a neighborhood too many days and a black man sleepin' in it means trouble. My car was all I had to my name. It took a lot of work to get to where you see me now. I own this house. No one's takin' it away from me."

We nod, and know there is nothing we can or should add. We listen.

"You know what these kids have to look forward to? For a lot of them, nothin.' This country's left them behind. Go up to Utica, Troy, you see girls all alone, knocked up by one guy after another, and they are stuck raisin' all these kids, four, five babies before they are a legal adult. Cops would sooner lock up the daddies for years for possession of an ounce of weed then put a dollar into rehabilitation. There are troubled times ahead."

"Maybe President Clinton—"

"Clinton ain't liftin' any weight for us. Jails across this nation are full of young black men, lifers for rocks in their pockets, or a lot less, standin' on the wrong corner. Lifers. Make no mistake, once you go in, you're a lifer. A young black man gets put away and his family got no money to get 'im out. Life hardens you. Last time I was in Troy I ran into a young woman I know who wouldn't let the daddy of her babies live with her because if he did, her food stamps would be cut off, and those babies need food. You know how poverty works in America? The offices that are supposed to help you…these helping hands got poison in 'em, eat away at a man's sense of self, eat away at a family. It's my duty to help…because I can."

He waves his hand at the window.

"It's so quiet out here. Don't know if I could ever get used to the city again. We got some churches that give out food, but here in the sticks? These kids' families got no money, very few of the farms you see are breakin' even. White kids whose families aren't makin' enough money off crops, they see the land they grew up on bein' bought out. These young white boys? They don't want to follow their daddies, growin' corn and apples. They watch their daddies fail right before their eyes. They don't see that shit on television. They want to be macho, go to the city and pack heat and be runnin' around like teenyboppers 'til they hit thirty."

While Fabio and Geoffrey share a joint I walk over to the place where baseball cap boy and his pregnant girlfriend sit, cuddling on a throw blanket laid across the floor. In the other room I hear pencil-mustache playing a video game, loud protestations at the screen when he loses:

"Boooool-shit! Bool-to-the-fucken-shit!"

"Hey we heard you might be a witch, or have some magic," says the pregnant girl.

In her stretched-out cable-knit sweater, two inches of black roots that match mine, hormones making her face explode with zits, and eyes like a teddy bear—I feel her volume, her hunger. She needs to believe something.

"I don't call myself a witch, but I do have cards with me."

I pull the tarot cards out of my bag. They are folded in a piece of purple metallic cloth.

"Please, please, can we see? Would ya…tell our fortunes?"

I shuffle the way I learned when I was a child and my grandfather and I played gin rummy. I put on a show for the pair, flipping and sliding the cards until my hands move with a hypnotic rhythm. I tell them to focus on a question, something they want to know.

"This card is the past of your situation." The *Sun*, children dancing, a card filled with rainbows and light. "This is the heart of what you are asking about..." Images of rusty swords dripping poison, a card of *Justice*, blindfolded, one of a man in armor, a plow, chalices filled with green juice.

"This one is *Strife*, and connected with this card, it shows that you want something to work well, but you have fear eating at you. There's something you know can go wrong and it's gone wrong before..."

"Shee-it, she knows..." the boy says, looking at the girl, as if the blood has drained from his face.

"Yeah, yeah, but will it be okay?"

Surgery

When I was ten years old I watched a classmate dismember a small plastic Smurf figurine over the course of a day. I didn't actually see him with scissors or a knife. He did it privately, this surgery. I dug my nails into my palms over and over again to stop from hysterically laughing each time Mark, that was his name, silently, without fanfare, displayed a new Smurf body part at the top left corner of his desk, as if displaying a trophy. Neat, like a gin drink or eugenics. It was a neat display. The best one was the Smurf's tail, a small blue circle that could easily be mistaken for a Tic-Tac. It sat there, lonesome as a cloud. Later on, Mark became a drug and alcohol counselor. There is a moral in all of this somewhere.

Cam Girl

First of all, hair is important, and I know because I have spent a lifetime trying to make my hair important, but it stubbornly resists. Her hair is frosted a lavender-white, still within the bounds of seducing farmhands rather than styled for a Swedish music video where a singer is in a harness with her genitals dusted, every so chicly, by the fluttering of a holographic ziploc bag.

"O I am so sorry I missed u sweetie," she types into her phone. I am sitting right behind her and on the midnight bus I am able to lean my head ever-so-slightly forward and read every word she taps with her thumbs, their nails shellacked in shades of Cosmos and Black Dahlia.

She continues: "I stayed at bar as long as I could, now on bus. I could only stay half an hr."

"So bummed to miss you." the man on the other end types.

"Oh that's so sweet, hon. I hope we can meet up next time I'm in."

"Was hoping to see your beautiful face."

"You're too sweet. I'll have new photos up on Monday. Going to edit them in the next five hours. I'm sooooo cashed and glad to get home. Did two shoots on Mon and Tue one of them in Tryon park, soooooo cold. Other one in alley and dude jacked my blanket."

The man types emoticons of hearts and eyeballs.

"Sorry to hear about your blanket. I bet you're gorgeous in them."

"SO sweet," she types, "U get them on Mon with 2nd tier. But just for U I can send a bonus pic tonight."

"Thank you gorgeous."

She is in skinny jeans and her wrists are covered in a fine layer of glitter. Her legs are folded, yet her foot, in a wooden platform clog, nervously swings in the air. Through a cloud of her perfume, gone stale in a way that makes me think she applied it well over twelve hours ago, I read on.

The man says she is gorgeous and sweet and so kind and so sexy five more times, while she finds a way of translating noncommittal and business-related information, her finger robotically scrolling galleries of hundreds of photos in her phone's storage, past bikini and lingerie shots, settling on a folder of professionally-lit "candids" in tight cotton long johns and yoga attire, the sort of shots that any news anchor or talk show host would LOVE to have as publicity stills; blonde and sanitized yet with a faint whiff of vodka martinis and two-way penetration if you say pretty please; the fictional woman in these "candids" prefers to sleep naked, drink coffee naked, would do everything naked if society got sane and said YES. She selects one, in which a cup of coffee steams at her bare midriff. She is leaning forward in a crop top, a pair of short-shorts, moccasins on her feet. Her golden legs stretch on for miles. Selected, and sent!

"You wake up beautiful, you go to sleep beautiful. You simply are beautiful," the man types.

"O sweetie, U made my night," she types.

I see a long list of messages cropping up from other men who need to receive her typing, her sweeties; her commentary that is neither truth nor lies, and a part of me wants to stay on the bus and compare and contrast her responses—how easy or hard will each man be; how demanding?—but it is midnight and my stop is coming up, and I have been awake a long time, doing my version of what she does, and so I walk through her cloud of Victoria's Secret Feathered Musk Number One body lotion—through the back door and out of our tame tin theater, to be swallowed by March's werewolf-breath, Longfellow branches, moon.

Deep-Fried Retribution

My cab driver was a sassy man in Jackie O sunglasses who spent the whole ride telling stories.

He wants to be a chef. He deep-fried three turkeys for Christmas last year but it wasn't enough. He'd like to open a 24-hr breakfast nook on the outskirts of the city that serves deep-fried turkeys.

He says everything is getting expensive. He says the city is spending a lot to make concrete Suicide Guards on a bridge we passed.

"There are jumpers at the mall, too."

"Of all the final places you could choose to go, imagine wanting to do it in a shopping mall," I said.

"Man, especially with kids around," he added, "that would traumatize a kid for life."

And this led into a story he told about his neighbor. When he was thirteen he knew an older kid, a guy in his early twenties, who was having an affair with his neighbor's wife.

The neighbor caught him and said, "If I catch you with my woman again, I done gon' kill you."

Desire grew fatal. The young man returned and was caught again. The neighbor took out a gun and chased him out of the house. Just as the guy was getting into his car, the neighbor shot him in the shoulder. His car door was open, but the gun was powerful. The impact spun him in a circle and he fell on the ground.

"Don't kill me," he pleaded.

"Wha'd I tell you? I tole you I done gon' kill you if I saw you here again. Now I done gon' kill you."

The neighbor shot him in the head, dead. The cab driver's mamma called him to the house but he was close enough to hear and see everything.

And I wondered how often the man in Jackie O sunglasses tells this story, if it is a talisman, a way to remember who he is, a way to test who he meets.

As I exited his cab I was left to do what I could: Wish him luck with his deep-fried turkey emporium.

Cut it Out of Me

They pass me at the bus stop; glistening in the heat, two bored children in tow whose feet drag, limbs thin as licorice sticks. Both ladies have seen better days and cackle as if drunk as they devour fried chicken from a clear plastic box that crinkles with the rustling of their fingers.

"FUCK me, this chicken is too good, whut the fuck is in it?"

"Chicken? Who the fuck knows, it's probably CAT!!"

"Ahm so MAD! I could just kill 'im I'm so mad. If I'm knocked up again I'm gunna march right to the doctor and say CUT IT OUTTA ME! No MORE, you're gonna have to cut it OUTTA ME, and if they don't I'm gonna have to do it myself with a kitchen knife."

And they cackle so loudly that pedestrians a block away shift course to not have to confront the savagery and power of the ladies' eyes.

"God-DAY-UM this cat is delicious!"

As the bus makes itself apparent, moving with the slow incongruous progress of a parade float or the melting of an ice cap, the ladies make noises of displeasure as they rise from their seats and wipe their hands on their back pockets and make grunting noises at the children to make their way to the curb. I hang back, allowing them to sidle past me, and as one does she looks me up and down and frowns and makes a "HUH," noise at me. The effect of her noise is THIS: Who the FUCK do you think YOU are, girl. You'll have to try harder. Your race, like mine, is RUN, and as she looks me up and down I am conscious of every wrinkle and roll and the way my eyebrows are uneven, and I will never, I will never.

The ladies sidle to the back of the bus and I am in the middle. I hear them spread out, make all the air-conditioned office people nervous. These passengers, in their silk-blend office cardigans and wilted oxfords don't even listen to their radios as loud as these ladies talk. The children are moot.

Three stops up I spy a gorgeous teenaged girl with heavy booty, wasp waist and a pale cream scalloped crop top. Her eyebrows are drawn on with the expert touch of a laser; her lips are frosted pale purple; her skin is honey, gladiolas, the lick of God. She does not walk, but ROLL on and sidle towards the back where she sits across from the ladies.

"Mmmm-mmm, it was gettin' stuffy in here, but I feel so much better now to have eye candy like YOU, baby," one of the women says to the teenaged girl. "Dayyyyy-um, you're gorgeous."

And she is, she is, for every one of us on the bus; the ones who eat cat and the man in the Downtown Clean and Safe vest who tries to answer the drunk ladies' questions on where to catch the Max with his wild afro and his small wire spectacles and his earnestness that means nothing to them.

For we court youth, and mourn youth and seek our answers from it, like a man who has jumped from a building and can only see the ground.

I Want to Believe

By the shiny new fence two people sit, one old, one young, and they are homeless. The man is white and in his thirties with a brown beard and a face that reminds me of a Sufi who has spun too long. He rubs his fingerless gloves back and forth against an empty strawberry yogurt drink.

"I know a place to get feta cheese pizza every night. With peppers, mushrooms. It's just a little mashed up."

"Tell her about the alien," the girl says. She isn't more than twenty and looks like Snow White but with golden-brown skin and freckles on her nose. Her shelf life for being holy is five minutes. She is high on youth, on more. "Tell her, the alien."

"I did...I found an alien once. An alien in a garbage can. It was very smooth...wrapped in...a...tablecloth."

"It wasn't an alien, it was a BABY," the girl says.

"It was not! It was an alien. I do not have to prove it to you."

"Fuck, he's so fucked he prob'ly *dreamed* the whole thing, but if it happened, I bet it was a baby."

"What did you do with the alien?"

"I brought it to the fountain and the witch took it. She...had...a black dress and leather jacket."

"Which fountain?"

"Hahahaa! You said Witch Fountain!"

Which version is better? For who?

I start to think of the *X-Files,* the slogan that grew popular so long ago. Isn't it what we're all doing?

I Want to Believe.

Jeezus

I was twenty-two years old and my bones were unfamiliar with the city. I was three-thousand miles from my home, sleeping in the basement of strangers, my shirt-sleeves at the cuffs smelling of a fine mold that entered every garment I washed and hung on a metal pipe. I trolled the streets in Cleopatra makeup and street punk rags, wanting to be laid bare, gutted like a fish by a random encounter. I was in Old Town, surrounded by bars at 2:30 in the afternoon. I felt a need to go in.

Old Town was made of halfway houses and pebble-gray junkies, yet it had the glints of Oz about it. Squares of purple glass were embedded in the concrete, worn to a softness that resembled wood. They cast light on a network of tunnels where sailors and whores and bags of rice were once pressed through stale air, the floors of each tunnel an amalgam of sand and spilled ale.

These were called the Shanghai Tunnels, a name meant to designate the port of call where American sailors were drugged and delivered, locked into labor on whaling vessels, in brothels, never again to see Little Jenny and Mary Sue, a thousand Little Jennys and Mary-Sues left in small towns where pigtails and scrap metal were the common currency, the hallmarks of sanity.

Nearly a century later, Old Town roasted in afternoon sun. An archway starred two Chinese dragons, their haunches pocked with red paint. They felt out of place above a woman in a rain poncho who rolled beneath a claw, her skin tootsie-roll-black and eyes bloodshot. From the ground, she whistled at men as they passed.

The bar was too well-lit. Pink curtains rustled in steam, turned a shade of yellow by nicotine.

Ten bodies sat in the room, bodies of an indeterminate age, their skin grown loose like bandages fallen off and replaced many times. Someone couldn't stop checking to see if the wounds had healed, and the wounds had not healed. Spirit tried to escape bone like the cigarette ash jumping from the patrons' hands, coating pull-tabs, making dirty snowdrifts of eggs on abandoned plates.

I sat at the bar and ordered a coffee. I was just getting started on it when the blonde collapsed two seats from me.

Her hair was a frizzy mess with five inches of black roots, the kind of roots that made me wonder what happened five months ago; what made her give up on the labor of presentation? Her body was shaped like a gumdrop in faded sweatpants. Her eyes were pale blue and wide like windshields, a network of veins broadcasting she had been up for days, or cried not long ago. A plastic flower was tucked behind her ear, an affectation which, if she was younger, would have given her a exotic air, evoked a plotline of a maiden about to be sacrificed to a volcano.

She was not alone, but in a way she was always alone.

She had dragged the man into the seat next to her and ordered two beers. The man methodically swigged at his, gazing into the distance as if the blonde wasn't there.

As they drank, the woman found excuses to pluck lint off his sleeve, smooth the mat of black hair that snaked across his head.

His hairs were thinning, long, nearly reaching his shoulders. His skull reminded me of a buzzard. His eyes were melanomas absorbing light.

It was then that the blonde stopped humming and picking at the man's shirt and noticed me.

"I lub this man," she said.

"Pardon me?"

"He has a destiny."

She smiled, and I nodded my head, mostly yes.

The man gazed into the distance, puffed on his cigarette as if oblivious to her words. Was she even there, or was she perhaps a ghost that haunted this bar?

"He's really special. I think he's gotta, ya know, magic."

"What do you mean?"

"Magic pow-er. I feel it just sittin' here. Can't you?"

"I'm not sure," I said, caught in the glare of her eyes.

"Feel it!" she said, stroking the man's hand, "He jus' radiates it. He's jus'…" She petted the seaweed fronds behind his ear. "I know he's gunna do something special. He and I are gunna get married."

I sipped more of my coffee.

She shot me a gummy grin. "You know who he reminds me of? Guess."

He looked like Charles Manson.

"Maybe Johnny Cash?"

"No, better'n that. Jeezus!"

The man slid his ink-dot-eyes my way.

"Don't you see it?" she said. "Yeee-ay-uh, the mother-flippin' son of God. This might be the Second Coming."

"With the hair…" I said, "I think I can see it."

I was halfway through my coffee. It was bad coffee, the sort of coffee that makes you feel more exhausted after you drink it.

"Sweartagod I never met a man like 'im. I don' even know what he's gunna do, but it's real big. The world's gunna change because uh…" she stroked the nape of his neck, skin turned loose and red like the glottal flap of a turkey, "What's inside this man."

She didn't mean turds.

"What's inside him?"

I couldn't help but ask.

"Well…I mean…I can't hardly sit in this seat because of the power…whoosh, it's like waves comin' outta him. Come on gurl, you gunna tell me you can't feel 'em?"

She shivered, shut her eyes. Both hands gripped her seat. She made a noise like the revving of an engine.

Jeezus-man's eyes flicked on me again, then drooped, moved to the horizon. He was not entirely there while this woman was MORE than present.

From across a room, I heard a woman make a tsk-tsk-ing sound: "If dat man is Jesus kah-rist, then AHM a monkey's uncle."

The blonde kissed the man's temple. She wasn't listening.

Two men at the end of the bar were dressed like truckers. They had stubble, fishing caps, unmanicured hands. One leaned in to the other and said, with a definite swish in his voice: "The only miracle that man's gonna perform is getting hard enough to find that bag's cunt."

I was young, thought every gay man tried to look like Adonis, but here, in the once-woods, almost everyone went incognito.

Jeezus-man's eyes were rolling back in his head. He was nodding off. This gesture of frailty brought the blonde to caress the veins on his neck. He was her Jesus and her baby at the same time.

"No man has ever made me FEEL like this."

I sat there and thought, how many times has a woman uttered this? How many times has the love eroded, leaving reality pocked as the paint on a Chinatown dragon?

What is in us, implanted in a woman's womb, her blood, that makes her feel incomplete unless she is loved by a man?

This blood, I wanted to rebel from it. Every time I broke free, I felt invincible, but invincibility is the worst drug.

You find another man to love. You tell sweet nothings to yourself. Things will be different this time because I have learned so much. Then you get addicted again.

I finished the coffee, not wanting to waste the dollar-fifty I'd spent. The clock on the wall said three. I was glad to get out of there.

I was waiting to see if a landlord would let me in a yellow brick building, the rent a tidy $254 a month.

I liked the idea of going incognito for a few months, maybe a year in this town before I returned to the world of superstars. I'd play my part, like the old men in the bar, my blue hair faded to a honey brown, my body in free-pile rags.

I walked up a hill with the purple glass squares, earth of the Shanghai Tunnels below.

I found myself in front of a high-rise, the front doors listing names of doctors in gold paint. So many buildings rose off of the ground, like rocketships, away from the earth and its shadows which tended to cluster together.

I kneeled on the ground and ran my fingers over the purple glass. The squares were warm to the touch. Chips in the glass opened like mouths to swallow rain, spit, my finger.

Who ever thought a city could swallow a person whole? Who ever thought a lover could swallow a lover whole?

Pray for it, like Jeezus. Pray to be bound, then pray to be released.

We say we are going somewhere, even as we're kicked. To learn, we race to forget.

Her Uncle's Kinky Shoes

Caresse was sick of being a white man's taste, a way to ease into a deeper understanding of blackness. She wasn't black enough in one way, not white enough in another.

"But let's get it straight. Even a little bit black is black to a white man."

She'd feel their relief in the elevator, when people would ask if she'd press the number five because she was closer and she'd smile, and their white faces would be spread in a rictus of gratitude, and she had learned years ago that her smile would make their body language back off a bit, but the rictus, it was their last defense.

"The more a white person smiles at you, the more scared they are."

Her brother was named Malachi, a name that means "my messenger" and he was a poet and all his friends knew he was working hard and saving his money to make his first music video, but one night his best friend shot him in the year 1985 and he didn't mean to and was sobbing when the cops picked him up.

Caresse ran to the sidewalk where her brother's body lay, and she knew there was a better place for all the blood that lay on the street, and that was inside her brother's veins. His body was already taken away but his blood lay there, and as the night was hot and the pavement still held the sun, she realized his blood held the sun as well.

She took a tissue in her purse. It held a few drops of his blood, and she kept it for two weeks before the idea of holding onto it sickened her and she burned it in the sink.

Caresse moved here and it is a long long way from Houston. She wanted to leave behind the heat and the blood and take care of her uncle and now she is a dental hygienist at a place out on a hundred and sixty-second, and before that she worked in a nursing home.

"I couldn't stay there any more, the things they do to people in there are evil. It is our god-given duty to take care of our elders, and the kids beneath me have forgotten. It's a short short time when we are strong and able to care for ourselves. We are babies at first and babies at the end."

Caresse's coworker is a blogger who goes on cruises four times a year and now has to take a number of immunity drugs because she contracted a mysterious "sickness of the blood" on a cruise.

"If you ask me," Caresse says, "I'd rather spend my money to have a big party for all of my family and friends. People get too into travelin' around, and they ain't ever getting their money's worth. In hotels where the air conditions like ice and people givin' you dirty looks, and you always take the wrong things in your suitcase. You wish you could sit down and…you don't even feel like yourself when all you got's a pile of clothes in a suitcase, and you're watching every penny. You start to feel like…a…ghost."

Her uncle was a cobbler. "He had a smile like this, that lit up a room. Now he is passed. I came up here and he was closin' down his shop to retire, he couldn't pay the rent no more. He would make these…fantasy shoes. He could take a shoe from I don't know… looked like the nineteen forties, and mix it with a disco shoe, or somethin' like a witch would wear, and he did these custom shoes for a bunch of queens, drag queens when they came in. He had a few women, high class escorts who loved him doin' their shoes. I think a few of them paid for their shoes with somethin' other than currency."

She takes out her wallet and shows me a picture of her uncle posing with one of his fantasy shoes.

Van Gogh Sex Kitten

"Like, I just don't understand why people make such a big deal about Van Gogh, like why does anyone need to know about Van Gogh and his squiggly lines?" says the teenaged girl at the back of the bus, her bellbottoms the finest in goth-reaper-chic, like bedcurtains of doom, like the sails of a vast Fellini galleon in a fever-dream, and her hair is reaper-schooner, too, the back half black, the front half burned a powder-white, toned gray as old bathwater, gray as a pensioner's underclothes. She is monochrome, her very physical nature waging war on psychedelic sunflowers and preternatural moonlight. She rambles in a smoky relaxed way, as if she is practicing for being immortal, to her dykey pal with a short pink do and a pair of madly-stitched overalls.

She knows she's on a roll: "Like—tell me one reason why I should even care about Van Gogh. Aren't we like OVER Van Gogh?"

The bus driver is one of those middle-aged men who are turning flat and dry as they press through the air, through time, itself, like living ironing boards. His face is pale. He has a slight flush to his cheeks. His hair is gray. His lashes, bouncing aloft pale blue eyes, are naturally lustrous, as if he is wearing mascara. He is the bastard child of Buster Keaton.

I keep sneaking peeks at the monochrome sex kitten and watch a small Mexican man get on, carrying an antique squeezebox. It is cloudy and getting dark. A rain commences.

The two girls stomp off the bus at Division, high on youth, high on each other, in a helium cloud of private power before the world of adults grows too near with its deadly gravity.

This Van Gogh business reminds me of being at a bar the other night and overhearing a man half my age talk about how Bruce Springsteen is irrelevant and how Bruce never really wrote "classic songs" whose lyrics you can remember. His main saving grace is that after Bruce, he starts talking about cats, and gets stuck on the subject, as if in his subconscious mind he realizes that he won't ever find another conversational topic as simultaneously disarming and engaging as cats, cat ownership, cat idiosyncracies, cat memes, cat selection and grooming and Youtube sites devoted to felines…for the rest of his natural life.

Yes, old folks, it is true: Your beloved Van Gogh and Da Boss are falling out of favor with the youth set, and soon enough, the kiddies will slam-dance against pillowed walls in their Google Glasses to a microtonal drone-jingle of the spheres.

Union Station, 2006

"The only side effect is how GOOD it makes you feel! It adjusts to every curve of your body! And honey, every curve of my sweet-ass body needs to be treated like a prin-cess. Mah booty is my business!"

She is hugging a four-foot-long body pillow that she has taken out of her suitcase rammed in one of the overhead compartments at the back of the Greyhound Bus. Our tube at large is a receptacle of white-bread sandwich breath, mossy flesh, shell-shocked break-up tears and eyes squinting shut as if the sheer force will bring sleep to deliver its blank knell faster to all fifty-one of us.

"I got my Gucci suitcase, mm-mmm, mmm-mmm. Honey I got that thing stuffed with forty-four wigs. Damn, I got no room for anything else in there but my makeup and some itsy-bitsy underwear."

She sashays up the aisle with her enormous body pillow bouncing on the arms and headrests of each seat, bopping deflated oldsters in the eyes, appearing like a parade float to the children.

Everything about this lady is a parade float.

She does not move with bones tucked in, the screwed lips of the meek. She bounces in slow motion, allowing her flesh to jut and ripple sideways. She has high, impossible boobs, so high they look like they might strangle her, an ass filled with magic gas. Her gray sweatpants hang low on her hips, showing the outline of a bright pink thong. Her face is heart-shaped with a button nose, ferocious brown eyes. Her lips are thick and covered with glitter, her limbs perfected by the rays of a thousand tanning booths. Her hair is the color of spun honey, held back in a cotton headband.

From where I sit, I can just see the man with his face going hollow in middle age, dark skin and a trim goatee, a plaid cap propped jaunty on his head. He has a wise but hungry man's grin; he's got a teaser of the bus ride to come.

"Your body is your business, huh."

As she reaches her seat, he swivels his body to face her across the aisle, as if she is going to settle down. But she can't settle down. She has to fuss, patting and fluffing the pillow and shaking her booty in the aisle. All the bus is a stage.

"And what business would that be?"

"I'm a dream girl!"

"Ah, that could mean a couple thangs. Girl, why do you have forty-four wigs?"

"I got poor impulse control. No, I need them. Ahm a runway model. I do pageants, sportswear magazines. Victoria's Secret. No shit. I need every one'a those wigs to be what they tell me to be."

She sits at the edge of her seat, and opens a professional makeup kit, so all the bus can see her opening its drawers and sliding out brushes and palettes of color.

"Ooooh, ahm lookin' rough. Baby I sleepwalked on this bus. I wish my eyebrows were still here. Where did they GO? It took all I had in here to climb on this bus. Two kegs last night at the Hilton and baby, I wasn't gonna let them go spare. Why do you have that beard, *paw?* How can your ladies stand to rub their lips across it? I tell you, I like my men baby-soft."

The man is chuckling at her, watching her hands move like a robot, squirting a gel on a wipe and running it across her face. She stops, puts the makeup case down, gets up.

"Can you read my shirt?" She cinches it across her bust and waist. *"I'm all about me,* it says."

A man in a seat in front of her gets out of his seat to crane his head and read it.

She scolds him. "Ah, you been here the whole time! Make up your mind."

She starts in on the creams, rubbing pigment on her forehead in a circle. "I have a shirt that says *Stop Following Me. I Have No Idea*

Where I'm Going. Man I tell you I've been on buses all week, on and off, on and off like a gypsy. The last bus there was this little kid takin' the cigarettes in and outta my bag and I said stap-stap-stap, don't ever touch 'em." She dusts a pearly powder on her cheeks and bobby pins a blonde bouffant to the crown of her head, right behind the headband.

"Ah, that's better. Does my hair look good? Then this kid goes into my bag and finds my duct tape."

"You got duct tape?"

"I'm a model, not a plumber." She is drawing precise lines around her eyes and lips. Circle every part to make it stronger, make yourself a cartoon. In fever dreams, in drunken sieges, through any haze they will see you. Across a crowded bar, a stadium, three blocks away—you cannot be lost with cartoon face intact.

"Depending on the job, I tape my tits, thighs, ass."

"Hoo, doesn't that hurt?"

"Man, it hurts more to be out of work. They tell you ahead of time what size they need. Coz if they say the ass is thirty-six around you gotta make it thirty-two, tape it down so it's thirty-two inches." She puts down her brushes and stands up to act this out: "Bikinis, now bikinis they like this beeeeeg," she pinches her fingers together, "like two lines, like my last shoot, little dots here and here, and tied around the back and this guy says, shit, that looks great on you, and I say WHUT does, my SKIN? The shoot before that I wore tees on top, white shirt, pink shirt, they all say stuff like this."

"Your ode to sloganism," Plaid Cap across the aisle says.

"Huh?"

"Duct tape," he adds.

"Mmmmm, you know how to talk to a girl."

He laughs, "You doin' the talkin'—all I'm doin' is sittin' back and relaxin'."

"My friend Columbia and me we get in so much trouble... eatin' Wheat Thins and EZ cheese, and hey we gotta lose six to seven pounds in one week and we do the chapstick trick. Rub it across your teeth and you don't feel like eating food at all, but your body needs somethin' to fill the gut. I do bags of soda crackers. I live on crackers, four bags a day and do this for two weeks. I get a ten pound ass change, just like THAT. And that is pretty damn good. I don't know how many models can do that in two weeks."

She grabs a huge white binder full of photos from her duffel bag. "This is my portfolio." She flips the pages. "Look at THAT. I mean let's DO IT, baby. How much ya gonna make on that, girl?" She jabs at her curves in the pictures, proud of what she's wrought.

"That girl…is that you?" Plaid Cap asks. "That's hot."

"That's me and my bestie Sierra. See we're up to no good there."

"What the hell kinda friends do you have?"

"Those two are Turkish twins. They're identical."

She lets the binder slip deeper in his hands, lunges across the aisle to go through the pockets of her coat. She readjusts, sitting crosslegged on her seat, broad pink glitter smile.

"Open sesame! I got more photos in my wallet. Awww, look, there's me as a baby. See? I came out perfect. That's my brother'n his friend Donny. They were arrested in a Civil War game for smokin' a bowl. They love those re-enactments. I love gettin' high. It just makes me want to get more high. Justin Stockwell, that's my brother, I miss the big baby. He's into Civil War shit, I'm not into all that. He's got Irish pride, you know white pride. He's inked all over, like an SS tattoo on one side of his neck, and I got mad at him coz he got to callin' my friends fags and I tell him *that's crazy talk*. He calls everyone with brown skin Osama. I'm tellin' you, he's off his rocker, but he's my brother. I shot him in the face in naked paintball. Two in the mornin' and he say bitch, I'm gonna punch your lights out. When he *gives* it—shit, I give back. That's somethin' I bet you would never guess, me bein' a model."

"What is that I'd never guess?"

"I'm an army brat. I been in the military since I was ten years old. Me and my big brother and sisters popped out our mama's pussy holdin' rifles. We were stationed all over the place. You ever play paintball?"

"I have not pursued the sport of paintball, dear."

"Ahm a big girl, ah take shots well. Shots…*and* shots! Aren't I funny? Five shots uh tequila and some coke and wham, it's 2 AM, I got my face mask *on*…and I'm naked runnin' around goin' 'kat-kat-kat-kat' and bam! My bro gets one in by the side of my head. I get up and grab my gun, climb up a tree waitin'. Kat-kat-kat-kat-kat. I got laser sight. I'm down and runnin'. Another guy is waitin' on me, but this big ass o' mine climbs and runs like greased lightnin'. Motherfucker got me, though. Had a bruise this big on my thigh for a week. Well this one guy has it in for me, I say all right, I can *play* that. I got a gun in my hand, you *better* not cross me. My mama threatened to shave me bald if I kept playin' paintball, and she did, held me down and got crazy with the clippers. She got a ponytail down to her ass-crack like Crystal Gayle, but she's goin' with those clippers like a fly on shit to my fool head. Looked like a Cabbage Patch doll for a month, had to wear a floppy hat in the family Christmas photo. Mmm, I'm all *sweaty*. I'm changin' into my leopard print pjs right now."

She bounces to the back of the bus and drags her suitcase off the rack and goes digging. I peek and see it is a long metal box, looks expensive. When putting it back, it accidentally slips and hits a kid's head. She pats the kid on the head, and he appears to go back to sleep. She disappears in the bathroom for ten minutes and comes back, rubs her arms and thighs.

"That's better," she says, "That's what I'm talkin' bout, baby."

She stands in the middle of the aisle, arms raised in a dramatic stretch. "We ain't been properly introduced. I'm Christa."

"Duane."

Next to Duane is a man who comes from Germany with an enormous skull which reminds me of a cantaloupe. He is pale with a long nose, heavily-lidded eyes that pronounce without speaking. A puffer jacket hangs around his shoulders. It is midnight and he is on his cell phone.

He says, "Mohammed, say hi to my sex-ee friend, Christa," and hands her the phone.

"Halloo? Huh? What's your name? Nah, I have a Turkish friend named Ahmed. Oh, my name's Christa. He is, we're on the bus. We're on our way out of here. We were in Portland today. Me? Fayetteville, North Carolina. From the country. Yee-haw!"

She turns to the man whose phone she's holding, says, "He says I have a mix of accents. Ah, like this? This is my Gucci Runway Voice when I'm working Portland…Mohammed, no. No planes. I take the bus when I do runway work. I'm terrified to fly. Oh, how old am I? Nineteen."

"Bullshit!" a man's voice calls from a seat I can't see.

"Ahm ALWAYS nineteen, son, and no sumbitch can take that away from me. Oh. My accent? It's Australian and Southern. Mohammed, sweetie, I'm an army brat. My daddy and his daddy too. I was born in Russia, mah mamma took me to the States when I was two. We were stationed all over. I learned more accents in modeling school. Hells yeah, a model and a dancer. Mah closet's all shoes and six cases of makeup and a shaker of baby powder. Belly dancer? Yeah, a belly dancer, Mohammed. Oh yeah, and in my closet I also have an Xbox and a half-ounce hidden in my secret penny cheerleading shorts. And luggage given to me by Gucci with a bb gun in the back. Oh, I'm provided for, baby. My ex sends me six-hundred forty-five a month in alimony."

"Mohammed? Yes, I'm his sexy friend…he's about to fall asleep on my lap…oh, oh…" She hands the phone back to the German, rubbing her low-cut pajama top close, which partially wakes him up.

Duane says, "Too bad it's dark. He doesn't get to see you."

We have been on the bus for five hours, heading out of Portland and through the mountains and high desert of Eastern Oregon. Forty minutes out a Latin woman with a life-earned face points to an eagle and we, even those on the wrong side, crane our heads to see. The bird is a speck of black in a sky of fading gray, flies with the bus, toys with the idea of highway before veering to terraces of sagebrush and snakes, and we, the pilgrims, along with earth, descend into darkness.

I think about the eagle, why not? I think about its wingspan, how all of us, no matter our ages, our rises, our falls, tried to see its wingspan, catch a single feather as if sight of it would give us something, we, the holy takers.

Midnight nears as we cross the Idaho border, and it is snowing. The bus gets stuck on a hill in a small town where a tavern is visible, wooden shingles of a broad Edwardian house. The bar has a name like Paddy's and already looks closed for the night, but many of us feel our stomachs leap, formulating a plan to escape the bus for a minute, just a minute, for a shot or a beer. Several passengers jump off to smoke cigarettes, and Christa is among them.

The party crew is just getting started. Night time is the right time. Tempers flare. The bus is stuck in the snow for an hour, and finally it starts up. The arches of a McDonalds are visible ahead and Christa is going:

"McDonald's? Can't eat there anymore. Might as well glue that shit to my thighs. Mah homegirl Tanya puts hooks in her thighs. It's nasty! She and her husband, they're into suspension. They get a high hanging from hooks."

"What do you mean hooks, Christa?"

She rubs her stomach. "No, that shit makes my stomach turn. It's so nasty I don't even want to say!"

"You've got to tell us now."

"I mean exactly what I said I mean. You pay to go to a club where they got chains on a ceiling with *hooks* on 'em, and people put the hooks in their backs and arms and other parts and just hang…"

"You're telling' me people pay to hang from hooks?"

"Oh Duane, they do…and dayum, I seen 'em on those hooks and they stay like that for half an hour some of 'em, and it's sick-nasty-disgraceful!"

"That is some *next level shit.*"

"How bored are you? If you gotta be mauled with hooks for kicks? Ah said to my girl Tonya, 'That's just sick, you out of control, ain't no sense in doin' that to your body, specially when you lookin' good in the first place,' and Tanya says girl, you gotta try it once."

Duane holds his head back and smiles.

"I been told by all these people I got perfect nipples for piercing, but uhnnnt-uh. Ahm not messin' up perfection."

Two seats behind her a child wakes up, one of many traveling with a grandmother who is sound asleep, mouth open like a paper bag, gray hair pulled back in a bun. The child fusses and reaches for a purse hanging from the seatback and finds a plastic-wrapped stick of string cheese. He wrestles with it, face knotted in frustration. Christa zooms over to him, strokes his hair.

"Ah baby, what is this?" she opens and peels the cheese, placing it in the child's hand, "Aw, shhh, shh, baby, mmmm, string cheese to please, yes, yes to baby."

She returns to Duane and the German. "Just shove it in, just like with my daugh-tuh!" She drags out the word. Duane does a double-take, looking at her tits and stomach and back up again.

"You have a daughter? What age?"

"My baby's two and a half."

"Gee…"

"She's at Fort Bragg. She's been diagnosed with OCD. She has to always have peanut butter with her cheese, and has to touch everything three times. My therapist caught it two years ago. My little baby Shaqueena, I call her Queen coz she prances around the room like a little queen…coz that's what she is. I was gonna name her Shaneesha, was nine months pregnant and ready to pop but you'll never believe it, I got this revelation, she has to be *Shaqueena*, and it fits! She and Ezekiel mah stepson and mah man all waitin' for me at Fort Bragg."

"You've got a husband and a kid; you're full of surprises."

"Oh I have to have a man. Can't live with 'em, can't live without 'em. Ah fell in love with mah dog, too, but I can't take it with me. I can't *wait* to get off of these buses, make my baby some barbecue ribs. I have to work mah money-maker on the road, but damn it can be hard. I go all the way out to Denver on this bitch. ABC models got this ass-backwards. I got a job in Denver then have to backtrack to Sacramento and Fresno."

"Why do they have you backtrack like that?"

"It's the model's life. Bein' in the military trained me for it, I reckon." She does a jig in her seat, raises her head above the headrest and peeks back at the rest of the bus. "Can't wait to get home and get me some double dips, muthafuckah…Mmmm, you heard me. My husband's first of the 5042nd airborne black berets. He's a green beret now, special forces."

Duane asks, "So how do you like hell month?"

"He's deploying on the 26th and I'm like biiiiitch, what you dunno won't weigh you down. I'm tellin' you, a girl gotta get some double dips."

"Ah Christa, how can you?"

"Oooooh, I found out mah husband cheated three times with me. I'm like, you still with me so I must give you better. He's like so long, goodbye, and then blink. You, Duane…Blink! He's at the door. I tell him, My pussy's better, so you back!"

She toys with the wig pinned to the back of her head, makes a growling sound. "One A-M! " she sighs. "Duane honey, I grew *up* a military brat. So now I'm a military wife. You know what a military wife is? An easy life. If the man says you better vacuum that? Basic training: I'm try'na find my kitchen knife. If I get quiet, you better be gone. I beat my husband with a sixteen-inch frying pan right off the stove, six times. 'Ah, so you're finally gonna shut up?' I say. Well he had to, coz he got his jaw wired shut! Then he broke the closet door with his knee!"

"Oh, you're bad."

"What's bad? Honey, the higher-ranking the husband, the meaner the wife. I don't like people. Most of 'em are boring and a waste of my time."

"What rank are you?" asks a man who is dressed head to toe in fatigues.

"Mah husband is 37-F, which makes me rude, obnoxious, mean…ah don't give a damn about people's feelings."

The man in fatigues has an overly sharp nose that reminds me of a wedge of cheese, forgettable white-blonde hair, face coated in a fine load of freckles, forever-squint. He looks at Christa earnestly, then at Duane, says, "Those are the best type of women for us. They keep us in line, no mud on the floor."

"You know what it's like to party in Fort Bragg? I'm tellin' you I head to Korea Town, the low tens to zero, go to the strip club. I spend eight-hunnerd dollars every time I'm in there. And really late at night I run naked on the lake. The left side is the Asian whorehouse, right side is strip clubs. I tell you when I'm stationary, I pray for nothin' but my nails, my hair and my toes. Mah husband leaves his credit card for me on payday. All's quiet 'til Friday night, then everybody goin' to everybody's house. We get drunk togetha, we get sick togetha, every one of us, every single one of us is shit up in each others' business from the first to the fifteenth. My brother's in the navy based out of Indiana. He come down and visit and get a tattoo, and the woman doin' his arm say I've got some fucken whacked out soldiers on this shift. I would never marry a jarhead. Army, tho—that's my cup of tea."

"Marines are bad," the man in fatigues says earnestly, "I never met one that made sense."

I think back to my marine-neighbor who said he competitively ate hot sauce, found a secret U.F.O, and got locked up for assaulting a female superior until her face was silly putty, and I am inclined by this one example to agree.

Christa goes, "I'm sayin' marines are cuckoo-cocoa-puffs batshit bugnutz and my whole family are marines. My dad was in 'Nam and he remembers bits and pieces. My bro came back from Iraq and fuck he won't be talkin' bout it for a while. I come from a line of whackadoo motherfuckin' jarheads!"

The squinty-blonde tells Christa about his time in Fort Benning, but there is no sex and no drugs and she starts idly going, "Oh, yah, Oh, yah," until she can tell he is winding down.

"Now, an army man I can possess. Unlike the navy they gots to have constant physical and psych evaluations, get their body mass checked alla time, along with their brains. Mah husband, he's thirty-eight now, he was a born athlete, track star in high school. He carries gear in a two-mile run, whoops ass for eighteen years and becomes sergeant. I love a man in uniform, when he comes home with his guns and gear and BB's, his automatic, and he tell me there's nothin' like destroying an attack briskly, that's when missiles start launching, let it rock. Thirty ought-six, nineteen with a thirty-three round mag, twenty-two hunnerd sawed-off, twelve-gauge, nine and deuce-deuce. My daddy just got a ninety-nine. My daddy has two SKs and he took me out to the shooting range. He takes me out and I'm terrified thinkin' this thing gonna blow my arm off. My thirty-thirty hurt my shoulder. SKs, you can bang in, immediately fire 'em, AK-forty-seven, Kat-kat! Whirl around. I'm the bomb! I'm the bomb. You know what else I'm the bomb in? Word searches. That's what I be doin' at first, while my husband's away. Then I find out military wives are not innocent. What you can get, baby. Does it look like ahm busy? I be paintin' my toes and my husband puts up with my punk ass for five years 'coz he got no chains...and knows it, too."

I just can't believe she has forty-four wigs in her suitcase or that she's hot off modeling for Gucci, or that she is talking without the use of amphetamines or madness, but what do I know? At any point when I think Christa's out of her mind, I think of why I'm on this bus. I didn't just break up with a junkie with eyes like glass beads, I pretended to be married to him for three years and just got a restraining order because he followed me around my apartment holding a steak knife that he refused to put down, and worse than the guilt and confusion of going to court with a man I already broke up with, I didn't even get my knife back because it is stored in a file as evidence in a skyscraper covered in metal shapes that sometimes look like bars and sometimes look like deco ghosts, surrounded by cherry blossoms.

And when I am single and alone for the first time in years, I get an email from a guy I dated for two months when I was eighteen, the first man I fell for in a way that I couldn't get up. A man who rode motorcycles and had a cop father and a halo of thick black hair that, like his libido, could not be tamed. He needed to date three women at a time, be on the run to another state to be satisfied. And what is satisfaction? You cannot blot out emptiness by becoming a song lyric.

"I'm in construction."
"I work in a vintage store."
"I need to ditch this popsicle stand. I have the wanderlust."
"I'm omnivorous for the new."
"Let's go on a road trip. Let's make history, Jen. I'm buying you a Greyhound ticket. It's been too long. You hear me?"
"Oh yes, I do."

And without having shared a conversation with this man for fourteen years, I pack a bag with a leopard-print skirt and hiking boots. My hair is freshly-dyed purple, and I don't know if on certain days I am real. It may be that Christa is more grounded than I'll ever be, at nineteen or ever.

"Oh I been hardened," she says, "I seen all kinds of stuff. I did my bizness on the twenty-first block of Compton. Two AM to five AM talkin' to guys. I hustled, if you know what I'm sayin'. Oh baby. It was rough stuff, I got a gun to my head. I was a lot of things to a lot of people. I seen all sorts of mangled bodies in war. I been hardened. I do what I was born to do—use men and be pretty. I love myself. I can't help it, I'm glad to be Russian and not white, coz whites have nothin' to say."

"I'm a thirty-nine year old black man, and I try to tell white people I have issues with them."

"Preachin' to the choir, baby. But goin' in battle, it's not what

I'd choose to do unless I had to. My gramma used to wake me up with a broomstick every day, both she and my mamma agree I came out swingin'. It's safest that way. I know how to give a bastard a machine-gun haircut, fully-automatic spring loads like a big girl. I's jus' visiting my sister after Gucci. You know my goddam fuckin' sister's like a hundred seventy-five pound black girl and one arm'a hers big as my neck. We goin' at each other in the front yard, that's why I have this busted lip. See the bruise?"

"She squared up good and whooped your ass," Duane says.

"My sister and I…one time we clip each other and both got black eyes. My mamma, I was blessed to have a mamma who was lookin' out for me. She got me into pageants early. You know what I learned early? Don't *talk* it. *Be* it. You know I did a photo shoot in a bikini and stilettos and I was all worried I'd get in trouble for havin' a tattoo on my buttcheek, but you know what I got for it? A Sierra Leone diamond. My next shoot I was on black silk sheets and the room was cold as a witch's tit. They had four big ass heaters goin' and the girl next to me her lips is turnin' blue. It's a harsh business but ahm a greedy girl, I gots ta eat. After my daughter was born I had to eat soda crackers to get back to a size six. Soda crackers and vitamin water. That's mah hair, string cheese. Who am I? Rick James! Mah favorite shoes, ah got shoes in my bag that I shouldn't even be tellin' you about, they cost more than all's yours rent. What I need now is vitamin water. Ah loves vitamin water. I got every flavor: Lemon, raspberry, and cherry. It tastes better than regular water. You get tarred of drinking regular water all the time. I got my niacin and biotin, and Vitamins b, c, and d, honey I got everything but the kitchen sink with me. Next year ah don't know, I may quit modelin' to just be a student and military wife. Mmmmm…I'm hangry! Where's my chocolate?"

No one can stop Christa. No one needs to. The truth is, she IS beautiful. Every part of her is perfectly in proportion. Her face, her hair, her breasts and brows and every line is drawn to exacting specifications. She has been trained, to a militaristic degree, to exude sex. Her body absolves the crimes her mouth commits, and its pardons extend years into the future. She could murder the bus driver, suffocate the kids, and still, the circle of men who ooh and ahh in a domino effect several rows in front and behind her would carry her to safety, to a secret nest, just like the secret penny pocket in her cheerleading shorts, all to hold, to lick, to siphon an all-redeeming truth from the symmetry of her body, manic hyper-life squirming like a greased rabbit beneath their hands. For surely one who shines so bright is not only beautiful; she is holy.

She digs in her duffle bag, comes out with a prize.

"Mmmmm…It's my favorite chocolate in the world. It's Dooooove…it, I dunno, melts. You know I love junk. Ah been addicted to EZ cheese since I was a kid. EZ cheese and Dove are gunna be the death of me." She flops her bouffant over her eyes.

At times of the night I hear her words phase in and out of my consciousness and I take notes as if I will be tested on every word she speaks in a pink notebook, smooth plastic covers. My fingers in their speed cannot afford to cramp. The small Latina girl who has fallen asleep on my shoulder leaks a heat like the Earth's core and this may be the closest I get to being a mother. Christa's words flow over me like music:

"I got kicked out a nail salon. Oh cha cha cha, hee-hee-hee, me and my homegirl we were talkin' some racy shit and we start laughing, makin' noises. Normally Oriental ladies are *thees* big, you pull 'em out of a shoebox and save 'em for later, but this one was *huge*, she kicked me outta her store and ah say, 'I don't pay this time!' and she just come stormin' up to me sayin' 'YOU GO,' and I say, 'Scuse me miss, the buffet is THAT way!' Well she got pretty pissed, and she all huffin' and puffin' front of me with her lip doin' gymnastics like this, and I notice she wearin' a crop top with this little belly button ring, and I say, 'Whu'd you get that ring for? To push you away from the buffet? You cut off at the chicken fry!' Ah tell you, I give sass back, you try to fence me in, baby. Now she freaken out and I say, 'Sorry, no chicken strip here, you can eat my finger!'

She waggles her middle finger back and forth in the air, until one of her many admirers says, "You're shameless!"

"I tell you ah get kicked out of a lotta places, like Denny's on mah eighteenth birthday, I couldn't walk straight I was so tight, and it was takin' all I got to just sit in the booth, order me some food. I sat myself up and looked at the little waiter, 'Give us some fucken peeeen-cakes,' and he go, 'Pardon me?' and ah say, 'Fucken flat peen-cakes, I want the kind that are round and purty, and I can shit out easily,' and these Asian guys walk by, gimme a look. 'Oh you, what you want?' 'Yer loud!' they say, and I say, 'Yer little. Yer fat. Get out of mah face.'"

She pauses, and says, "Ooo, cha cha. Ooo, cha-cha-cha. I'm not nice to people. Really I hate people. I'll look at someone I don't know, say you're ugly, badly dressed, ah just don't like yer voice, you make mah fucken ears bleed! I could use a lifetime's supply of valium to deal with the lot a-you."

"But you like us, eh Christa?" a man says from a seat I can't see.

"Passably. I back up mah mouth with *these* guns. One time I rode this bitch up the ass and had eight uh her teeth stuck in my knee. Right there. See that scar? Ahm all pullin' it apart and pushin' it together, and I tell you military does hand out prescriptions like candy, I was poppin' percs like skittles, y'all, and I betchoo I was perky. But you know, I gotta get my act together. Ah think I'll stop modelin' and go into Playboy…"

"Yer old man will be pissed with that," the infantry man from Fort Benning says.

"No, he's okay with shit ah do, bikini stuff and titties. As long as I don't do porn. See, porn is different. I want to feel like a sock in a shoe, not a hot dog in a hallway! Oh man, that reminds me of Cheddar! You wanna know why? We got this long-hair emo guy in Fayetteville we call Cheddar, skinny-assed like a girl, and he do anything to get his rocks off. We be outside the whorehouse and say, 'Hey you go in we'll give you five bucks, you bang Jessica, and you see, Jessica she ain't got much goin' on in the facial department. He goes in, with his face so white like this…and when he comes out he's got this look, and we say what's the matter with you? There was orange goo between his fingers. He hooked up with a girl name Crystal who be banging' herself with carrots, and he go back and throw a bag of carrots at her the next day. Oh yeah! I'll give you *my* secret blend of herbs and spices! That was pretty *naaaas*-ty. I tell you on the road you get used to ramen…but hot sauce fixes anything."

Duane has a friend on the bus who got into a car accident and was paralyzed from the neck down. Duane's brother was hit and killed by a drunk driver and ever since then, he buses to conferences for the survivors of drunk driving accidents. I can't see the man in the wheelchair, but I hear Duane tell Christa about him, and sure enough, she bounces up to the front of the bus, where the friend is strapped in.

She slides in next to his body, says, "Now you might be stuck in that chair but I bet there's still a lot you can do."

Ten minutes later, she is telling him about her taste in chewing tobacco: "I'm grizzly wintergreen, long cut really. AH tell you, everyone in Fayetteville dips. No one goes to jail for drugs, but I do for driving without a license. We gots a guy called Jerome the Gnome has a meth lab...and mmm-mm-mmm, the sheriff is bought. Whenever there's s'posed to be a bust the Gnome is gone the next day, movers comin' in...everybody's bought and ever-body fucks ever-body. You be fishin' somewhere and you runnin' into your own son or cousin all the time. We got this LA cop come in, the informant said he started to deal, two cops shot dead, only the internal investigations guy walks out. Somethin's happenin'. They don't really disappear; they just move far away, like the Salinas's. You know what they ship inside those trucks? I went to school with Jake and he'd tell me the cop got in the back of the squad car with him and with a fifteen year-ol' girl and a garbage bag fulla weed and they split it. Better to split it than let it sit on a fucken shelf somewhere. Cops smoke bowls and let 'em go, but I get busted for not havin' my mothertfucken purse with me!"

A man walks up to Christa and says, "This is the fourth time I've told you to stay in your seat. Nobody needs to see your ass."

She looks up at him with her long fake eyelashes, and bats: "You *dumb*, buddy. You mean. Why you talk that way to me? I don't want you given me no fraquito chaquito. I speak very good Spanish when I want to."

"Why you talk like you're from Africa?" the man asks her.

"Ahm from all over the place. I speak ghetto, Russian, and Spanish fluently."

When he goes back to his seat, she mutters, "Ah just hate people. They're so mean. Cha cha cha..."

There is no chance of getting sleep. There is no way my ears can stop listening, no way my hand can stop taking notes. Christa goes to the back of the bus, waits to use the bathroom, a belligerent bounce to her butt after being scolded. When a little old man wearing overalls comes out of the bathroom she winks sweetly at him and asks, "Did you wiggle dry?"

At 3 AM the Mexican family get off at a stop in Burley, Idaho, leaving an empty seat next to me, still warm from the heat of a sleeping child. I feel a loss. I will never see her again, feel the trust she had in a stranger. The bus is cold, tastes like Christa's soda crackers and steel. Christa is moving up and down the aisle, looking for an opening, and flops down next to me and my pink notebook.

"Hey, you pretty. Wanna see what else is pretty? Mmm—mm-mmm, mm-mm-mmmm. This weddin' ring."

"It's nice," I say.

The stone is huge, almost as wide as her finger. She tries to start up some chit-chat, but I am at a loss for words. I find myself paralyzed, as if I work in a museum full of dinosaur bones, and I'm comfortable walking around the bones every day, but one night they come to life and walk around me. She's holding a bag of M&Ms in her hand and offers me some.

"I'd offer you more, buts I'm a greedy bitch." She pours the last of them in her mouth. "Melts in your mouth, not in your hand! Hey, you a student, writin' in a book?"

"Yes," I say.

"Ahm goin' back to school, that is if I don't model for Playboy." She's up and back in her seat.

"Ah promise you I don't smell like a bed a roses, but ahm not tryin' to fight it. To be brutally honest with you, Duane honey, I bet I smell like hell. Red Bull gives you wings!'

Duane is shaking his head. "Just when I think I've fallen asleep. Ain't nobody stoppin' you, is there? You are a powder keg."

"Duane, honey. What you like in a woman?"

He lets out a long sigh. "That depends on the woman. What do you like in a man?"

"I need a manly man, not a five year old boy, a man who can throw me up against a wall, not pull out a chair for me. Ahm a *woman*...not handicapped. I can fend for myself. I got a *name*, fool."

At times the bus gets quiet and the smell of onion dip and old pillows and feet fills the chamber, a choir of mammals snoring. I peer above my headrest and see a woman with her head wrapped in a turban with a baseball cap on top, her hands, which were once folded, now fallen to her sides, one on her neighbor's thigh. I see the women with sensible cardigans and graying hair. I see white men with wheat-color hair and skin like paper who look religious, men who look like ranchers, a group of Native American kids.

On their dim night setting, the lights installed above the windows make me feel that we have been on this bus forever, and we are no longer traversing the cliffs and winding roads of Utah; we are barreling through outer space, and *have* been for the past thousand years. My wrist hurts from masturbating, which I did before packing for the trip, and I wonder if it is time to learn a new way of masturbating, because as it is I do it the same way I have since I was eleven years old. I wonder to myself if Raphael and I will have sex. I know it's foolish, but I imagine the way our foreheads touched when I was eighteen and he was nineteen, and it felt like a cosmos was tingling and created between us right above the bridge of my nose.

"I'd like a woman's opinion on this. Ah'ma gettin' two of mah wigs. Ah used to have long platinum-ass blonde hair, when I'd do it up in a bun it was bigger'n my head. I got sick of the blonde jokes. Why does a blonde wear green panties? Cus red means stop! Oh, no! I gots ta comb this one out. Ahm gettin a different one."

Duane turns to me, says, "You've been awful quiet. What's your name?"

I tell him, and he tells me about how he lives in Chicago. He was down in Dallas, and then San Diego, and Portland. He is traveling with the handicapped man, going to a string of conferences where all of the people who attend the conferences have one thing in common: drunk driving. Mothers, fathers, grandparents, and thousands of injured souls, some who lost half their faces, some, like his friend who can no longer walk.

"My brother was killed by a drunk driver. Since then, I've been working with organizations to get a class action lawsuit going. We believe that knowledge is power. We believe a thousand handicapped people traveling to conferences and discussing the flaws in the vehicles they were driving, discussing the flaws in sentencing for drunk drivers, discussing the flaws in the medical system for treating addiction, discussing the problems with bars and liquor stores selling booze to people who are obviously impaired, all of these flaws in the system need to be pursued, so justice can be achieved. Now I'm on my way to Denver, then back to Chicago. But Chicago is a very cold place to be, even in the summer. It's a *cold* city, like most of the cities of the north. The people are cold, the buildings are cold. I find myself wishing…for the warmth of a wife."

Duane confides these things to me, and I write down his email in my notebook.

I feel like I am a stranger having taken Christa's place. Is there something I offer that Christa doesn't? Am I speaking to Duane longer than I normally would, to feel, for a moment, the power of Christa's woman-body, what a woman-body can see or hear or absorb like litmus paper if it moves around a bus, puts itself in front of men?

She comes back from the bathroom where she was brushing and trying on wigs.

"Oof, ah give up. Not a decent time to be rasslin' with hairpieces, five in the mornin'. Time's to get a snooze."

The bus hums and rattles, and on the rocky horizon I see an orange glow start in the East.

The morning brings Christa, yawning and squirming awake like a kitten, wetting a wipe and attacking her face, opening the brass clasps of her enormous makeup trunk.

"When this box shuts, I'll be pretty."

The group of Native American children, one in a sweater covered in pink hearts, another with blonde hair in an elaborate braid, another so small he speaks with his eyes and fingers rather than his mouth, reaching for the edge of Christa's makeup box and she is eating it up:

"This here color eyeshadow is called *Orange La Creme.* I know, it should just be called *Orange. Blue Shampoo! Petty Purple!* Ah think I like the sound of *that* one, *Petty Purple."*

At 4:55 PM the bus stops in Fort Collins, Colorado.

I have been on the Greyhound with Christa and Duane and fifty other souls grown weary with sitting in one position for fourteen hours. My hair is fried with dye and looks like something removed from a dryer's lint tray. I have done my best to touch up my makeup, jab a curl of toothpaste in my mouth as the bus rolls to a stop. I have Raphael's cell number to dial, need to find a pay phone.

My eyes are locked onto Christa and Duane, and inside myself I feel the preparations take place to say goodbye to them, even if with a nod or half a smile, but as I watch, the bus filling with gasoline fumes and sweat, I see each of us has turned off from each other, lost in private calculations of Where We Will Go Next.

Protect Your Investments

The myth of progress which is secretly stasis imposed over variety to produce singularity:

Growth Boundary

Amidst a symphony of construction noise; multiple hi-rises erected like a modern Stonehenge whose purpose is to celebrate growth unfettered from reason; amidst the hammering, drilling and clatter of massive sheets of metal, I hear a man sing opera with a voice as big as a bloody slab of meat. He goes for several blocks until the city swallows his din. This man's voice is a flower in the barrel of a gun.

Tony (Hula-Hoopin)

I met Tony at an office party where everyone was an ad executive or a dealer of vintage clothing. It was at a slick meat-market-type nightclub downtown that was a step higher than other meat markets by having deco mirrors and people who read Jared Diamond tracts and always had bubble tea straws on hand to serve as impromptu day-glo pipelines of cocaine.

This party was deliberately a 'seventies' party. I remember putting on a jumpsuit and a bolero hat and thigh-high boots before riding my bike downtown.

I was living with an ex-boyfriend. Now ex is a tricky thing to say, at any time. This ex-boyfriend was a junk hoarder and he hadn't shown interest in sex for over a year and he spent most of his time collapsed in a chair reading vintage pulp science fiction. The darkness of his eyes and the whiteness of his whiskers made me think of a pussywillow trapped within columns of junk. Parts of the house were devoted to his boxes that he cherished but never opened, and at times the boxes felt so much more real and heavy than he was, these boxes he was paying rent to keep and haunt, a pussywillow-headed wraith.

One of my girl-friends tried to talk some sense into me: "You ARE NOT having a romantic relationship. Why don't you just change your Facebook status to single so that you can LIVE again. You are a woman who deserves love…." Blah-de-blah-blah, and it was true.

My ex-boyfriend was invited to the party but he didn't feel like going. These were HIS strange adult friends who ran night clubs and drove cars. I was starved for any sort of attention, so I got dolled up and showed up and commenced drinking.

It was here that I met Tony, a guy wearing a platinum-blonde shoulder-length wig that made its wearer feel like a cross between Phyllis Diller and Veronica Lake. Despite his platform shoes, he was barely taller than I was. He wore a sequined jacket and black satin pants that showcased the lean contours of his body. A feather boa inflated and deflated around his shoulders as he moved, a living amoebic thing, and he would not stop talking in a British accent.

I was a sucker for men like this. Halfway through our conversation, he broke character and became an American schmuck.

I suppose this is the nature of costume parties, masquerades in general: You can start getting interested in a fiction a person creates on the spot; a fiction that may not correspond at all to what the person is or does on a daily basis. So intrigued was I by this guy's coked-out jumping, dancing and joking, so intrigued was I by someone being a POSSIBLE NEW BODY, one who might like to go out and LIVE with me, that I didn't put much thought into this man being prosaic outside of this character he was playing, which was a British rock star.

We danced for hours to Donna Summer and other disco hits that a deejay played. I had empathy for the deejay; I was like a double agent. I imagined that the deejay, a fat man with goggle glasses, greasy hair and a black tee-shirt, would go home to listen to Black Sabbath or some sort of obscure Singaporean psychedelic music for an hour to clear his palate of the tepid bass-guitar that moved up and down like a yo-yo on these disco hits.

I could SMELL the money and boredom in the room. A lot of people here were from LA, and I could sense a sort of inarticulate numbness when I looked into their eyes. To try to speak to them about raw existential matters was verboten. This room was all about SUCCESS, SUCCESS, SUCCESS!

At the end of the night I got Tony's number. I rode my bicycle on a meandering route through Old Town, past a motley assortment of crack addicts who wanted to make love to my hat. I rolled on a bike path under bridges and around the grunting forms of entire families in sleeping bags. People were mummified in bags to the point you would wonder where the breathing holes were. But the night was warm and fragrant, still—only a mild chill in the air.

I got home to find my ex-boyfriend reading a political blog about how the Bush family has been in cahoots with the Bin Laden family to orchestrate a new world order for several decades. A week passed and I decided to set up a date with wig-man.

Tony told me to meet him at his ad agency—yes, an agency he was the head of. It was in an old brick warehouse downtown between Powell's Books and the Whole Foods grocery store.

The idea of going on a date with this man after spending three years with a guy who had only taken me out to eat once, at a Taco Bell—seemed full of possibility. I dressed in a simple black minidress and platform shoes and got on the bus. There would be no bike-riding in these shoes.

It was a late Saturday afternoon, a steamy one in July. The sun was constant, intense, grinding down on the shoulders and backs of people in the streets like a sheet of sandpaper.

Once I was off the air-conditioned bus, I started feeling rivers of sweat pour from my armpits and between my breasts, as I made my way to the door of the warehouse where Tony would be.

I buzzed the door, a door painted a dark emerald green, and I thought I remembered a nightclub, an all-ages psychedelic rave-groove-out place occupying the ground floor of this space ten years before.

Tony swung open the door, without his wig. The first thing I noticed was the pinched quality of his face without the curtains of Goldilocks Dynel to cover it up.

He was tanned like an alligator suitcase. Set into his skull were deep-set eyes that swiveled with the mad gleam of Rasputin. He had short and mildly-gelled hair, fashionably baggy jeans on doll-legs, a long-sleeved cotton shirt poured tight on his torso, sporty stripes on the cuffs, leather loafers. The look was moneyed, yet casual—a cross between an Italian soccer player and a sharpened pencil. His glance at me, a reptilian glance that spanned from my split-end hair to my platform toes, was efficient; too efficient. It looked like he had swished me around in his mouth and spat me out before I even made it through the entrance.

"Ah! You made it! Don't YOU look nice. Don't trip on the stairs!"

Without looking back, he started bouncing up a narrow flight of stairs. This was no ordinary dating game. He was about to give me the tour of where he worked, and usher me once and for all into the Mind of the Mad Inquisitor.

The transition from High Summer to Office Utopia was complete. The second floor was air-conditioned. Tony moved so airily through his rented rooms, like a helium balloon covered in lube.

We passed through several mini-boardrooms, computers left on with lazily floating screen-savers of children's birthday parties and tropical fish. I was mentally keeping track of how many employees this man must pay as I piloted my way through a maze of dry-erase boards, swivel-chairs, cubicles covered in collages and post-it notes.

I was thirty-seven years old and still looked like twenty-seven. I was not wearing anything weird other than a Cleopatra-worthy shellacking of eyeliner. I had been on the earth a long time and had gone out with a lot of men, but every single one of them, even the ones from wealthy families, had eked out a uniform lifestyle as unwashed artists in basement garrets and rented rooms barely larger than bathroom stalls. I had never even CASUALLY gone on a date with someone who managed this type of money or real estate.

Of course, it is entirely possible that this man was just an employee masquerading as the boss when everyone was gone for the weekend! It was a relevant possibility to consider, but the thought didn't cross my mind as I attempted to follow this man to a room with a round, Victorian-era window that looked like it was more suited to a turn-of-the-century dance studio than a place where people designed slogans to sell ink cartridges and microbrewed beer.

Tony fell into a seat at a computer and saved something he was tinkering with. He invited me to sit in a swivel chair, and offered me a cup of water from a cooler in the corner. As he handed me the cup, he looked at me in an uneasy way, and I got the feeling that I was at a job interview rather than on a date.

Tony swept his arm in the air to indicate four words written on a dry-erase board.

"I have this here to remind myself and everyone who enters this room what is necessary for valid living."

VALID LIVING? What IS this horseshit? I thought to myself.

The words on the board read: AWARENESS, COURAGE, DISCIPLINE, LOVE.

"What do you think these words mean?" he asked.

"Well, they could mean many things," I said. "At least in theory, if not in action, they are mentioned in the dogma of hundreds of religions."

"Dogmas," he said, narrowing his eyes and licking his lips a little bit. His voice had a sing-song quality that alternated with the defensiveness of an asp.

"I am NOT talking about dogma, my dear. These are true and tested VIRTUES that a mere mortal can live by, and in the process realize the immortality within."

"The immortality within? Meaning what?"

The man rapped his knuckles on a desk, and on the armrest of his swivel chair:

"We are beings of spirit on complex collision courses with each other. There is a grid of energy that flows underneath every one of these surfaces, and if you can perceive this with the right angle of thought—you can penetrate the boundaries of matter itself. You can move ABOVE and beyond the laws of physics."

Now it was my turn to wag my arm: "You are asserting that if you thought about it in the right way…you could walk through that wall?"

"I can walk, dance, or FLY through it." He grinned. "You of little faith! If you allow every act to be infused by these four cardinal qualities, you will be fully realized, living the path of a spiritual warrior. All desires are attainable. The world will lay itself at your feet."

I didn't know how long this would last, but it definitely didn't feel fun. I could not just listen to this drivel without a fight!

I said, "Are you claiming that the folks you see in the street, homeless dudes and drug addicts and people with mental illness—all of the folks who appear to be losers, are simply not living according to these principles?"

"People always make things so difficult!" Tony exclaimed. "The answer to your question is YES. And do you know what makes everything overly complicated? I detect it in YOU, as well. You are a skeptic. You are a Debbie Downer. TOO NEGATIVE!"

A 'Debbie Downer?' I thought to myself.

"Do you like games? he asked. "Let's play a little game. It is a game that you will find, in the end, to be surprisingly revealing. I use it on all of the new people I hire. They don't always get it at first, but they usually thank me for it afterwards."

His aimed his pencil head and his Rasputin eyes at me with a gleam of contempt.

"From here on in…you are forbidden to speak in complete sentences. You must reduce, or refine, all thoughts and perceptions to THREE WORDS. We must try to have a conversation with only three words at a time. For example: YOU FEEL HOW?"

"Air conditioned thanks."

"More deep down."

"Curious awake here."

"Still go deeper!"

Yes, can you tell? This was ridiculous, and even as I tried to maintain a glib demeanor, I found this guy's challenge to be both insulting and inane.

However—I am not a quitter. If there was to be an adventure to come, perhaps one that did not involve mystical mind-games, I was willing to stick around a little longer to find out.

On our way out of the building, Tony escorted me to a scaffolding above a stage set where he informed me that he had just completed a shoot of a music video. This was his attempt to soften the mood. He rattled off familiar band names, information that would impress a different type of beast.

Did it impress me? I was here, wasn't I? Was I here as a tourist?

The first thing Tony wanted to do was cook dinner for me. It was a five-block walk over the freeway to reach the supermarket near his apartment. The walk was hot and awkward, filled with moments (I suspect) of both of us wondering if we wanted to continue with this. We passed a Burger King full of drug casualties in pajamas.

Women with chocolate-kiss breasts and dyed pink hair stood in front of the flame-broiled Whopper Palace, severe and immobile, as if they existed in a different time frame. They stared at Tony and I like chieftains gazing from the celluloid contours of photographs.

I was racing to keep up with Tony, but my platforms made it

hard. I was starting to get the feeling that I wasn't even living MY life anymore—I was an appendage, a spectral voyeur hovering invisibly over the pate of this madman's fizzling brain.

Once he was in the grocery store, Tony raced up and down the aisles showing me that he made the best selections regarding bread, greens, cheeses. The floor was freshly waxed and my blocky shoes kept slipping. Twice I fell to my knees, and saved myself in a drunken way, even though I had yet to take a sip of alcohol.

Each time I skidded to the floor, Tony grimaced and muttered "Jeez, what's WRONG with you?" visibly distancing himself from me, as if the denizens of the supermarket might accidentally assume he was preparing a meal for a smack-whore.

WHAT AN ASSHOLE! I thought to myself, while salivating over the cheeses and wine he threw in his basket.

The dinner itself was the best part of the evening. We shared a bottle of wine while Tony made pasta in a one-bedroom apartment in a building where a witch I knew once lived. He had a balcony,' tasteful leather furniture, hanging plants.

The sun commenced its syrupy descent, and at this mosaic-tiled table where I sipped glass after glass of pinot noir, I could almost pretend to myself that I had a different body, a different name—that I inhabited a different city, a different country, a different year.

Absorption and release—that is what moments like this were about.

Tony told me a story about his bedroom being haunted when he was a child. I told him stories of growing up in Syracuse. It was at this point in the evening, before we were exhausted and sick of each other, that something human came out—the faint fumes of genuine feeling, or whatever name you prefer to use for the finer ratios which humans contain.

When we killed the bottle, Tony decided we should have a night on the town. The sun had set and he shrugged on a leather motorcycle jacket. After putting it on, he seemed to acquire a newfound strut, like a boy who in 1977 who buys a Halloween mask of THE FONZ.

The elastic hits the back of his neck and contracts, white and snug: THE TRANSFORMATION IS COMPLETE.

As we passed over the freeway and into the meat-market blocks of the city, Tony interrogated me on what I thought of his "costume." He called it his "costume," as if to show me that he was aware of the interplay of artifice to artifice that makes up the social dance. Having spent many years selling new and vintage clothing, I told him that his leather jacket was modern and probably purchased for around nine-hundred dollars from Nordstrom's or Saks' Fifth Avenue. I gave him similar ratings for his pants and his shoes. He approved of all of this analysis, as if I were verbally masturbating him.

We were both drunk and Tony yowled that he wanted to move his body, he wanted to DANCE! We ended up going into a nightclub close to Burnside where we discovered ourselves to be the only white people in the establishment. It was as if we had broken an unspoken rule, but nevertheless we had shown the doorperson our IDs, and were allowed inside.

Once upon a time this club had been a rock club, and then a goth club, and now it was an anonymous place that gathered pick-up artists and frowzy ex-cheerleaders with hair like dustbunnies and lone deformed voyeurs with several levels to drink in, state-of-the-art flashing lights, a deejay booth. Two huge rooms had their tables shoved to the sides, and for as far as the eye could see, young professional couples who were either Vietnamese or Laotian were having a dance party.

I was conflicted on whether to stay. I stared at hundreds of faces and continued to get confirmation that we were the only white people in there. These young and well-dressed people, with their clean bodies and elegant shoes, they were obviously celebrating something or having a reunion for a reason which we would indefinitely show our ignorance.

I wondered if it was disrespectful to stay. Tony ordered drinks and shrugged his shoulders and grabbed my hand, and in a way he had of moving like a funky guppy, he insisted we launch ourselves into the middle of the dance floor to get it on.

I danced for an hour in those platform shoes, and didn't fall this time. It was as if I had a superlative sense of balance now that several white russians and vodka tonics were installed in my veins. After leaving this party, we went to a nightclub I had always wondered about, one that had life-sized statues of Greek nymphs and satyrs in various states of pillage and seduction.

This club—it had a name like "Paradise" or "Nirvana"—it set its scene with grandiose reams of plush curtains, Star Trek mood lighting, and a velvet rope outside where several women in crack-revealing mini-dresses and flatironed hair waited to get in with young-professional boyfriends. Apparently Tony came here a lot because he said we had "V-I-P" status, and we walked right past the lines of yawping, dry-heaving, yet freshly-exfoliated people as if we were related to the Kardashians. These were drunk people with money to BURN.

Inside I met several members of the Blazers (the local basketball team), each who had a bevy of four or five stagger-drunk groupies. I saw bionic women who looked as if they had Crossfit memberships and waxed earlobes and deodorized panty-lines. I saw an assortment of young Japanese women with three-thousand dollar Vuitton purses that would still resell at eight-hundred a pop. I was introduced to several horse-faced girls in their early twenties who called themselves fashion designers. Each of them immediately complimented my vintage belt.

Everyone was moving in slow motion, leaning their arms, knees, even their ankles in the right way, as if they had finally "arrived" somewhere. It was as if they were conscious of being extras, if not the stars of a music video. I even caught myself feeling proud that I, too, had PASSED—in this crowd of people with cars and hi-tech stereos and jobs selling insurance or distributing eyeliner, or being stylists for lounge singers, or whatever these people did.

Everyone appeared to SHOW money, but other than vague references to athletics and fashion design, I was clueless as to what they really did, and like most of the clubs that Tony and I entered that night, I noticed that the MUSIC was turned up LOUDER THAN EVER.

In my early twenties I went to dance clubs, and the music was played at a volume that still allowed for conversation. In the bars Tony and I went in, you had to abandon all hope of conversation, which I figured was a relief for what seemed to be a shell-shocked generation barely capable of producing unscripted "likes" and "ums" accompanied by furtive jabs at their phones. You could eternally be a voyeur in places THIS LOUD! No one would ever penetrate your veneer, or "find you out" as anything other than a sequence of dry-cleaned fabrics and designer scents.

After a point I realized that it was too late to get a bus home. The weekend buses stopped at one AM.

Once I accepted the grim reality that my original bus-escape plan was foiled, I relaxed into the meandering boozy pattern of the night.

One of the bars we entered was a hipster bar with a "beauty shop" theme—in this pink and sepia camp-shack I recognized people I'd seen at experimental music shows, which gave me a laugh. On "my" turf, so to speak, these artists and bitter alcoholics would wonder what I was doing with this guy who looked like he had been mail-ordered from the Sears Catalog, complete with his own food pellets and storage crate. In the hipster bar Tony and I danced, and we were the only ones dancing. our feet making clomping noises on a wooden balcony that sounded like it would capsize with all of our jumping.

Tony and I danced wherever we went—well, it was better than TALKING to the guy! I thought to myself: I bet this guy has NEVER met a woman who can dance as much as he can. Despite this, I felt as much attraction to him as I would to a blood-encrusted kleenex balled between the seat and the wall of an emergency room.

Even with beer goggles, even having not had sex for a YEAR—even though when he smiled, there was an impish quality to his petite nose, his cherub lips, his sculpted, doll-like chin, I felt no spark. Everything about Tony reminded me of a doll, a wind-up doll, the kind that plays a little set of cymbals.

I imagined that as a child he had been mercilessly picked on, which resulted in wounds that ran so deep that he, even in his mid-forties, was embarrassed to be seen next to a woman who slipped on the floor in a grocery store.

He *was* an asshole, but I pitied that in him which could never be fixed. Not even the belief that he could walk through walls gave this man inner peace.

The time came that we had drunk enough and danced enough that he invited me to come back to his apartment. Maybe we could hit some more bars on the way, he added.

I suggested we walk the ten blocks to his place, but he drunkenly exclaimed, "WALKING IS FOR LOSERS! Walking is for POOR PEOPLE WITH NO TASTE! Are you KIDDING ME? WE ARE TAKING A CAB!"

He would not let this idea alone. We got into a cab that was driven by an old African man, by which I mean an immigrant from Africa, a man who spoke very little English, and who was playing a cassette of folk music—chanting voices with the metallic notes of a thumb-piano.

This was the sort of African music I loved! The sort of music that rolls from the earth of Ghana and Sierra Leone! The sort of music that trills from Niger, and south from Kenya and Tanzania, and is made of the heat and the rasps of old women and the hormones of lean striated men.

I wanted to stop hearing Tony jibber and tell the driver how much I loved the music, but it was hopeless. Tony kept drunkenly rambling his new-aged bullshit about rising to one's proper level of power, and how some people were idiots, poor in spirit and money, who had no taste, and by walking rather than taking a cab, one slowly erodes one's spirit and no longer is able to discern that one deserves to be moving on a higher path…

It amounted to so much nonsense and I kept my eyes glued to the face of the driver, who would think that I, as a woman, and obviously a slutty westernized woman, was guilty by association of being as idiotic as this jibbering man.

Good god! Why did I care what either of these men thought? There is NO WINNING when you deny your own individuality by starting to worry what other people think!

As we entered Tony's apartment building, walking past nicely-arranged dressers and chairs in the lobby, up several flights of stairs, I heard strains of loud music that seemed to echo through two floors of the building. As we neared the door of Tony's apartment, I realized that the loud music was coming from inside HIS rooms.

He unlocked the door, and a song blasted us in the faces. It was a non-hit album track of a nineties Annie Lennox release.

The whole album was on repeat, and had been playing for the PAST FIVE HOURS that we were gone. So drunk and loopy were we, that Tony had played this saccharine music, and DIDN'T EVEN THINK ABOUT TURNING IT OFF as he threw on his leather FONZIE jacket for a night on the town!

Tony let the music play, and made us vodka cocktails. Then he got out the hula hoop.

"Just *try* it!" he said. "It is an exercise in balance—mental and physical balance, where your mind is forced into a state of relaxed awareness where you focus on your pelvic motion, and your breath." With the mention of pelvic motion, I could see him lick his lips and give me a little wink. "I HOOP it several times a day!"

And there, in front of me, as I sat in a leather lounge chair and took sips of a concoction that tasted like vanilla and vodka and rum, I watched this clockwork man start hula-hooping to Annie Lennox at top volume at 2 AM! I sipped my drink and watched him athletically HOOP AT ME for a full ten minutes.

The voice of Annie Lennox sang: "Whyyy-yih-yie—ee-yih-yie-yie-yie—uh-eye," and I could have asked myself the same thing.

At this insane man's goading, I picked up the hula hoop and tried to get it to work for one minute, the man studying the contact of the hoop to my hips the entire time.

"Aha…there you go! There you go!" he exclaimed.

I never had a hula hoop, or really, any toys as a child. I preferred to run in circles and draw pictures.

Next Tony said he had to take me to a 'special place.'

"But—oh, you don't look very interested," he said.

"What do you mean I don't look interested? It depends on what the special place is!"

"You are just SO negative!" Tony hooted. The drunker he got, the more he sounded like a secretary trying to maneuver dollar bills into the g-strings of a Chippendale dancer. "Jeeeeeeeezus, Debbie! Debbie DOWNER!"

"Give me a break!" I said, "You expect me to act excited about something and you don't even give me a hint of what it is. What kind of businessman are you?"

One who expected women to worship him for his power, and his ability to provide alcoholic beverages, no doubt.

The 'special place' ended up being the roof of his building, where some of the residents had set up a small tomato garden and folding chairs. There was a view of the downtown skyline and several bridges.

Despite the lateness of the hour, there was a balmy quality to the air. The lights on the horizon seemed to twinkle through turgid clouds of humidity.

It was here that Tony approached me, put his hands on my shoulders, and said:

"Why do you resist?"

"Resist what? You?"

"Resist everything," he said, "You are a closed-off being. You will not spiritually ascend if you remain this way. At some point each soul is faced with the choice of taking the leap—"

I could see where this was going, and I was right.

Taking the leap into a new echelons of status and culture was to start by taking the leap into Tony's bed.

Being far too nice of a person, I didn't want to tell him flat out that he was unattractive to me.

I ended up telling him that I was going through a break-up, and even though I was 'feeling out' single life, it seemed that I was not ready to take the leap into dating.

"This isn't dating, Debbie. This is the cosmos." He waved his arms at the moon above and the city lights below. "This is raw experience. No strings attached."

When it became clear that I wasn't going to KISS THE DUDE, he hit the bottle hard and started insulting me for the next half hour.

In a way I was far more comfortable with this, because I was off the hook.

I retired with him to his living room, where we continued to drink, with him getting exceptionally glassy-eyed, mumbling about how negative I was and how I would never graduate to higher levels of spirituality at this rate, which was a stupid waste, and a shame.

He was in fact getting so drunk that I took a notebook out of my purse and started writing down all the things he said, and he barely seemed to notice.

At this point, it was nearing dawn.

"I have to pass out," the shriveled creature said. "Are you going to stay here? " he asked.

"No, I need to take a bus home. I'll just sit here a while. The first buses should be starting up around five-thirty."

"Fuck buses! What sort of a trashy weirdo ARE YOU?"

He fished in his wallet for a twenty dollar bill and threw it at me. "Take a cab. PLEASE!"

I felt tawdry and ridiculous as I took the cab-ride home from Tony's Northwest apartment to my Southeast rental house. After this man had bought me drinks all night I felt like a hired escort, or a stripper—even if I hadn't had sex with him.

The sun was rising over the stunningly green trees. The sky was a deep oceanic blue. The air was filled with blossoms and birdsong.

I hated living in the suburbs with a strange man. I hated how he told me I would never 'make it,' and I believed him. I hated a lot of things about my life.

I was depressed and had lost touch with almost all of my friends. I quit writing for a year. I quit almost everything, and chose to live on credit cards and the sales of go-go boots.

I was a 'Debbie Downer'—but in ways Tony would never understand. In the same way that junkies can sniff out other junkies, was it possible that an actor had sniffed out my act?

Five years have passed since the events of this story took place—and a part of me wants to believe that there are aspects of our reality that remain as constants:

...That even if the Earth suffers a nuclear armageddon of tragic proportions, or is hit by an asteroid, or if in twelve billion years the Sun goes supernova...that...hovering on a mile-wide chunk of rock in space there will be a brick apartment building on Northwest 17th with deco accents and a rooftop garden and nestled in a honeycomb of rooms, a man in fashionably tight-yet-baggy jeans with Rasputin eyes and a doll-nose will be STILL listening to eleven-decibel Annie Lennox on CD-repeat, and swiveling his hips in the circumference of a pale blue Hula Hoop, just a slightly enlarged version of the child who saw a ghost in his room and was mercilessly mocked for a being a nerd, so much so that he had to one day convince complete strangers that he could THINK his way through the atomic latticework of walls.

Besequinned Poodle

Why yes, I did just pass a woman in a nondescript winter parka with fur-trimmed hood walking a poodle in a tight-fitting sequined tunic. The besequinned poodle was weaving all over the place, romping from puddle to puddle, determined to show me who ruled the sidewalk. The woman called the poodle's name to rein him in: "Kafka!...Kafka!"

Lonnie

Why am I attracted to people like Lonnie? Because life is fragile and it is easy to fall apart and people like Lonnie though you see them on street corners looking nearly dead are survivors of incredible joys and pains, have impacted several lifetimes in one shell and their eyes are seeking something simple and universal from you if you are able to give the sacrament of listening.

But first there was the bar.

I came from an expensive bar where I drank an expensive drink, and on either side of my stool were trim men in carefully-chosen shirts, precise colognes featuring notes of cyprus, steel, bodies made by machines, maintained by secretaries. Some were on dates and some were in town for business and the football game. In the din of drinking and the clatter of silverware I could barely make out which ones were in the film industry and which ones were in banking.

One man asked me how the duck was, and I lied and said exquisite. I had no interest in eating a forty-dollar duck, but I watched as he did, and he nodded appreciatively afterwards with his meaningful goatee and wire-framed glasses, and I lied again as he agreed that the duck was very finely done and usually they are too tough, and I said, "Not here; the flavoring permeates the interior."

On the other side of me a man with a shaved head told me he worked in law enforcement and his specialty was managing cases of lunatics and drug casualties. He moved his body like it was oiled, accustomed to command. His voice could be sold in capsules for every man who wants "insta-strength."

How long does it take to get a voice like this? A cross between a bark and whisper? A timeless caress. It dismisses as it embraces. It could turn ugly if you didn't do what it wanted.

I didn't think about it at the time, but he would have done a double-take at where I ended up next. When I walked out the door I knew that one masquerade would end and perhaps others would begin.

The night was coalescing in a light mist as the last humans drained from office towers and stood impatiently, uncertainly, for the seven and eight o'clock tin tubes back to posturpedic beds and serial British romances.

I paced through the rain, aimless as a compass needle when the aliens invade, watching as downtown transformed and the night shift began and party people disgorged themselves from cabs and silver bullets. Kids in hats with animal ears and tails walked arm in arm as if they were about to solve great mysteries, and I saw her:

Lonnie. She was in the 12 and 19 bus shelter. She was doing a dance around a man with a beard and a hoodie and a star tattoo on his cheek. She wore a trim black trench coat, striped moonboots. An enormous plastic tote-bag on her arm said Buffalo Exchange.

Her hair was long and fluffy and very clean, and I was thinking to myself: "Once again I see a person on a million drugs who grows better hair than I could ever get to sprout from my vitamin-enriched scalp."

Star-Cheek had a dour voice, as if he was scolding her. "You see—" he said, "With all due respect! I can't agree with you. I can't believe in a god. I can't subscribe to faith. That's just the way I am. I need *evidence*. That's no offense to you."

"But it IZ offensive to me coz yer tellin' me there IZ no God! I personally believe in a God and *all* the things he's done fer me!"

Star-Cheek made an impatient grimace and responded. "But there you are...talking about *your* belief system. I said *I* don't believe in a god. I'm exercising my free will. What I do or don't believe doesn't keep *you* from having your beliefs."

The little woman with a mass of hair that seemed bigger than her body jumped on him without missing a beat: "Well Gow-ad gave you the free will to do that. He lets you NOT believe in 'im!"

Star-Cheek gazed up the street for signs of his bus, his head moving with a bird-like quality. "*Tell* me," he said, "How do you even know if your God is a he or a she? I need *facts,* not faith."

The woman was animated before, but now her arms were flapping wildly. She was jumping up and down like an orangutan on all sides of the man; she was covering ground very quickly, talking so fast her words would blur together and sometimes the ideas wouldn't finish. She didn't sound angry; just excited—even playful. Her voice was high and curled around itself like a little girl in a beauty pageant, chanting this:

"God created this werrrrrrld with freeeee will in it! I know God does ex-ist! And ANGELS? I seen signs of 'em. I know God's acted in *my* life!"

Star-Cheek must've been a glutton for punishment. "How can that even *be?*" he asked, "that a god can create a world and give it free will? How does that even *happen?*"

She buzzed on: "...and the rule of law, and part of that is to respect other people, and their opinions, like you should respect mine, and that means treating others as you would like to be treated!"

"You have faith," the man held up his hands in resignation, "and I require evidence." He gestured to his bus which pulled up. "I'm not meaning to hassle you or tell you what to think."

"Or disturb that pretty lady over there!" the woman said, pointing to me, "and her pretty umbrella."

I thought I would linger as long as this discussion was going on, watch the woman's mad dance; that I would drift into the rain once it ended, but things didn't swing that way.

When Star-Cheek got on the bus, the big-haired woman fixated on me. It wasn't hard to do, because I was smiling at her.

To see Lonnie *is* to smile at her.

"Wow! You really are pretty. Can I see your eyes? Are those angels on your umbrella?"

"Not angels. They're cats. But you could think of them as angels."

"Wow! Your *eyes* are like a cat too!"

She was doing an aerobic routine with each sentence spoken: Arms, fingers, feet could not be still. A plastic cup of sundae was in her hand (don't ask me why I have seen so many people eating plastic-cup sundaes on the rainiest day of the year so far—but I have!) and as she gesticulated wildly about angels and the rule of law, the soft ice cream would almost flip past the rim, over and over again.

At moments I wondered what kind of speed she was on, or if maybe she had done so much speed in the past that she permanently moved this way.

Lonnie told me she had just come from the McDonalds where she had gotten the sundae, and a man asked her to watch his stuff, and he went away and was gone for twenty minutes, and she couldn't wait any longer and left.

She said she was staying in a motel out by 82nd, and it was part of her transitional housing, and she had a case worker and she just got these clothes from the case worker, and she was so glad to have sixty days in transitional housing, and for an extra fifty bucks she could have a room near a swimming pool, and she was going to do things right this time because she didn't want to be homeless again after being homeless for a year.

Lonnie said that she wasn't supposed to have men in her room, though she had a couple in there at times, but they didn't fool around, the men just smoked grass and she said, "Don't do that around me, I don't want to get in trouble," but all I could think is she's on more than grass right now, wow-wee, as she moved, like a mechanical serpent in the air, the world's biggest six year-old girl with her pale aqua eyes, so sweet, a sing-song innocence in that voice that said she loved her god and her men…but she was *careful!*

A cop car went by and Lonnie tried her best to stop jittering and stand still, but she had too much energy, let out a huge jitter and her coat ripped off her back, exposing an enormous pink cowl-necked fleece sweater that dangled on her skin and bones, making her look like a demented fairy. As the car slowed and rolled she told me cops had thrown her on the ground and tried to shove her head in a toilet and they always try to get you to admit you are using, but you never should, because then they have the right to search you.

After the cop-car left, she giggled with pride.

I laughed with her, because we were smoking and she was telling me about the man who took her laptop last night…and where on earth would she get a laptop?…and she wanted to get it back from where he's staying in HIS transitional room, but she thinks she should have her vet friend she just ran into join her because she doesn't want to risk anything funny going on by asking for the laptop alone.

Lonnie said she's learned to be careful around guys: Sometimes they want to make out, or fool around, and it's tough when you're living with them or alone with them, and you have to figure out how to not make them mad when you're alone, because you never know what they will do. She had a guy who had stuff for her and in exchange she could stay with him, and have stuff, if she'd be like his housemaid, and she cleaned his bathroom really good, but when he said it was too clean and didn't match the rest of the apartment she had to figure out the best way to respond. Lonnie has a lot of experience with men getting angry for the little things, not even the big things.

Lonnie stayed in motels for a long time, over a year, with a man who used to be a pro baseball player. When she described him, her eyes went mooney. She rattled off a list of places they stayed, hotel names sounding like a song, sounding like train stops, repeating.

"His arms and legs were muscular, he felt so good to be in bed with, fall asleep with."

In a trance from the recollection of his muscles, she went on.

The baseball player got addicted to opiates because his coach and manager had him play through his injuries. He and his teammates tore muscles and dislocated their bones all of the time. She said he was really sweet but he got her using again, and she was clean for five years, during which time she just went to churches and was really religious for a while, and her best friend was named Janet Fabio.

Janet was a recovering alcoholic and she and Lonnie would go to TGI Fridays and Applebees together but just order the food, and sit there for hours, not drinking, and Janet would look at the alcohol and groan about how good it looked, but she wouldn't give in.

And Lonnie had to go away, when Lonnie started using again.

Lonnie liked to have fun. And she didn't drink much, she told me. She mainly did other stuff. Well…sometimes…(she added with a sheepish grin)…she drank a lot…and today she was…backsliding. She knew it, but she didn't want to backslide and end up homeless again.

"But thank God my daughter doesn't use. She hasn't touched drugs once in her twenty years."

Her daughter was raised by her husband's sister. Lonnie's husband was dead. Lonnie tried to get custody, but was nodding off in court, and had been up for several days and her lawyer whispered, "I don't think I can win this case for you. You are going to have to ask for visitation rights."

"And it was better this way," Lonnie says. "I couldn't raise a kid at that time. I wasn't able to. Her aunt is religious, the right kind of family. My daughter is beautiful…like I once was."

"You still are," I said to Lonnie, and through her wrinkles I could see great beauty.

I wanted to love and protect Lonnie forever, but I knew this was impossible.

I asked Lonnie where she grew up. *California.*

"I rode horses and swam in the sea", Lonnie said. "My daddy was a drunk and my mamma was a junkie. She sold pills and smack and she was damn good at it. My uncle was in a hardcore crime ring, but let me tell you Jen we had good times, we had really good times. I mean even when we were all messes, my momma and daddy and uncle held the family together. We even had UPS deliveries at 3 AM on Christmas day, so we didn't do so bad for ourselves."

Lonnie got a B-plus in English composition, and she went to college after she lost her kid. She had a son, but he's in jail.

"*And* he doesn't believe in God! I think the boy's dyslexic. But what do I know? For years I didn't know what the difference was between fiction and non-fiction. Is fiction the one that is true? Or is it non-fiction?"

The motel Lonnie is staying in has a king-sized bed and a sofa that is big enough to sleep on.

At first Lonnie slept on the sofa because the bed was big and scary.

"When I lay on the bed, I felt shadow things like claws or hands creeping out from under it and wanting to steal my soul. So I took all of the white sheets I could find and made a white halo around the bed."

"A halo?"

"A protective white ring of sheets. And this ring of sheets helped me fall asleep…finally!"

She giggled after this, and said: "You probably think that sounds crazy, right? White sheets couldn't have helped me. It was probably my imagination."

I decided not to be Star-Cheek. Lonnie's life was too short for another Star-Cheek. I said: "You had an instinct. You may have had that instinct for a reason."

"Wow! Thank you! You think so? Thank you!" she said. Again I saw the sunny smile of a sixteen-year old Stone Cold Fox in California who either rode horses or shot up horse and does it matter which one under the sun, under the sun, and every atom of her was beautiful no matter how dark the vale.

A man approached us and showed us videos of a person on a beach using a jet pack. This man was very young, very much a nerd, and he decided from his assessment of us in the dim and the rain that we would be able to spill some of our enthusiasm onto his phone videos of jet packs. He told us that these jet packs were in development, and would be the wave of the future. We watched for a minute as a small black figure in a steampunk-looking scuba suit flew in a horizontal line above a beach.

I could tell that Lonnie wasn't impressed. She kept laughing.

Another man approached us and said that he just came from McDonald's and someone had stolen his sleeping bag.

"Oh, I'm so sorry sweetie," Lonnie said to him.

"How long ago did it get taken?" I asked.

"Only a minute ago." '

"Then he's probably still around here somewhere. He can't have gotten that far."

"Yeah I want to hunt him down and slit his throat. It's gonna be a cold night."

He took one look at Lonnie and said, "Jesus. *You're* solid."

"Yeah, it's methadone," she told him. "I'm on five milligrams a day, but I tripled up," she giggled. "Now I'm comin' down a bit."

The guy mumbled about something he took that should last him three days. He named an exclusive-sounding college which he said he graduated from. He told us that once he had been a professional man and had a wife and children. He had been head of marketing at a car dealership, but then his life fell apart.

"Why would you give up all that?" Lonnie asked.

"My wife left me. I have nothing to live for. I want to put a gun in my mouth every day."

Professional gray-haired people at the bus stop looked over at this conversation with worry in their eyes, and then studiously looked down.

We talked a little longer, and the wannabe dead man said he better hunt down the guy who stole his sleeping bag.

He shook both of our hands goodbye, and Lonnie peeped to him: "She's got a boyfriend!"

She turned to me and said, "I'm lookin' out fer you. Us girls gotta stick together. You're my new friend! I don't have many friends."

I made sure to get Lonnie's number, which she gave me in a sing-song voice. Over the course of our talking, I let many buses go by, but I finally got on one, Lonnie waving to me and singing: "Goodbye, Jen, my new friend!"

I sat on the bus as it passed Pioneer Sqaure, where, in the misty rain, a large stage had been erected with blue-gelled spotlights aiming at a vast emptiness; a non-concert for a non-crowd—and I contacted the part of myself that would have stayed and walked around in the rain all night with Lonnie, hearing more of her stories, and maybe telling more of mine.

If I had stayed, would we have sat under the misty gel-lights of that blue stage? Would we have ended up walking across bridges? Sitting in parks? Would we get in conversations with an endless string of strangers, brief encounters? Lonnie never hesitated to give a sweet word to passersby.

She was a mother and child in one, and neither. You could call her a phantom, or a fake, or a haunted house. You could call her anything…a long line of yous who have your knowledges, your angles…but I felt a love for Lonnie, whatever she may or may not be.

"I will call her number in two days. I don't want to lose track of Lonnie," I said to myself, a burst of blood leaking through my pants and making a small red stain on the bus seat.

When I got off, I held an umbrella in front of my crotch so no one would notice.

A part of me is still with Lonnie. Or maybe that is a lie, like my comment to the man about the duck being exquisite is a lie.

Who are we, and how do we rub off on each other? How different are any of us in the end?

Pissed

It's 90 degrees and the streets downtown are filled with passed-out bodies, some using garbage bags as pillows. The nerd homeless play *Magic: The Gathering*, their asscracks splayed to the sun like meat pancakes. In the shadows burned and battered forms assume the cast of a Goya painting.

An Asian man in a wheelchair is covered with scabs and a flannel blanket that is more hole than blanket. A bulldog-faced man with short hair and a black golf shirt sits in a puddle of his piss, one pant leg rolled up so that he can adjust his artificial leg. He starts screaming at me for looking at him and then starts yelling to the entire street about his piss and that we should all fuck ourselves, and I can't blame him.

I duck into the airconditioned temple of Office Depot where I'm assaulted immediately by a blonde middleaged ex-cheerleader who droopily asks me what I want and when I say an ink cartridge I'm militaristically directed to a very large and pale clerk with bloodshot eyes who rambles a five-minute speech about the products and services they offer before giving me my receipt at which point in exhaustion she can no longer look me in the eyes as she mumbles goodbye. When I leave the store, the pissed peg-leg soul and his motormouth have gone. Once his leg is on right, he moves fast.

On the bus uptown a woman who has a laugh like a squirrel and a lint tray of hair questions the driver about earthquake preparedness and learns that the driver is saving her money to go to Antarctica. The driver promises to bring back a souvenir. What would a souvenir of an uncivilized ice reef be?

Squirrel-voice has eyes like cracked ice on a windshield and at times she speaks so loud and so fast I think her voice can act as a scalpel and sever my eardrums from the rest of my head.

They all mean well...enough.

Future Hymns

Overheard on the bus: "He opened up the bottle; yah, the big bottle and put a straw in it and handed it to me, and then I just disappeared for a couple days. I made friends with a sea lion during that time. His name was Morris."

She goes on about a man she knew who dismembered a woman and burned her body in a desert, and in a matter of seconds, she is giggling about her work schedule again.

These are future-hymns.

Fuck Waldo

Teenaged boys on the Max:
"Where's Waldo?"
"Fuck Waldo!"

YOUNG
GOD

Young God

I think of American arts and culture over the past 300 years and how so much of it can be analyzed as the behavior of a young god who has slain his mother.

Mother is dead! The god makes loud myths trashing her name, uses her hair to stuff pillows, lights bonfires of her flesh and boils broths of her fingertips. Her body stretches on forever! Her legend must be forgotten.

The young god finds a wife and has children and must provide for them. They need food, known as culture, a religion made of Paul Bunyon and Davy Crockett…riverboat men, hustlers, gamblers, and pioneers. They bow beneath the dangerous gaze of Lady Liberty. These babies sup on tales of industrialists. They pray for a new kind of security. They pray for the Future.

Mother is forgotten. Her bones are no longer visible. The young god and his children have forgotten how their energy and industry were born of the gap her death created. The young god is now a senile old god, grown fearful of the Future, of his own reflection. He no longer knows if he has the strength to go on. He and his children bicker, they watch *COPS*, they no longer talk at the dinner table. They no longer dream big.

Big is a lie for other people, people who have more, are born with more. Big is a lie for *other* people, people who are born with less.

The young god is now old and has forgotten his name and wets himself in the grocery line. The kids put the young god in a trailer outside the house where the nonsense he speaks, a disjointed series of what he calls facts and figures and warnings, is no longer audible.

Months pass and they figure he is dead but don't bother to check. They are afraid of the mess they would find. They have no desire to deal with the smell.

A flash flood comes and the bones of the young god's mother poke from the ground. His children are old, too. They no longer use language. They point at clouds. They point at foil pouches and indicate want.

The old have become young and the young may as well be old, for the young and old are equally confused as to what is real, what year they live in, what is fact or fable, who they can trust.

Mother's fibia sings in the wind a savage tune.

Diet Tips

Eat cheese bagels while web browsing photos of plastic surgery disasters until you lose your appetite. (I have a thing for plastic surgery disasters. From Pete Burns' lips to Priscilla Presley's Permanent Morticia gaze, to the unholy muscles morphed beneath the mug of Carrot Top! From Kenny Rogers' ruined eyes to Lolo Ferrari's radioactive (and now deceased) zucchini-shaped tits. From the simian collagen-mask of the Duchess of Alba to the scotch-tape skin of Mickey Rourke. Have you seen Burt Reynolds lately? He's outdone Cher, but he waited 'til eighty to do it...I can't get ENOUGH! Madonna has mysterious dents, as if her face gave birth to a face and then digested it subcutaneously. And I just discovered Michaela Romanini, the Italian socialite who morphed into a He-Man doll with lip-liner! There's the guy from Rio who went to Dubai to get his ribs sucked clean. They vacuum his back fat and shoot it into his lips, but he played with his nose too much, it's hit the point of no return. He looks like a portrait of Matt Damon rendered in candle wax and Kaukuna Port Wine processed cheese. There's the practice of women getting labial trims, I mean the SKIN, not the hair, so they can look as if they are made of bubblegum stretched on a pinky finger...wet with a preternatural spittle! From the extravagance of Almighty Orlan to Donatella Versace's transformation into the female Iggy Pop...I can't get enough! I can't get enough!)

It's Like Clockwork

Visitors to the waterfall crossed the bridge and marveled at the moss, the spray, the majesty of rocks below, rocks that seemed to grimace and roar as the rushing water hit them, however today there was an unwelcome sight in the basin. With foam lapping against its sides, the body of a naked woman appeared: young, lifeless, stiff. The body bobbed back and forth, seeming to be trapped in a cluster of boulders.

A ranger was called to assess the situation, and with a few magical words, the public's alarm transformed to laughter.

"It's the local fraternity. It's a terrible thing to do, but those boys do it every year 'round this time. It's like clockwork. Some years they use a blow-up doll, and some years they go all out and get a department store mannequin...They haul 'er up the bridge here, and toss 'er in."

Visitors to the waterfall remarked on what a lifelike mannequin this was, and shaking their heads with emotions they could not quantify, they moved away from the grisly view.

After three days the mannequin began to change in appearance; it grew softer, grew strange. It appeared to have been bitten. It changed size.

The laughter ceased.

Gold Knows It Will Prevail

Indigenous rights activist Winona LaDuke says: "If you make the victim disappear, there is no crime."

In 1637, Massachusetts Bay Colony governor John Winthrop, a Puritan lawyer who waxes long about building a "shining city on a hill," starts a holiday. He proclaims "Thanksgiving for the successful massacre of hundreds of Pequot Indian men, women, and children."

We observe this day of Football, Macy's televised parade, 100-foot-high helium-filled mice; Spidermen and clowns and pumpkin-spice lattés; antacids and DUIs, collections of pink bodies who must pop pills to tolerate each others' company, protected by pink insulation in walls; rows of dollhouses filled with the smell of roasted foul.

In the Phips Proclamation of 1775, King George II calls for his subjects "to embrace all opportunities of pursuing, captivating, killing and destroying all and every of the aforesaid Indians."

Bounty hunters are paid 50 pounds for adult male scalps, 25 for women, 20 for children under twelve.

The 1814 "treaty" with the Creek Nation has an aim to break up communal social structures. The conquerors select a handful of men to bribe with land, leaving others out—creating a caste of untouchables, spreading Western capitalism along with measles, smallpox, typhoid fever.

Starched collars, violin rosin; city on the hill lined with blood-filled spitoons.

The Creek-Muscogee, known as mound-builders: Their Southeast cities, look like pyramids with the tops lopped off. Some for burial, religious practices, platforms for dancing. Some hold houses and observatories. They go back a thousand years, archaeologists say, but stopped around 1600, when Europeans came.

The Creek-Muscogee territory spans Tennessee, Alabama, Georgia, Florida…

Does it not feel like it goes on *forever?*

Seized for King Cotton, the Creek avenge their dead, lost fields and trees and streams and children, which impels future-president Andrew Jackson and his men to slaughter with rebounding fury at Tallushatchee.

"We shot them like dogs!" shouts Davy Crockett, *King of the Wild Frontier.*

As the white invaders surround their town with hatchets and guns, Creek women smother their children before the soldiers reach them.

One mother starts to kill her young and she is slain and Andrew Jackson plucks a baby from her arms.

Soldiers deliver the child to his wife Rachel, to raise as their own.

Jackson has dreams of sending him to West Point, but the boy, named Lyncoya, prefers to tend horses. He dies of tuberculosis at eighteen.

After Jackson's victory at Horseshoe Bend, a treaty is drawn that requires the Creek to surrender 21 million acres of land to the conquering army.

Jackson Sez: "Friends and Brothers: By permission of the Great Spirit above, and the voice of the people, I have been made President of the United States, and now speak to you as your Father and friend, and request you to listen. Your Father has provided a country large enough for *all* of you, and he advises you to *remove* to it. There your white brothers will not trouble you; they will have no claim to the land, and you can live upon it you and all your children, as long as the grass grows or the water runs, in peace and plenty. It will be yours forever. For the improvements in the country where you now live, and for all the stock which you cannot take with you, your Father will pay you a fair price…"

Andrew Jackson is the ultimate consumer.

From 1830 to 1840, federal troops escort 60,000 people—Choctaw, Creek, Cherokee—from the East in "exchange" for land west of the Mississippi.

The West or your death.

They are led at gunpoint. Marched from rich green hills and swampland to plains of scabrous rocks, tall yellow grasses: Tribal elders go slowly and the wind is barren, and they no longer feel their fingers and they fall.

Thousands die on the Trail of Tears.

Under Lincoln's rule, military officials hang 38 Dakotas on a raised platform.

4,000 whites with picnic baskets camp in the streets to celebrate the spectacle before the bodies are moved to a shallow grave.

In darkness doctors raid the grave. Their burning desire to study the bodies of aliens knows no bounds.

Armstrong Custer and his 7th Calvary, which he boasts is composed of hard-drinking Irishmen, advance through the West. Custer says: "They are no match for us," and he orders his men to leave no breathing one in villages of sleeping women.

Overcome by certainty, he dies at the hands of Crazy Horse's warriors on a hill.

The Lakota, Northern Cheyenne, Arapaho: There is Spider-Above and Spider-Below. Spider Below, when weaving in and out of human spaces, plays games, hides food, brings about murder. In some translations, the name, Nihancan, is stated as White Man, but Spider wove before the pink arrived to force the tribes away from their Great Lakes and south, to a land of ghostly sage where air presides over rock without contest.

The Ghost Dancers of South Dakota: Wovoka, their leader, has a vision during an eclipse of his people returning to the old ways.

He says it is wrong to sign treaties, to plead, to assimilate, look for mercy in the white man, as your reservation is carved in five pieces to make way for white homesteaders, then made smaller for seekers of gold.

Ghost Dancer Sitting Bull resists, is shot between the tenth and eleventh rib in the moment of his arrest.

Navajos reject the Ghost Dance. Blood has tainted its name.

The Blackfoot, the Cheyenne, the Sioux: Ulysses S. Grant says the extinction of the buffalo is the solution to the country's "Indian Problem."

30 million bison are slain to ensure that the nomads of the plains go hungry. One expedition, featuring celebrity sharpshooter Bill Cody involves an army-supplied escort of 25 caravans of fresh linen, silver, and a traveling icehouse of chilled wine.

Express trains surge from the East promising a safari unlike the men inside have ever known:

In baggy pants, eyes red with liquor, teeth loose from sweets, collars soiled with the sweat of traveling in a tin car through long stretches of 100-degree heat, men drop their cards and pick up guns. They shoot from open windows at the first broad-browed bulls of spring, and being poor marksmen, their shots render each bull's hide too damaged to fetch a price.

Mothers weep. Sioux Hunters Weep. Comanches weep. Death closes in on them from every horizon as if they have been cursed.

In the course of two years the buffalo are driven to the brink of extinction. Millions of carcasses are left to rot, their deaths too plentiful to be itemized for profit.

Skulls are stacked in piles three stories high, resemble candelabras. Starving tribes are left to collect the bones and sell them to homesteaders as fertilizer.

White settlers are filled with a sense of foreboding to enter the plains.

The Indian Appropriations Act of 1781 states that the United States government will no longer recognize the sovereignty of tribal nations.

"A war of extermination will continue to be waged between the two races until the Indian race becomes extinct." —*California Governor Peter H. Burnett, 1851*

The State of California in concert with Papa Washington spends $1.7 million on campaigns to empty the territory of every member of every tribe.

The rush for gold rots brains and makes hands crumble like dust. The goldfields of Northern California lie in the ancestral lands of the Karuk, the Wintu, and Miwok.

Army and cavalry detachments surround and kill 800 men and women of the Pomo tribe. It takes five days to lift the bodies from the land.

Women with wombs slashed, arms raised to plead for mercy, arms broken. Eyes protected only by hair and midnight rain, proximity to final night. Hundreds are taken as slaves. Gulches stacked with bones; hunters compete for who can best hit the children who stray from the herd.

Cavalrymen wear fetuses on their shoulders like epaulettes, female genitalia on their hats.

Testicles are turned to tobacco pouches; fingertips mailed to wives and sons as trophies.

Reservations where men are fed less than bread, and their skin grows so thin on their bones it is as if they are made of paper and yet they are given more paper, told they must move.

White ranchers track a group of Yana to a cave and shoot thirty men.

"In the cave with the meat were Indian children," says a witness. One of the ranchers "could not bear to kill these children with his 56-calibre Spencer rifle. It tore them up so bad. So he did it with his 38-calibre Smith and Wesson."

Sacred land remains, barely. Driven to the places of cold and desert and no arable ground, children stolen by social workers for the final act of relocating the young, should the natives choose to procreate and the forced sterilization that took place with "check-ups" until the 1970s does not hold:

The reservation at Standing Rock is filled with trailer homes and heroin.

Banks refuse to give loans on the property. The emergency room is shut down for unsanitary conditions.

The bounty of freedom, "as long as the grass grows or the water runs, in peace and plenty"—the forever, *forever*, did not come through.

Private security firms paid for by petrodollars surround the tribe and pellet them with a bounty of rubber bullets, tear gas.

Oil knows it will prevail.

Gold knows it will prevail.

Social media is filled with images of shattered arms, hypothermia, elders thrown on ice.

Social media shows attack dogs, a treaty signed by Obama saying *we will honor your ties to the land.* Then the water cannons come.

The Dakota Access Pipeline is a $3.78 billion construction meant to shuttle crude oil across Sioux burial grounds and the Missouri River to a destination in Texas.

The corporations vested in its completion are Energy Transfer Partners, LP, and Sunoco Logistic Partners, LP—38.2%, Enbridge—27.6%, Phillips—66-25%, Marathon Petroleum—9.2%.

The investors in the pipeline are Citibank, Wells Fargo, BNP Paribas, SunTrust, Royal Bank of Scotland, Bank of Tokyo-Mitsubishi, Mizuho Bank, TD Securities, ABN AMRO Capital, ING Bank, DNB ASA, ICBC, SMBC Nikko Securities and Société Générale.

One year after the pipeline has been in use, it has sprung multiple leaks, but not so many as to get in the way of profit.

One year after the pipeline has been in use, the men and women of Standing Rock cannot look in that direction to see what they have lost.

They are supposed to die.

December 2017: An announcement by President Trump on Monday in Salt Lake City. Two national monuments will be portioned and sold:

The Bears Ears National Monument will be reduced by 85%, and Grand Staircase-Escalante will be reduced to half its current size, a total sale of 2 million acres. It is the largest cut to federally-protected land in U.S. History.

"Some people think that the natural resources of Utah should be controlled by a small handful of very distant bureaucrats located in Washington. And guess what? They're *wrong.* Together, we will usher in a bright new future of wonder and wealth." *—Donald Trump.*

Gold knows it will prevail...like General Armstrong Custer.

Cuckoo Clock

Jeff Bezos to spend $42 million turning a mountain in Texas into a cuckoo clock that runs for 10,000 years, says this will INSPIRE the human race to have "long-range thinking," tho I personally think sinking this amount into the nation's public schools as a "Bezos Subsidy" to improve literacy might be a better example of long-range thinking, and insure a handful of Americans are left to read all the books Amazon sells. But seriously folks, in my opinion our government would LOVE to phase out brick and mortar schools altogether and replace them with standardized test prep taught by state-mandated personalized droids (at heavy consumer cost) to pod-children who will be allowed 6 hours a day max wakefulness and spend the rest of each day sedated in virtual reality coffins. THE FUTURE IS NEARLY NOW.

As American As . . .

As American as Napalm and Four Loco
As American as bottled water and rivers of fire
As American as getting dental work done in Mexico
As American as a landfill of Barbie doll heads and broken bb guns
As American as bath salts and Honey Boo-Boo Weight Loss Tricks
As American as funding ISIS so oil stays at $30 a barrel and Lockheed
Martin stocks rise higher than the sun
As American as the Unabomber and John Henry
As American as Malcolm X
As American as embryo porn and the 700 Club
As American as Tammy Faye Bakker's Ghost
As American as Diane Arbus and Vivian Maier
As American as the nuclear reactors that must be maintained for
another forty thousand years by priestly descendants who will not be
here, not be here
And Now Let Us Praise Famous Men as the Earth Burns
As American as an oil rig given the Utopian name Deepwater Horizon
As American as swiping right and ordering ramen on Amazon Prime
It is never too late to become new
It has something to do with an eternal digital afterlife, and pralines

Masculinity 101

A car goes by with a bass that makes the windows in the building shake in a lazy tune, a tune that sounds like five-foot-tall testicles stuck in an alley, stuck in a doorway, rolling in the refrigerated custard aisle. Five-foot-tall testicles slap against our cheeks, have nostrils and birth certificates, need to vote, get government subsidies, buy their own island. Five-foot-tall testicles are forming a band, taking growth hormones, making private inquiries about electrolysis. Five-foot-tall testicles dream of a day when they grow so large they shift the magnetic poles and make the moon crash into sea. Five-foot-tall testicles need to know you're the one and the only one, all seven billion of you.

Aqua Rave Headphones

The lonely man on the bus with a shaved head and aqua rave headphones is casting his net far and wide. After I get on, his gaze lingers on my head and shoulders a long time while I gaze out the window and do the "It isn't going to work" posture. His gaze lingers on every female between the ages of 16 and 60, finding no fruit or fate in the seventy-something immediately in front of me with hair tinted a green-toned umber; hair so sculpted and translucent in its froth that it reminds me of a macaroon on display in the window of a boulangerie. The old lady's nails are glossy, manicured a cherry red. Her jacket is a Chanel knockoff.

The man in aqua headphones wears sunglasses on top of his head, as if he has an extra pair of eyes up there to search for women who may be on the ceiling, too.

He resolves his focus on the woman immediately across from him in the "reserved for elderly and handicapped" seats. Neither he or this woman are elderly or handicapped from what I can see. The lady is somewhere in her late thirties with long black hair, aviator sunglasses, and clothes that in their trendiness perfectly match the beige and denim hues of what the man has on. She is holding a thick leather purse on her lap and chewing gum.

The man starts telling her how it is such a beautiful day and he was wearing a coat because he didn't expect it would be so warm and how he was just working out at the gym and hanging out with "buddies" (I somehow don't believe the latter part with how starved for attention he seems) and...hey girl, what are you up to on this sunny afternoon?

She is smiling stiffly, answering each of his questions with monosyllables. As he proceeds to question her, she takes on the glazed quality of someone at a job interview, or even worse, she is forced to make nice with a dental technician who is flirting with her as he scrapes a chrome pick across her molars (which has happened to me, on this planet everything has happened at some point) and her nail polish is the same aqua color as his rave earphones, maybe they are a match made in purgatory.

He comments that her bracelet must be new and then he says, "Hey sorry, am I giving off a weird sex vibe?" which would make a lot of women say piss off but she is not that kind of woman, and she nervously smiles, and he asks if he can get her number and she says, "perhaps," and she is very nervous now.

He says, okay, okay, well can I give you mine? As if on a tether she painfully crosses the bus aisle to sit next to him so that she can enter the digits of his number on her phone and I bet this dude cannot believe his luck, he just got a woman who clearly never wants to speak to him again to sit next to him BECAUSE SHE IS POLITE!!!

Believe me, I know the ladies who were raised to be exotic flowers and handmaids, believe me I know how the choker of politeness bites when men ask for anything from you, and I delight in a strange way at this man's surprise that her warm body is right next to him; I suspect he doesn't get much success, and beneath his bravado he is a forty-something child who is aging well with the studious application of moisturizers and despite what both of them are projecting these two may be very good for each other in the end, but they will never know because she will not ever, ever…call him back….or will she?

Sideways Lightning

She grew up in mound country and no matter what happened with her parents she could go to her grandparents' house which was built on the biggest mound of them all. The oldest civilization of mound-builders in the nation thrived here, however conquerors can only speculate on what the purpose of these mounds were; whether or not the mounds were for ceremonies or for farming or war, or they were portals for spirits to congregate before moving to other places.

Her grandmother had a red face and a blue boy under the stairs, and when she visited she could feel the blue boy with his glowing face follow her with his eyes.

Corners of the living room floor would sink and maggots spilled from the holes in ways that could not be explained, and she grew up and went away and flew a sign and many men wanted to tame her, and the sideways lightning was paid for and passed through her veins, and something to be in the future means nothing in comparison.

It went too far and she needed to be tied to the bed, and she sweat and she screamed, and it took many days of every cell in her body filled with the sickness, and she made sounds like childbirth and peeled the skin from her arms, and her granddaddy was downstairs and his legs could barely work, but he could not bear what he heard issue from her throat so one by one he crawled up those stairs on his elbows because his love was vast like a constellation and her pain was breaking his heart, and it is like a ship, the house listing, listing on the largest of the mounds, and it rumbles and it contracts as if the confines of its occupants' bodies cannot bear the magnitude of their souls.

It's a Small World Adderall

She works in the circus. She travels half the year and when the winter comes she stays in the north woods and hunts and eats her own venison, tries to provide for her son, but he is hooked on easy opiates and adderall and whatever his friends can get a bead on because you are old and dumb if you don't realize that one out of every four kids has gotten into oxy or cocaine or at least LSD before their first wet dream.

In a land of megachurches and selfies, we need a fix that's nearer, gets under skin.

She grew up on the border of Nashville and everywhere else and her uncle built a fallout shelter in the heart of his home.

"One day he took me down to the bunker, included me and mine in his doomsday plans. I grew up believing I was destined to be a country singer. He said, *When war begins the enemy will hit Oak Ridge first. From the time you see the explosion you will have two hours to get to this bunker. I have added all provisions to accommodate you.* Well I said *thank you, but when the end comes I'm not staying here. I'm going with all those other people. They aren't leaving me here.*"

And the bomb hasn't dropped but there is fallout everywhere.

Bearing Light

The go-cart drivers have gotten off their prime time airport shift. The oldest man does stand-up comedy about the people they are obliged to ferry and how poorly they tip, and one driver commences to discuss the ways in which young black women of this generation need to be "tamed" because they have expectations of men being abusive like on rap videos, rather than filled with a Christian Family Man's love. He thinks Tupac was a genius but walked with Lucifer, the glamorous "shining angel."

"People think Hell is darkness, a sort of darkness like we recognize darkness in this world, but it is not. Lucifer is the bearer of incredible light…and his hell is made of light that our greatest Earthly cities cannot produce."

Circus Bike Girl

I was at the intersection, rush hour traffic, and buying a coffee. As the machines whirred my liquid to life, I watched the progress of a woman with purple hair and a floral-patterned sundress on one of those twelve-foot high circus bicycles that make a person a sitting duck as the cars try to literally drive over each other to get to the homes their drivers resent having to pay for and die in. And this woman, she was on this bike and she was a-teeterin'. The heat, the sweat, the purple hair, the gleam of metal that cannot in itself be angry, yet it feels so during rush hour: All the sunburned office-hawks in their air-conditioned pods, and this woman suspended so-so-high in the air, the bike quavering, seeming to almost crash into every car that passed, but she smiled like a trapeze artist, like an astronaut, and kept on fluttering through. She made it, and pumped away. If she wasn't smiling, I bet she would've got a hundred honks. A few years ago I saw an entire family, a mother duck leading her ducklings across this same rush-hour intersection, and the speeding bullet-hawk-machines stopped in their progress with awe and confusion, the same way they did for the purple-haired circus girl.

Runaways

The old man is Irish, his body has emerged, fully formed, from a 1968 National Geographic exposé of the Aran Islands like Venus from the frothy shell.

His balding pate has a fresh scar. His sweatpants are highwaters; any pants on his nearly seven-foot frame would be. The hollows under his eyes are violet. His sneakers are nuggets of coal. The green-haired barista girl eyes Aran Islands with suspicion after her bearded coworker serves him a delicate China cup of coffee.

He has a shaking disease. Sometimes his bony hands cling to the hem of his enormous t-shirt. His body rocks as if he has been strapped into a roller coaster. Sometimes he holds his own hand and whispers words that sound like raindrops over the Japanese pop that plays here.

He was across the room, then he plopped down beside me, smell of mothballs, eyes closed in private vision.

A brunette girl in a miniskirt and clean white sneakers asks him how he is. She is somebody's granddaughter, will one day be a mother, and she invites him to sit at her table in the sun. He takes a moment to escape his fugue, return to the world of talking.

Now they are together, his smile, her skateboard, her maraschino red puffer vest.

The girl asks steady questions about his life, asks if he has enough groceries. He tells her he usually eats frozen foods.

They run out of words, but smile at each other.

Eventually they find more words, about his record player, and rock and roll, the voice of a female singer fluttering in the air like a feather a kitten bats across a room.

"I really like the Carpenters." she says.
"Oh yes. Oh yes, I like the Carpenters."
"Do you like the Runaways?"
"I don't know, but I've heard the name."
She points to his plate, and says:
"Don't you like cream cheese with your bagels?"

Standing Cock

The work day is done.

Manny and his coworkers are letting off steam. When the conversation turns to current events, he finds that he has to speak up:

"Why isn't there a porn out named *Standing Cock?*"

It would be timely. Think of all of the scenarios that could be explored in a ruggedly natural setting involving faceless sadists, bondage, and rubber bullets! And the tender yet forbidden embrace of a *local* Romeo falling for an out-of-town protestor-Romeo but having to keep it a secret from his conservative Republican family!

Manny's voice rises with excitement and he claps: "I want to star in that! I wanna be in a porn before I get old and fat."

The Fake Thing

Sometimes I don't want the real thing, sometimes I want the fake thing, all of its flavorings and jingles, all of the stuff I made up in my head. I can paper my nest with it. I can spritz it on my chest and lip-sync the lyrics and strip and use two mirrors and trick lighting to turn myself into a budget version of it. It can make me think of my mother, and a time without death. It can make me think of the snow before global warming. It can sound like Broadway musicals, it can sound like locker-room rap. It is the smell that comes from teenagers' mouths. It is q-tips and lace. It is man, what every man is with bedsheets of five-month sweat and cum and the pubic hairs of forty women, some who only slept there as "friends" before you live like a married couple, the fake thing is what we are before we grow up, before we use the words "I'm in love," before pap smears and the cancer and the online requests from the child molester who makes noise music but can only play two notes on a piano. The fake thing is pop hits and Victoria's Secret and the real thing wonders if it can write grants or sell plasma to buy another bag of coffee and the real thing is slumming it and the fake thing makes us scream to a canyon at three AM:

"This is the real me!"...or was that the real thing?

ORPHANS

Our god is Manifest Destiny. Our religion is a dick pissing on a corpse.

Breathe Deeply

Breathe deeply…when your berth is sixteen inches wide. You sleep for eight weeks in a space that is never still and filled with the smell of dying.

Breathe deeply…in the stream, under reeds. You have been under water two minutes and still you hear the shout of men with dogs above your head.

Breathe deeply as they hurl your body to sea: Descend a ladder of bones, climb to the floor where your brother, your mother.

The collar is made of ragged iron and bites his shoulders. His bones have a pulse and he cannot sleep unless he leans into a clump of hay.

His thoughts foam; they fever as he puts into account the steps he took to escape, every turn right that should have been left. The evening he dozed on a bed of moss. The hour he failed to find the North Star.

When he rose from the hay he saw spikes radiating from his collar like a dead man's arms. They made hollows, so the hay-bale appeared to have eyes, stare back, stare mean, a trickster's grin.

The foreman pleads with her to return. Says master is done, but when she comes, she is tied to a post, taken to a space where pain makes her eyes see white.

Forty lashes. Go to the kitchen and ask for salt, the master says to her son. It makes wounds crawl. It makes the sobbing dearer.

The wives are as rough as their husbands, and more so. Word comes of a wife so mean she cracks a child's head in half. She wants to see cheeks branded. She wants to see legs break. She wants to be baptized in the cries of women young enough to be her daughters. Her hunger is tight as the ringlets on her cheeks.

This mother is beaten in front of her children with a handsaw, blades to her back, and yet she holds her mouth. She refuses to give them cries.

The final river to cross, how is it that the trees are so still and the sky is made of maggots?

These children see their fathers beaten until they no longer bleed.

These children run and bite and hurl rocks at the overseers and hide in straw bales and hold candles for their mothers and get photographed for posters selling "alligator bait."

Their mothers' dresses are ripped to the thigh. See them sold, see them run, and the dogs in pursuit catch up, and masters call to the dogs to bite until the nursing woman's breasts are gone and the baby has to be suckled elsewhere.

This one disbelieves the wounds, does not want to think any man is possessed of a hunger that must be fed by intestines hung on grass.

Breathe deeply: A dead man's hand, fingers so fine as if they are about to describe the flight of a butterfly.

This child was alive when you last took a draught of water.

This man had a look in his eyes as if he was alive since Bible times.

This girl could draw a picture of any lizard, any white man, grandmother, grandmother.

Sharing meals and asking ancestors and pleading with the bark, learning how to read when no one knew the reading was taking place.

How to read a room, a field, a face with precision in order to stay alive and yet remembered as animals, as children, eyes that glow in the dark.

Even after you reach the Union you must buy your freedom, lest any man with an eye for silver turns you in:

He's gone fifteen-hundred miles and made it to Pennsylvania where the farmer claims to have pity, but calls in constables to inspect the barn, the hay, the rafters, the price a man can get for restoring escaped slaves to their masters.

The slave runs, but in a circle. While the cops and farmer are chasing trails by the river he returns to the farmer's wife, demands bread and produce in a bag and she gives these and he travels further north, to Canada where the incentive to return an escaped slave dissolves. Poof, like gnats when sunset comes.

To be in a nation, no matter how "free" a state means veins filled with poison. How do you temper a poison which runs so deep?

1525 to 1866: Twelve and a half million Africans shipped to a World Named New. Two million die, chained in rows, side by side. The cargo hold of this ship takes four-hundred but is jammed with seven.

The ocean wears a necklace of bones.

Cabrini-Green, Bloody Sunday, Jim Crow means feet leave red tracks in snow. A child sees his father covered in gasoline. A Vietnam vet brings his white wife home and he is bullwhipped by men in hoods in front of his parents.

This is no admittance. This is white women clutching purses in the subway car due to fear of black anger, black knowledge, black space. This is fear in the white soul that the grandchildren of slaves, when no reparation has been made, will grow strong enough to strike.

Paid to sing a song in a restaurant where you can't buy a drink. Taking a knee to redlining, gerrymandering, pawn shops and lead on walls, no water in Flint, Blackwater cops shoot men searching for food after Katrina, call them looters, call them *kills*.

No admittance. A wall so high that under a black president prisons take in more men of color for smoking pot and broken taillights and walking in broad daylight with a cellphone in hand.

This is no schools, no trials, no jobs, no homes, no exit.

Breathe deeply: A man after dark wonders how to hold his hands. He wonders how quickly to move to his knees, how to hold his keys in a way that does not look like a gun. He wonders how to turn so the shots hit his shoulder instead of his lung; what to say before they get him in a chokehold and words can no longer come.

His mother and the mothers of a million black men: Children old enough to walk, but they do not know if they will be allowed another day standing.

Breathe deeply, kids on corners who are going to school, and the ones who are using and trying to look like men.

Try to get over the wall, try to be heard, find out in a book or a video or every stranger's eyes that Martin Luther King was killed because he started to see that sitting peacefully was not the answer, that acknowledgement of class war might bring together whites and blacks rather than divide them.

Breathe...the inside jobs which reek like a sewer opened.

There is a monster that is accustomed to swallowing everything.

Emmett Till, Tamir Rice, Kendra James, Freddy Gray, Trayvon Martin, Antwon Rose Junior, Phillando Castille, Amadou Diallo, Keith Lamont Scott, Sandra Bland, Keaton Otis, Aiyana Jones, only seven.

Eric Garner says "I can't breathe" eleven times on video as a phalanx of cops press him down, use *all* of their weight, trained executioners.

The coroner's report says homicide yet the cop who did it is still on the payroll.

It's called "broken windows" policing. Kill a man for pissing, jumping a turnstile, selling cigarettes, and in this way you discourage "larger crimes."

Breathe deeply when for-profit prisons enforce a "lock-up quota"—a jail must be 90% filled or the government pays the company for unused beds.

Tellers tremble when a black man walks into a bank. They force smiles, like saran wrap across their faces.

Breathe deeply...with low wages, no loans, no homes, no teachers, no hope.

You ask why a man burns down his jail cell rather than painting pictures on the wall to make it more bearable?

Candy Cane and Macedonia

Her face was once a sexy Bob Hope Halloween Mask. Her floppy brown hair dangles at her chin line, swishing back and forth on the collar of the camo jacket, a man's camo jacket from a man's war, and it drapes over her frame hiding her woman parts, along with the baggy jeans, the blunt black galoshes, the shimmy-shimmy-shake-shake of the galoshes in a flirty way, a way that informs me that YES, this lady-sack was once a stone cold fox, yes, that Bob Hope Halloween Mask was once filled with baby fat and optimism, wore hot pink lip gloss and drank moonshine in someone's big brother's backyard, and she did everything to get too old while too young, and now she is on the streets.

She is sucking on what looks like an oversized candy-cane, and it may have been accompanying her for many moons now, the tip or ridge of the peppermint stick having its barber-blood red stripes sucked away, so it is bone-white and pushed in and out of the space where her two front teeth used to be.

Her peppermint stick fits through the gap perfectly, as if she lost her teeth on purpose to better facilitate the eating of phallic sweets.

She leans into the personal space of a tall mentally-disabled man with a blonde-gray buzz cut and a crisp oxford shirt and velcro sneakers and a baseball cap with a huge letter T on the back.

I don't know what the T is for, only that his eyes are like marbles and when the woman stops motormouthing for a second about a guy who had two bus passes worth ten dollars but she didn't want to go near him and get them or do something worth ten dollars to get them, and so she walked off into the night, tho' it was cold, and how she loves candy canes but even more digs cotton candy, and when she stops and the guy with the baseball cap and shattered-marble-eyes opens his mouth it is in a slow California surfer drawl, quite unexpected for his sober frame.

Parts of him are missing and the woman's conversation floods over his invisible spaces.

The bus gets more crowded as it eases downtown. A man with a long gray ponytail and a small black backpack and a canvas cap asks the two where he can camp for the night.

The candy-cane camo woman says she's headed to Tent City, and the man asks where this tent city is.

She tells him it's right on Burnside and it fills up fast for the night, but if you get there in time you've got a place to sleep, and if it's too full you can get a bus out to a waterfall where another tent city is. She asks the guy how long he's been homeless.

"I am not homeless" the man says with a serious voice, a gunslinger's squint. "I am a traveler."

"Ohhhh...a traveler, huh? Where ya from?"

"I am from Macedonia."

"What are you up to? Where ya headed, huh?"

The ponytail guy shrinks a little and looks away: "That is not a conversation I want to have."

And then without missing a beat the woman turns back to slow California man and keeps gumming and slurping and talking about her love of candy, and idly rubbing a few sores on her face, and she is both younger and older than she looks.

Hiroshima at the O.K. Corral

I went door to door in lingerie and painted mental pictures of PVC plants studding the shores of the Mississippi like poison pearls. In combat boots and cut-off shorts I told the tale of Dow Chemical buying cemetery plots for townsfolk who died of leukemia and bowelrot from their all-devouring factory sluice. Visualize a town gone six feet underground; no babies crying, no food on the table, tongues absent, breathless, night.

In glitter lip gloss and a black satin g-string I spoke of the Hanford Nuclear Reactor where barrels buried in the dirt held five hundred-thousand gallons of spent uranium waste—strontium-90, technetium-99, iodine-129, arsenic, chromium, chloride, fluoride, nitrate and sulfates slithering from corroded husks like a league of b-movie demons with the power to alter genes. See stage-prop barrels rusty as old swingsets, chintzy as a set of Mardi Gras beads, and the children are our future.

No, the children are not our future. We cannot claim them. Our pride yields a leafless tree.

With a tattered lace ribbon tied around my neck I talked about dioxins found in steelhead salmon, how the making of Barbie dolls and gasoline and hair gel delivers low sperm count and bum nerves in every order of life.

Our hormones are off. The frogs are disappearing. I don't believe they are at a private party.

In a bra with busted elastic straps I helped strangers visualize a liquid bomb of pig feces from name-brand farms filling freshwater streams from Virginia to Illinois: *Anaerobic death-water! Doom!*

In a silver leather bustier and rave rings I whispered of inner-city asthma, garbage barges, dolphins in fishing nets, five-hundred chemicals off-gassed, heavy metals, agent orange, floods, fracking, rivers on fire.

In torn fishnets I got biblical about coal mines, silver linings, palm oil factories, poached chimpanzees. I prophesied steep decline for starlings and bees.

I stood beneath nylon moth-proofed American flags and made old ladies cry in a window of acceptable grief before they'd close their doors and eat canned peaches.

I complemented the geraniums of a drugged-looking Swedish woman whose husband did the talking for her in a mansion shaped like a horseshoe. They offered me a San Pellegrino fizz.

In a rhinestone dog collar I walked past camper vans and garden gnome collections in Republican-rich suburbs as if I was a guerrilla in enemy territory. To be honest, America was enemy territory to me. Then I met her.

Once I read a story about Hiroshima:

Twenty years after the armistice, America's greatest scientists were sent to Japan to introduce nuclear power plants to the country. Their crucial and strategic problem? How to make nuclear power friendly to a population where almost every living person had an uncle or cousin or sister vaporized by the force that results when uranium and plutonium isotopes smash.

Imagine the alarm, the awe, the sleepless nights of America's greatest scientists when they learned how to imitate the power of the sun's core—with the press of a button. Imagine the awe, the alarm, the sleepless nights of those kissed by imitation sun.

The survivors were turned into walking biology experiments. See this man, his head so overtaken by tumors? You no longer see his eyes. He looks like a walking crimini mushroom.

A mascot is drawn: A cartoon child who has the chubby cheeks of a Pillsbury Doughboy. He is the mascot of nuclear power. He is named Atomic Boy.

Symbolically speaking, his is a complex position. He is an avatar and a beneficiary of nuclear power at the same time. His smiling face is mass-produced on brochures sent to every prefecture in the country.

I imagine: Breakfast. The sun rises over a cherry tree in full bloom. An old woman rises from her prayer mat and pours tea. Her eyes quickly pass over her husband, who is studying a brochure about the magical properties of nuclear power.

Now it is better. Now it is safe, and the chubby cheeks of Atomic Boy are proof of this.

Godzilla is released. Bicycles are replaced by cars. Laughter fills the air.

When I met her I wondered: Does she know about Hiroshima?

We left the office, equipped with maps of the day's turf. One by one we were dropped off, exiting the sliding doors of a white Ford Aerostar selected for its anonymity. Cramped in the back, our bodies filled with nerves and rage and sour tortillas, my van-mates cursed the world they were about to enter.

These men, with their wild Scottish faces and t-shirts hand-washed in Dr Bronner's soap, with their addictions to microbrews, disc golf, and fermented lentil recipes, had been doing this for the past twenty years. They were *lifers*. I knew they had been in the war too long.

I was dropped in the West Hills, the base of Forest Park, facing a maze of charming cottages painted primary colors, their residents once journalists and actors, or at the very least ad-men whose wives took pottery classes—a liberal populace who treasured their veal along with their oats. Over the course of doing my rounds, I walked down a dirt path, and saw the Victorian lanterns, cobbled sidewalks, and bamboo gardens grow scarce.

The sun was a celebrity playing a well-loved role. It poured honey-color light on the firs that filled each yard. It was late afternoon, moving precipitously to night.

The houses before me were set back from the road. To reach each house I had to walk on planks, down stairs, on bridges and over creeks, then press buttons on official-looking intercoms, rap doorknockers in the shape of lion's heads.

These people liked their seclusion—but they also had serious cash.

With four hours to make my quota of one-twenty, this was a lot of extra walking. The odds were slim that I'd get a sympathetic donor, let alone an answer.

You see I had rung the doorbell three times and when she answered the door I had to question, silently, whether she knew about Hiroshima.

I don't know if she knew about Hiroshima or the Suez Crisis or Steve Jobs or Mister Mister or the Charleston Chew or Where's the Beef or the hit-jobs of Kennedy, Kennedy, X and King.

She was dressed head to toe in a prairie bonnet tied at her chin, a long floral-patterned dress with a high collar, sleeves that tapered to lace cuffs, and an apron. Lace-up boots secured her feet. Her hair was long and brown, and her face had a pinched quality, like a golden Sun-Maid Raisin.

With her dark brown eyes she gazed at me, mouth agape for at least twenty seconds before I launched into my explanation of why I was there.

As I spoke, my eyes discreetly locked on the furnishings of the room behind her. As with her bonnet and dress, everything in the room—from the oriental carpets and stained-glass windows, to the player piano and the succulently-fringed lampshades—was dated no later than nineteen-hundred. I saw no television, no stereo equipment, no wires. She appeared, with a serious level of investment, to be deliberately and perhaps permanently living in the nineteenth century.

A dozen scenarios ran through my head: Was she in a religious sect that had forsaken the modern world? Was she some sort of mail-order bride who came from a rural area of one of the more obscure Soviet Bloc nations, and due to her inarticulateness of American culture, she had no idea that she was NOT living like her contemporaries in the Utopic West Hills?

Perhaps she, being of a certain age, had listened to too many Eagles albums, come into money, and bought herself a number of dashing Jesse James clones to live in her stagecoach harem forever and ever, until the robots inevitably invade with a royal flush of fluoride and autotuned future-hymns.

Or perhaps I was overlooking the obvious: She was a paid escort hired to dress up like this to realize a wealthy man's fetish, and in the next room he was ball-gagged and overdue to be bullwhipped underneath a portrait of Sitting Bull.

My words tapered off. The room was as solemn as a church. I apologized for interrupting her afternoon. We stood in a silence that grew minutes long, gazing at each other. Without speaking a word, she nodded her head "no," and closed the door. I heard the lock turn.

I was on a bridge made of wooden planks. A stream bubbled under the bridge, and the air was very cool and green on this summer's eve, and a part of me wished I could pass under that threshold and spend a much longer time with Prairie Woman's lampshades, her player piano, and her cold, dead eyes.

Fireflies

Summers in upstate New York are long. The entire month of August is filled with thunderstorms. Like a plant that grows taller and taller and collapses under its own weight, the humidity grows; the soil is swollen, turned black with peat and the tree roots thirstily drink and ease through the grass, their earth-knuckles showing, calloused, severe, alerting the humans to how temporary our blood-sacks ultimately are. You find yourself shifting your posture every few minutes because the sweat won't stop dripping down your nose. It is as if your cheeks, your shoulders, your armpits, your awkward shins—they are parts of a flesh-tone water slide.

When night comes, the fireflies rise: From the cedar branches they favor they move in lazy columns, small orbs of green-glow-to-white.

In a world where people are still saving up to buy color tee-vees, the fireflies are truly a spectacle. Old couples in metal rocking chairs sit on concrete squares they call their "porches" and stare into the shadows beneath their backyard trees, the metal joints creaking, their breathing slowed to a lizard's pace, and they wait for the fireflies to rise.

Children stop what they are doing, in awe of the columns. How do the insects know to form in spirals such as these?

They glow like quartz, like sentient clouds. They glow as if they are projected from a distance, perhaps from a beam deep underground.

There are rogue fireflies separated from the others. Unlike the ones suspended in the air like sequins on a burlesque curtain, these rogue fireflies blink on and off in erratic waves, and when you wait, your breath held, wondering where each rogue will be when it flashes on again—it is all the way across the yard!

It is blinking above the clothesline! It is something you cannot define.

When I was eight years old, I wanted to catch a firefly and keep it as my pet. I washed out a clear plastic container with a lid. It was essential that I be able to see through the plastic to make sure my firefly was inside. I poked a few pin-sized "breathing" holes in the plastic lid, and put a couple leaves inside, presumably because insects need to chew on something green—and I waited.

I waited through the sunset on a night with air so humid that it felt like a naked breast rubbing against my side, my neck, my eyeballs. In terrycloth shorts and pigtails and a body hyper from growth hormones, I waited by the back door, at the very edge of inside and out, hoping that I would let the spirals of fireflies emerge from their trees undisturbed by a body even three feet away.

When I saw them emerge from the cedar boughs, I pried open the lid of my container. I held the lid in one hand and the jail cell in the other. I was ready.

Stealthily I went out the back door, tiptoed across the grass and approached the thickest column of fireflies, what looked like fifty or sixty of them rising in the air, lazily flashing at each other, emitting the brightness of a full moon across my face. With my plastic jail-unit ready, I slammed it onto one of the flashing, diving forms, sealed the lid, and went indoors.

I had caught an insect with wings. Under the kitchen light I could see that it was dull, and brown.

"Whatever you have in that container, you can't keep it in the kitchen! It could be carrying diseases," my grandmother said.

"It's just a firefly…or at least I think it is," I said, but doubt was creeping into my head.

The insect in my cell was not lighting up.

I decided to go down to the basement and turn off the lights and wait a couple of minutes, to see if in a darkened room, the firefly might flash its light. It didn't.

I was positive that it HAD been a firefly I had stalked and captured in my cell. It was flashing right before I caught it…my eyes did not deceive me!

"Maybe it needs to calm down and chew on its leaf," I thought to myself.

I left it in the basement, peeking at it every hour or so, with no luck. The thing would not flash in MY darkness!

The next morning I went downstairs and checked on the insect. It was dead.

I was positive that the insect I caught was a firefly, surprised that when examined, it appeared so plain.

Its wings were a textured bark-color. I could barely perceive two dots, or nubs, where the "luminous agents" would activate under the right conditions.

Later on I learned that a firefly's flash is dependent on ambient temperature and barometric pressure. All of this information would be exciting to me—that is, if fireflies were still around.

In ten years' time, things changed. My grandmother and her neighbors used chemicals on their lawns for an *evergreen look,* with nary a thought to how the little flags that said "Keep children away" could also mean "THIS KILLS EVERY LIFEFORM IN ITS PATH—some lives just take longer than others."

By the time I was twenty-three visiting the trees in the backyard where I grew up, I would only see one or two fireflies flash in a night.

Ten years later, I stared into the blackness for hours, hoping to see even one. Now the fireflies are all gone.

I no longer live in Syracuse. The fireflies and I seem to have left around the same time.

Arcane Orbits

Humans look for narrative in everything: A hurricane in a fingernail, a voodoo curse in the way a stranger picks his nose. I want to add that lonely humans especially seek connections in faraway objects. The personal affairs of Channing Tatum, Bette Midler and Jeb Bush affect the way I spend my morning as much as a cyclone in the noxious clouds that churn across the surface of Saturn, yet—yet!—I receive a phone call from my mother in which she tells me that Madonna is crying onstage during her World Tour because her ex-husband is fighting for custody of her son, Rocco, and she is afraid that Rocco doesn't love her anymore.

"You know honey, when she took Rocco on tours with her in the past, she forced him to have his hair long and in two ponytails like a little girl. When he turns eighteen he has the choice of getting ten million dollars from Madonna, or living with his father, and he wants to stay with the father. Ten million dollars aren't important to him. So while she is onstage, on her international tour, Madonna is breaking down in the middle of performances and crying. You know, I feel sorry for her, honey. I feel for her pain. I understand a mother's love."

Clover

Her name was as unisex as her look; a skull like a wedge of ice topped with shiny white spikes, her neck and arms striated with leather cuffs and collars, a constellation of rhinestones and studs. Rub against any part of her, the wrists, the thighs, the cheeks, the gelled confection of hair that shone like a prized macaroon under the lights of the marquee, and you would be gored like a toreador. Her jaw was wide, her eyes cold, her soft waif's body hidden under oversized smocks of black lace, trash-bag vinyl, the kind of clothes that make you think of aquatic life caught in a net. The lug soles of her boots bounced before us like gobstoppers of doom.

Clover.

The Paris was managed by a guy who seemed very old to us at the time, what some people would call a shady motherfucker named Hugo. He liked to be called Senor Frogg. The dance nights he put on were always prefaced by the phrase, "Senor Frogg Presents," in which he encouraged drunk strangers to do things "froggy style."

He hired someone to make a logo of a cartoon frog in gangster pants and rave sunglasses—which is what Hugo wore on a daily basis. He had an air of pride when he convinced someone to actually *address* him as Senor Frogg.

Urchins would glom onto Hugo and crash in his party pad, a series of desolate rooms inhabited by motheaten couches and balled newspaper which you climbed a narrow stairway to reach. To pass to that upstairs zone felt like spleunking.

The rooms were behind the marquee, lit by neon, filled with a buzzing noise. It didn't feel like people lived here. They took drugs and moulted here.

Once a cabaret friend of mine was exhausted after a show. She crashed on one of these sofas and awoke at dawn, one of the cloudy, mirror-colored, fractured dawns northern towns have, to see an invisible force moving her keychain across the room.

Clover! Clover dwelled in Hugo's upper rooms. She was the general of an invisible goth army.

Egyptian symbols snaked across the lobby, painted by a guy who later asked me on a date. I went to his apartment by a shopping mall where he played me a Stranglers album and showed me a doorway where his roommate pulled him from a noose.

In 1972 the Paris commenced a two-year run of playing Deep Throat. This hall has housed a sex club, a gay cabaret, rows of glory holes, anime porn: A damsel in a red slip, perfectly conical breasts and a yellow perm painted by the door, Crayola-peach arms clamped on a stone windowsill, Rimjob Rapunzel waiting for Jizz Charming.

Burnside and 3rd: The speedball cocktail of meth and heroin gives this block its all-night reputation. It makes these boys and girls instant groupies of the strangest souls: Guys in cheap business suits, turkey-breast loners who pretend to be bikers, Hollywood producers, "inventors," Luciferians who know about MK Ultra, stolen sperm for a test tube army, each gatekeeper-Svengali pontificating in motel rooms, speakeasies, backs of cars.

The kids move like robots, a flesh parade of bones not fully grown, fontanelle pudding-caps yet to seal and blot out cosmic radiation.

I did the door and sold candy cigarettes. I sat on those barstools of torn glitter vinyl and dented chrome, and heard the life stories of a thousand kids who ran away from their parents, who were raped at ten, who heard spirits in their heads. One girl said she had nightmares of tropical insects as wide as her chest. She would have a recurring dream of being in Thailand and the insects would come out of the walls and cover her body. She rarely slept, but she stayed alive.

Boys ran away from Mormon fathers. Some came all the way from Utah and Tennessee. I fell for a punk with a pageboy; his hair was an organism that reminded me of John Fogerty.

Between the slowly-shifting shore of human sediment, sharks shuttle from cars with seat warmers, champagne, ringing in a Happy New Year every night, following a timeless human rule:

The nouveau-riche travel to the places where poverty and sex intersect. They dance in ruins. They must remind themselves of where they came from, or where they could end up if they play their cards wrong.

Face tattoos, men in witch-skirts and trenchcoats as long as Oz, the Puerto Rican guy in drag that made him look like a secretary. The limping oldsters who don't want to hear more stories. They scan your face an extra second to see if you have a chink, a hole, a way to wedge in with the stealth of icepick need.

One night I was cleaning up after a show. The floor was swept. The money was counted. The toilets were returned to sanity.

I watched Clover turn on the rack of lights above the stage. Instead of the colored ones, she turned on the ones that gave tones of rock candy, ice. She put on a song with a glacial beat.

Industrial music. European. Cold. It coursed through the speakers on either side of the stage, speakers as tall as I was, taller than Clover. She cranked it up, and in a jerky amphetamine way, she raced to the center of the empty stage, an ice priest in harness, wagging her legs in baggy pants, making her arms move like ropes.

She was in the center and dancing as if she was struggling to free her body from her rags and spikes, from the breasts too present, from her breath, from her veins, from her pinhole mind.

The smoke machines smelled like cotton candy.

Alphabet Lives

In the Bowery they fixed up the buildings because they needed a place to live: Black Panthers, Puerto Ricans, acid freaks from the rural zones, commune kids who wanted to have urban gardens, and the dojo master; boys touched by their teachers, girls locked in closets, left to get rat bites in their feet, fractures in their skulls from fathers who burned with Old Testament flame.

One hundred years past this bar was the Billy Goat, two drinks were sold for a nickel to every man appearing between five and five-thirty in the morning.

This one a chapel. This one a dry cleaner. Look very closely and you will hear horse brass, hit the reek of rotting hay. Rouged cheeks are practice-fever.

Do buildings have souls? Do buildings work like tape recorders? Could you cross your legs or hook up electrodes? Could you roar in the key of c or tie cotton twine from wall to wall and pluck the building like a harp and unlock the times, all of the times that took place: Lutheran holiday dinners, sock hops and counseling vets. Now there is tinfoil and David Bowie painted on this wall. They have patched the holes and tapped into the city's electricity. Barricades and secret entrances. Jugs of rainwater and drawbridges and graveyards of pigeon bones.

CUANDO, CHARAS, Bullet and ABC No Rio, C-Squat and the olfactory spunk of concrete and brick powder and urine and wires and one room decorated in airplane parts and another filled with hairpieces and a futon mattress dragged into a tub in a room where a door will close.

Here was a rooftop pool, deco glass, tin tiles on the ceiling, marble erodes.

Johnny the junkie had been still for days before they found him and there was no choice but to brick him in the broom closet because some fates are better than being on the street.

It may be said in death:

More tender effort was put into protecting his presence than in life.

Oxy's Midnight Runners

Most people assume that when Marillah says she likes older lovers she means men, but she means women. Marillah is sixteen and her face is shaped like a sexy peanut and though her hair is dyed white and shaved around the back and sides, she says she is a quarter Choctaw.

We are sitting in a parking lot staring at the river and the overcast sky. Marillah says her friends are going to come soon, and she thinks alcohol is boring. She gives me a pack of pills because she says they are no good but as the hour progresses I feel her soul burning a hole in the pocket where the foil-wrapped pills are, and I know she wants them back, and she will rifle through my folds should I lose consciousness which I won't because I have snorted fine white dust with her in the dressing room of a store selling novelty glasses, hoop skirts, and posters of dogs wearing hats.

Kade comes, and he sees through me until Marillah tells him I am cool and he starts sneaking glances at me and he says I can be useful, and I ask how.

"You can get things for us," Kade says with a hangdog smile and he runs his fingers through his hair, fixes it again and again in the driver's side window of a minivan. His hair is wavy and black with the tips turned yellow, and his eyes are pools reserved for a chosen few.

"Shit, the cops," he says, and indicates a gray van, and then a white one, but their drivers to my adult eyes look like normal and frazzled business people hoping to get out of the French Quarter.

Marillah has green pills and Kade has blue pills and we walk in the cold to the voodoo store and stare at a shrine of a goat god who is the same color blue as Kade's pills with breasts and slanted eyes and a pentagram on its forehead. I want to buy and hold and know the goat god but I'm stopped by a sign that says **No Photos, Please Don't Touch.**

The essential oil is whack. The sandalwood smells like fabric softener.

Marillah and I pick up books about witchcraft and she chokes on the prices and stares daggers at the dreadlocked thirtysomething behind the counter in hiking boots and an asymmetrical poncho. Marillah says she has hexed enemies many times, and sometimes she also hexes friends because a hex doesn't doom you, it only makes the bad things that are going to happen to you happen faster, and then you have them out of the way.

Marillah and Kade and a friend called Creeper Steve who is forty-five and trades them a small bag of mushrooms which may or may not be psychedelic for other things in their pockets move through the French quarter, often walking in circles in a way that makes them appear lost.

We take a train to the cemetery and talk about memory and why the sky isn't green and Kade wants to tell us all about a rapper who he wishes he could listen to right now because the rapper is so deep and feels so much that he'd understand the meaning of these buildings and the dead flowers on every shelf containing skin-flap bones, and inside this crypt is a metal tray that must have held wreaths and it looks rusty and Kade jumps on it and rolls back and forth on the marble floor and at the last minute keeps himself from knocking a vase off a shelf with a name like Henrik carved so serious and so extinct.

The doors to this crypt are like those of a bank. At the end of this hall are windows of yellow stained glass. I find a small blue rubber duck someone must have deposited here twenty years ago as it is dried in the sun and covered in dust, and no one dares dislodge this blue rubber duck from the spot where it is propped on this eternal windowpane; the dead have claimed it.

We run on the grass and we slip down fine black holes of mud between each plot, some plots with walls, some plots with sphinxes, all of the stones like butter cookies crammed against each other and we are in slow motion now with a gentle buzz because we took the blue pills and are floating minds with feet that only get in the way.

Marillah tells a ghost story which she says is a borrowed ghost story from a woman she slept with who was a college professor and this woman lived in a shotgun shack at the north end of the city and was always talking to a ghost who she said she was in love with even though the ghost was two hundred years old.

"Shit, what kind of ghost hangs around here for two-hundred years?" Kade asks, "What is a ghost even made of?"

"Who was the ghost?" I ask.

"She said he was a Union general, and she has no truck with northern bitches, but this one got under her skin."

"What does that mean, have no truck?" Kade asks.

"My grandaddy used to say that all the time. He'd list all the people he had no truck with: Law-men, tax-men, the Pope, men in ties who who quote Cheech and Chong, and people who use the words 'shock and awe.' Also he hated those jeans that make muffin tops. He held no truck with women who wear girdles in the wrong place."

"I saw a dead body once," Kade says.

"Shit, what, on the *Walking Dead*?"

"No listen, listen."

"Shit, I WAS TALKING ABOUT A UNION GHOST and you wanna barge right on in with your fake dead body."

"It's not a fake."

"I'll be the judge of that."

"*I'll be the judge of that,*" Kade says in a prissy voice.

"You know I was goin' down on her and I felt this thing race above my spine. Like, above my spine, like somethin' was fuckin' flying through the air, and she told me she didn't have any pets. It was HIM. She said he was jealous, and even worse, a heathen woman to be taking a 'flower' so young. And I said flower my ass, I'm like a diamond ring. I'm like a stone that's dug up from the ocean floor, something that's been underground a long time."

Kade is shaking his head to the rhythm of her words but then he breaks the mood.

"You think being a rock is better than a flower? You throwed, girl."

"We're surrounded by rocks right now," I say.

"Is she always so quiet?" Kade asks.

"Shit, she's here to write a book. She wants to know about us."

"Then you're going to want to put my dead body in your book. It was my uncle. He was shot dead. I didn't really know him well, so it didn't fuck me up."

"I'll hear you in a minute," I say to Kade. I turn to Marillah. "Do you ever worry about a ghost following you home?"

"Shit, as I see it ghosts are following me home all the time, but I don't know the hundreds of 'em that are there, so what does it matter if the soldier joins 'em?"

"Well he's got it in for you, personal," Kade says. "He don't want your bony ass around gettin' in the way of his professor-lovey-dove."

Kade's hands play with blades of grass until his fingertips are green. Crows caw at each other from trees to our right and left. I think to myself that there are crows in the south as well as the north.

I say, "Access is everything."

"Speaking of access," Kade says, stumbling closer to Marillah. He reaches a paw for her bag. "Hand over those shrooms."

"Back the fuck *off*, Taz."

Kade dances away and trips over his feet, making a *doof* sound as he touches the ground. "You crazy, bitch!"

"I don't wanna do them yet. Boy you just don't have any patience. You want to gobble down everything at once and what's the point of that? Don't you want to have something special for later? Oh don't even answer."

Day 2

Marillah has left five messages on my phone. She says that I need a 'part two.' I take the trolley to what friends have told me is the potter's field—a cemetery for those who cannot afford polished marble and concrete angels. Instead of gravesites there are burial mounds, licorice-dark balls of soil piled in heaps that rise to my knees, and some higher. Each one is labeled with wooden boards, penants for the Saints, names and messages to the dead written on impermanent cardboard.

Marillah sits by a row of graves covered in wreaths made of Four Loco cans. A bottle of Jim Beam is left as a devotional object on a grave. The bottle is covered in flecks of dirt, but the label is not faded. Kade dares her to sip a clear liquid inside. Marillah lights a joint instead.

"You do it," she says, and Kade demurs.
"It's probably just piss anyway, or rainwater."

Kade hasn't slept in a day, but he's gotten naps. He took a nap at his friend Welles' place, and he took a nap on the trolley, and he took a nap in the trailer where Marillah sleeps. Marillah is leafing through a "Book of the Loa," and Kade is doing fake karate moves in the grass. It is cold enough to see our breath, but the rays of sun make Kade shake his head like a dog.

"My dad and my step-dad died of tar and I had to live with my grandma, and she kept my daddy's urn in her bedroom and it freaked me out."
"Well why do you have to go into her bedroom in the first place?" Marillah asks.
"I was stealing her arthritis pills. Percodan, Vikes. She had so much of it. I mean there was more than she ever took because she was trying to be you know, careful, and so she would get new bottles before the old ones were done. So I borrowed Welles' pill press to make aspirin look like her pills so she wouldn't know I took so many."
"So you'd rather get dopey than let granny feel good."
"She feels good, but she likes feeling good with company, you know. She plays video poker with her girlfriends and they get shitfaced on Captain Morgan's Spiced Rum and Malibu."
"Malibu? You gotta be kidding!"
"She gets through half a bottle of Malibu and she's OUT." Kade impersonates her on the sofa. "She ends up lookin' like one of those pug dogs, shit, with the tongue stickin' out the side. Once she was wasted and I went to her room to her 'hiding place.' She had a script for Norcos and I was ready. I saw my daddy's urn start to move, fuckin' move, like this, and I froze."
"Fuck. You never told me that one. You savin' it up for the guest."
"You know what it looked like? In real life it looks red, plain red, nothin on it. But I'm tellin' you my fuckin' heart turned to ice and

then shot up my throat and out the back of my head. See that hole? That's where my heart went. Never to be seen again."

"What happened with the urn?"

"It had all these ghosts on it like Japanese girls in kimonos, and they were dancing and turning into clouds. I saw the top of the urn become fangs, like a dog's fangs, and my grandma is super clean in her room but all of a sudden I saw food on the floor and raccoons were coming out from under the bed to grab it with their hands."

"You mean paws?"

"Hands. My daddy didn't want me in there, I could feel it, and I wanted to tip the urn over or throw it in a pile of pillows. I mean, then it would be under the pillows and not see me, or have fangs."

"Shit, from what you told me about your dad…"

"He ain't really my daddy. I mean, how can you miss something that's never there?"

"Like people who are born blind," Marillah says, "People ask the blind all the time if they miss seeing and the blind say SEE WHAT? We never saw a goddam thing, what shit you smokin? How can we miss what we never saw? Like I see that as a good opportunity to develop other senses. Like psychic senses."

"Fuck!" Kade goes. His fingers reach for the sky. "Did you see that? It was a comet, but shaped like a star, a cartoon star. Ooo, that was a good one."

"What did you do with the urn?" I ask.

His eyes go wide as he remembers.

"I was tryin' to step closer to it. I told myself to focus on the sound of the upstairs neighbor's dog because he's all barkin' and the guy is having a fight with his girlfriend. Those two *always* fightin' and listenin' to shitty country music. I say to myself if I can focus on their voices then the urn can't get stronger. I just have to get up to it, grab it and throw it under a pillow…but I just can't. I had to run over to the corner by the window and sit like this. I tried to breathe for a while, and the urn starts to be red again."

"No more fangs?"

"Aw man, not that day. But another time I was crashed on the couch and my grandma she was out with her girlfriends and I hear that floorboard creak. I felt like the air was uh, tight, cold. I didn't know WHY I was awake, I mean girl, I had five Klonopin and I couldn't move my legs, not even my mouth would open. But I heard the floorboard creakin' in Grandma's room, and I knew it was the urn. The urn was comin' to get me. This was before I went to live with Welles."

"Well fuck, you're standing here today so I guess the urn didn't get you."

"Welles' sister," Kade says, turning to me, "slit her wrists and his mama said it would be good for me to be around after that."

"Did she die?"

"No, but they put peanut shells on the floor for a week to get out the smell, I mean the blood. Bleach didn't get it all. Welles' mama said she just kept smellin' the blood, and she didn't want Tiana smelling it again."

"So peanut shells are better?"

"They didn't have her stay in that room for weeks. But Tiana ran off with the guy who got her pregnant and uh, lost the baby and they found meth and oxy in her system and Welles feels guilty because he thinks she stole it out of his drawer.

"Speakin' of which. Welles and Dee at midnight?"

"Shit you sure she's not a narc?" Kade says, aiming his eyes at me.

"Does she look like a narc?" Marillah says and passes her joint to me.

"I'm a nerd, not a narc."

"Nerd, come. The sun is gonna set in three hours. We gotta use the light. Come with us."

We take the trolley past ancient oaks dripping with Spanish moss, like the abandoned shawls of an army of Stevie Nicks impersonators. We pass shotgun shacks painted purple with green gables, villas with wrought-iron balconies that would not look out of place in Spain. We pass mansions with such elaborate displays of columns and turrets that I imagine their residents swipe right on Tinder in powdered wigs and hobnail boots.

A man who is a Southern History buff sits behind us and blathers on about the campaigns of Stonewall Jackson to a companion who goes "mmm, mmm-hmmm." All around us are mothers and babies and tourists bundled in cashmere sweaters and down jackets and stocking caps that they never anticipated they'd need to wear in the city of New Orleans.

Kade watches a video of a man drinking Robotussin on his

phone. The man on the screen has greasy brown hair and wears a hat with hunting flaps. Kade shoves earbuds at us. "Listen to him. We can listen at the same time." The man is drinking and singing and all of the sounds are in slow-motion like a 45 played at 33 and a 3rd.

We get off and approach a man named Tree in front of a minimart who is tall and in Carhartts with copper skin and tattoos of arrows, x's and stars that rise like cords from his neck and over his cheekbones to the edges of his squinting eyes. I think to myself that if he continues to squint like this his eyes will become assholes. He moves around me to have a conference with the others. They agree on which parts of the neighborhood they are going to, that they will pool what they find when they are done.

"You can come with me," Marillah says, and Kade jumps up.

"No, she's comin' with me! I need her more than you."

"What do you mean you need me?" I ask.

"I'm a Pee-Oh-Cee, a cop magnet. They won't bother me if I'm with you."

The cold makes us move faster. Late-afternoon sun pulls shadows from our bodies like brains pulled from a mummy's nostril.

Five trash bags are lumped at the edge of the curb. Kade gives me a wide-eyed glance and rubs his hands with enthusiasm. He starts opening bags and asks if I'm going to join him.

Kade finds a water bottle half-full of whiskey, a bottle of Adderall with eight pills at the bottom, a bottle of migraine medicine, a ton of antacids and aspirin that he says he can soak in chemicals and sell to college students who don't know any better. He tells me he can engineer a high like a scientist, one that will give just enough of what anyone needs while hoarding the best for himself. His eyes light up with each bottle, even if it takes twenty minutes to go through a garbage pile to find it.

We find Viagra which he tosses on the curb, but then changes his mind. "I can find a buyer for this, too."

We find a bottle of Ativan with two pills left, a full bottle of something called Sonata that gives a person waking dreams, and more allergy pills than we know what to do with, though Kade has plans for them as well.

He deftly sifts through each pile, with a sixth sense for when he's getting to what he calls "bathroom bags"—in which used and unused sanitary napkins, q-tips, razors, unopened bars of artisan soap, stained facecloths, busted curling irons, eyeshadow, and a treasure-trove of "expired" pharmaceuticals are.

I savor each collection of bathroom waste as a poem about the previous owner.

Every once and a while Kade has to toss something so grotesque to the curb that he says he needs a acid bath to feel clean.

"Down to your bones?" I say.

"Better'n *these* bones, " he says, kicking a pile of gnawed ribs and chicken hocks across the frosty grass where they remain like runes that could tell a fortune if one knew how to read them.

I find a lifetime's supply of birth control—and leave it behind. I find laundered clothes that are cleaner than mine ever are, and tuck some in my bag. I find black lace underwear with the tags still on. I find a lot of things I'd like to take with me, but I don't have room for them now or on the plane which will take me away from the nerves and needs of baby wraiths.

I think of the homeowners who will in an hour or five walk to the ends of their driveways and find their bags torn open as if by bears: Who or *what* passed here, they may wonder. Why did everything have to be so *scattered?* And the phrase rolls through my head: What is and isn't *scattered* comes down to hunger and cosmetics.

I find an opened bag of pizelle cookies and an artisan yogurt that comes with tumeric powder and a personalized plastic spoon. The yogurt is still cold.

"Gross! How can you eat food someone put in the garbage?"

"How can you take pills someone left in the garbage?"

"Aw girl, I saw you grab those undies. You don't know what th-fuck *touched* those!"

"You don't know who sat on your trolley seat. Laundry fixes everything."

I offer him a cookie.

"No WAY!" he says.

I offer him the women's underwear.

"FUCK no!"

It is night. Kade looks increasingly frail as the hours pass; his hands are filled with earthquakes.

When we reconvene with Marillah and Tree, a fourth person has joined us, a woman in jeans and a windbreaker and a face like an albino crow. She is a street thirty-five, has black hair, missing teeth, a laugh that is too easy.

Kade tries to do a cartwheel on the curb, and when he does, a noise slides out of the woman's mouth, a loud "AHHHH-hah-hah-ahhhhh…" that tapers at the end like equations that calculate smaller and smaller divisions of space until infinity is held within the dwindling last syllable of her laugh. Her laugh is a saw; her laugh is a beacon and a warning, her laugh is every joke about Lorena Bobbitt; her laugh is the last thing you hear when the bars close or when the moon is covered in blood.

"Ahhhhhhm comin' with you!" she says. Marillah looks like her patience is being tried.

Tree moves toward the woman and with force in his arm escorts her across the street and speaks to her there. We wait for five and then ten minutes, but the conversation between them has grown long, and the woman's arms rise and fall in the air as if they are telling time. She lets a crumpled paper bag she is holding fall on the ground, and starts kicking it.

Finally Marillah darts across the street and says something to them both, her white hair flopping in the air like something fresh and bought in a novelty store.

She waits for a pulse of traffic to move, then returns to us. "Not our problem. We'll see Tree later."

Marillah and Kade show off some of their finds to each other, agree they have part ways to "do things."

Kade is headed to the university to find buyers. On a night this cold I question his certainty that he can make a hundred bucks in the next two hours. I weigh in my head how my fingers have gone numb, how much energy it takes to bob beside these lives and listen to what they need, a need that is there even when they aren't talking. I think about where I'm staying, and I think about where I could go, and I realize that there is no where to find peace.

Marillah's trailer is in a yard of a friend west of the city and too long a slog to bother taking trolleys or buses at this hour. She tells me she might hang in a cafe, or walk around the square in front of St. Louis Cathedral. Sometimes she hitches where she wants to go. She says it tests her instincts.

"People are more good than rotten, despite what you hear…oh, everywhere. Fuck, I've had some psychos get on my back a few times, but I'm confident I can talk or fight my way out."

We are on a trolley headed to the French Quarter. Our car is full of tourists and rush hour commuters. We are cramped on a wooden bench. Marillah's legs are spread wide, and her huge canvas backpack is held like a baby between them.

I ask, "How do you fight?"

"Oh, mind control first, if I can help it. People aren't that hard. Once you accept you can see what they want, you're no longer scared of their wants. SO many people are bettin' on you being afraid of 'em. They go OH SHIT when you're not. It's kinda like being a surgeon. Once you're no longer afraid, you can move their skin flaps aside and yank around the veins and muscles in there."

As she talks, a halo of bark and rubber mats and medicine flies around her head. Her eyes are bloodshot and she has new fuel.

"What if they choose to fight you…or test you?"

"Oh, they test. Look at this. Punch it." She yanks the denim jacket down from her shoulder to expose her bicep. She stands up and grabs the leggings around her knee so that her thigh muscle bulges out of the stretchy fabric. "Miles of walkin.' Lord I think I've walked to the Moon and back a dozen times. Punch it."

"I don't have to punch it."

"Your loss."

Ronnie Hightower is his name. He is a thin man with a face that is boy-band handsome and feathery light brown hair. His entire body is slumped in clothing that reminds me of wax paper, discarded gloves; brown lace-up shoes that look too big for his feet. He says he is thirty and his mother's on vacation here and made he and his sister come.

"How long have you been here?"

"Almost four weeks."

He tells me that his mother took him here to clean up because he loves heroin too much, and he misses his baby, both of his babies.

"My girlfriend she's seventeen years old and so beautiful. We had a really, really special thing, but I have problems." His voice drifts in and out like a radio station incompletely tuned. "We have a little baby and she and the baby live with her mama, which is a good thing, a better thing. I only met the baby once…but I'm gonna go back and make things right. Her mama don't think I can. Her mama takes care of them both. She's an administrator in an assisted care facility. I tell you…when I met my baby…held her in my arms… she's so tiny, it's somethin' that just keeps haunting me. Do you know what I mean? Do you have kids?"

"I had one when I was nineteen, but I gave her up for adoption."

"Why? " he asks, his eyes coming alive for a second.

"I was too young. I was a kid myself."

"Aw man, it's so hard," he says. "Then you know…you know. It's in here," he says putting his hands to his ribs. "I jus' can't get over it. How can something so small take up so much of your heart?"

The trolley is going through a dark stretch lined with trees and fewer houses. Ronnie starts to look nervous like he doesn't want to miss his stop.

"Hey, how old is your kid now?"

"She's almost grown up," I say.

"Shit, no. Grown up?" He looks me up and down and peers deeper into my eyes. "How old are you?"

"Thirty-five."

"Shit. I woulda never known it. Girl, whatever you're doin', it's working." He looks embarrassed. "Do you get to see her?"

"Yes, it's an open adoption. We're friends."

"You're so lucky."

A paper parade halo has formed around myself and the Lost Boy with a boy-band face and pale blue eyes. When the train slows for another stop, he gets nervous, and starts asking neighbors where his stop is, and they tell him.

His time here is nearly done; I see our halo ripped to shreds by invisible fingers. We will never see each other again, which feels like an amputation.

"Hey, I'm glad I spoke to you," he says.

His eyes are no longer calm as he gazes through the glass,

through his own reflection to the tree-lined streets outside. There is something he needs to get to, bad.

"Be safe," I say.

He is a bundle of nerves disappearing from the gold berth of the car.

I turn to Marillah.

"What was he on about?" she asks.

I tell her.

"Fuck, he's lyin' his ass off at you. Why would his mama take him here? The French Quarter to clean up? Four weeks? What the fuck's he really been doin' all this time? Fuckin' scum liar. And why'd you tell him you have a kid? And you're thirty-five? You're not really that old."

I'm even older, I think to myself, but no one believes me when I say it, so why wreck a good thing?

The eyes of a deer so hazel in flaps of skin remind me of oiled eggshells; a doll-face, a baby animal in a zoo. Welles has a mustache on his upper lip, I can count seventeen hairs that make up the mustache and he doesn't blink twice when I enter in the company of Marillah, Welles of the dreads that are thick and the skin that is golden-brown. I see freckles across his nose, freckles that compete with beads of sweat. I don't want him to think I am someone off the street looking for a high, but as the hours pass I realize that my desire for a high has grown greater than my desire for a story.

Marillah's Ritalin, Marillah's corner store ephedrine, Marillah's caffeine pills when the rest runs out—sitting like virgin and crone spitting distance from the fecal grove of palmettos that line the shadowy hinterlands outside the cathedral. Marillah gets into a fight with a rat-faced woman who is hanging off a busker. "Throw down for the music!" rat-face yells to a stream of fat white tourists in windbreakers bearing sports logos.

At the sight of Marillah, rat-face flies into a spitting match, accusing her of flirting with a white man with a face like a pelvic bone and thin blonde hair that hangs to his nipples, suits his playing of a violin. Rat-face grabs at Marillah's arm and wrestles for a moment, but stops when a squadron of potential donors moves our way. The fiddler redoubles his efforts to play a gypsy melody along with the bongo player in army fatigues and an African beanie.

"Crust-punks think they're in what? Fuckin' Poland or that shit? Where do gypsies come from? I think I read they were originally from India."

"Untouchables," I say. "That's what the DNA testing says. Modern Roma came from India. Their ancestors were of the untouchable caste."

"Girl, you said it. I wouldn't tap his fugly noodle ass if you paid me, anyway that bitch has been followin' me around for two weeks sayin' Kade traded her shit codeine syrup for a mother-of-pearl brooch that he gave his grandma as a Christmas present. That has fuckall to do with me. I hate downers, downer people are a dime a dozen. Downers can be good mixed with other stuff, but shit, not alone. This is everything:"

She snorts white powder off her hand and holds it up for me to do the same in a corner far from people; too cold, too cold for many at this hour—a handful of fortune tellers bundled like Russian infants in the age of Chekhov; so many layers of nylon and mufflers bearing the omnipresent Fleur-de-Lis huddled over folding card tables decked in purple fabric: Crystals, palms read, even though it's so cold you can barely make out their faces and hands through their impromptu snow gear.

"Twenty-nine fuckin' degrees. You picked a time to come."

"How'd you start? How did you figure out this is what you wanted to do?" I ask.

"What I want to *do?*"

"The way you live."

"Well how'd *you* start?"

Marilliah thinks this is the way I am, as if I came out of the womb this way.

"I could tell one look at you, you like a high. You like lightning in yer hair."

"I'm here to hear stories. I'm sick of telling mine."

"Fuck that's *your* story all week. I'm not a trained monkey. You know what Bernadette told me? She's my *teacher*. She's got the finest ass, like an apricot. She's flat like this, and her body makes my hand feel like…my hand, I mean every part of me like heaven when I rub her bones, fuck I'm getting' all twisted up just thinkin' about her. She said I was descended from 'a noble people.' She said after the Civil war the Choctaws up and down the Mississippi were surrounded by the army, forced to move to Oklahoma. Their farms been' stolen, cattle killed, homes burned down. That was the trail of tears. And the Choctaw tribal leaders heard that farmers in Ireland had their fields go…uh…what is the fuckin' word…when they can't grow shit."

"Barren."

"Yeah, barren, and couldn't grow shit, and the Choctaw, who were treated like fucking punching bags, could barely feed themselves, donated somethin' like two hundred dollars to send to Ireland, and now there's a statue of a Choctaw in Ireland. Fuck, you'll never see that here."

"Empty plinths," I say. My friends in town have shown me empty plinths where statues of Confederate generals were taken down ten months before. Even on cold nights like this, lone picketers draped in Confederate flags make busy with bottles and spray paint to show their loyalty to the now absent General Lee and Stonewall Jackson.

"My people were slaughtered here. It's a funny feeling to say you know what you come from. Do you feel ancestors in your blood? Who's in *your* blood?"

"I don't know much about my father's side of the family, but I feel that I take after them. They are French, live in France. I've only met my father twice. I met him for the first time when I was seventeen. I saw a photograph of his mother. She was a concert pianist, so I heard. She had a wild smile in her photographs, an artist's smile. I feel she is in my blood."

'Hmmm, an artist's smile. Yeah, you got that. Well I didn't know my daddy, either. I was in a teen rehab center in Miami. It was fuuuuucked up. Like a maximum security prison. I was thirteen years old with these cholo bitches with no eyebrows who said they wanted to fuck me up, and shit, they scared me. Those bitches had scars."

"Why were you in there?"

"My mama had me when she was sixteen. She was staying in Baton Rouge and got with my daddy, and that lasted two minutes. She still don't remember his name. She was beautiful at first: High cheekbones, these wide-apart eyes. She wanted to be a model, even did a couple shoots with pervs who had her in lingerie. She would show those photos to me and every guy she could get in her room, as if she was proving she was once pretty."

"Where is she now?"

"I lost track. She was a fucken crack whore. I can't blame her for that, but I blame her for the assholes she let in our apartment. She'd be gone for a week sometimes and I just locked myself in the bathroom. I tried to squeeze myself under the sink, but I got too big to fit. She brought guys back who were fuckin' demons. I mean trash. Won't insult demons. They did stuff to her, and she let them, and sometimes not for money, just for the shit in their pipes. She let them tie her up. I had to fuckin' clean her own shit off her, more than once. I was born with fuckin' rocks in my blood but I swear to you I'm not gonna shoot ice like Welles and Kade. Those boys got garbage pail blood. They'll do anything."

Welles' mother does custodial work, but when she gets home at 2 AM she is too tired to clean her own house. Welles of the sandalwood hands and the freckles painted on, sweat beads and smooth motions; a dining room table covered in coffee mugs and pills. Side tables with framed photographs of smiling kids, one that looks like a smaller Welles on a bicycle, a girl holding a coal-eyed terrier dog who may be Tiana, who slit her wrists.

The hardwood floors are bare, and the overhead light is on. Fluted glass lampshades blossom like flowers from a fixture on the ceiling. Like everything else in this building, they are old, may have hung here since the forties, giving off their powdery, sperm-color light. These tall windows which look like the building's eyeballs, this green-hued enamel paint. A heap of dishes are shoved to a far corner of the floor, and partially under a sofa.

Kade is running back and forth between the kitchen and down a dark hallway. I hear him grabbing things and swearing, "NO, No NO! Fuck!" He doesn't have shoes on; only clean white gym socks and shorts. His shirt is off, showing a slippery Buddha-round gut and bumps that snake down his left arm which look out of place with his kid's face. He comes down the hall saying, "That blue-hair girl is still in the tub trying to tattoo Connor."

Marillah looks at him and he slows down.

"You know the one you called a skank. That stripper. Mika."

"Let me guess."

"No, I'm tellin' you. She wants to baptize him a 'lost soul,' and he says yes. I don't get it, why he'd let her, I mean she's not hot. Those fake tits look like basketballs, and they're the same color as basketballs, too. She's done 'L-O-S' and that's on his left hand, and there's India ink all over the tub."

"I want to piss. You come with me," Marillah says, tugging at my wrist. She is clutching her bag. The darkened hall smells of fried food and pot fumes and feels increasingly narrow with Marillah's mountain of a bag bumping against mounted picture frames.

The bathroom door is old, made of a solid wood, and open a crack. Bright light leaks from the other side, and with the light comes the sound of a woman's voice motoring on about chipmunks in her boyfriend's backyard. Her voice sounds like an ashtray.

"And I told him I always wanted a pet squirrel and no I wouldn't allow him to shoot at the chipmunks because they're innocents. Mika knows about squirrels and chipmunks, and how they all have spirits. She's got a shrine of bird skeletons in her living room. What are all of the critters you got? You have the one that is on a nest and you have broken blue robin eggs in it, and then you have the one that's a cat skull painted pink, and whenever I see it I'm thinking I should be feeling it's scary but the way you have that pink and the glitter on it and that striped part on the tail, it's so…I think the word I want is respectful "

Marillah says, "Knock-knock," and shoves the door open, where we are face to face with a middle-aged woman with dyed blonde hair and a face that looks like a ball of clay smashed between two heavy palms, bearing the lines of palms—life-line, romance-line, mount of Venus; the forehead carved with fingernails, two hollows poked for eyes. Her jaw is square and her lips are determined rims that pucker to emphasize a point. She is wearing office slacks and brown loafers, and over this, a long white canvas trenchcoat is tied at her waist, the belt cinched so tightly that she appears to be an ornament hung by her belt, in this case, hung on the edge of the toilet where she is sitting. The expression she gives us when we open the door is that of a sublime mastery of everything.

I turn my eyes to the tub, where the young man is moaning, attempting to communicate with the woman who is straddling him. The clawfoot tub is big enough to allow two people in easily, but the man is tall, his brow heavy, his eyes nearly hidden under it, and the way he moans, "What letter we on…" and shuts his eyes again, he reminds me of a mutant fruit.

Mika is a robot; I am convinced. The way her spray-on bronzed skin covers her skull, her long toned arms and her 24-inch waist, her legs waxed and coated in a pearl powder that shines all the way up the robot-sinews of her thighs pumping a rich indigo robot-ichor to the basin of her crotch, which is covered by a strip of pink nylon. Her skirt is hiked over her hips. Two strips of pink nylon stretch over her basketball-round breasts, which are, like the rest of her, bronzed and then dusted with pearl powder, a powder which, depending on the way the light hits it, sometimes shines green, and sometimes tangerine. Her eyes are bloodshot yet lined impeccably, first with a pale white line on the innermost lids, then with a series of blue and purple stripes which race up her temples. Her false eyelashes are like barbed wire surrounding her eyes. When she blinks, they move in tandem with an industrial determination to deflect observers from falling, like stray hairs and insects and dust in the wind, into her depths. Despite the largeness of her breasts, the rest of her is undernourished. Beneath her pancake makeup, her cheeks look pocked and bruised. Her hair is dyed white, with feathery aqua streaks that spread from her widow's peak and look as if they have been professionally curated in a salon, shellacked with a bankroll of powerful styling products to approximate immortality; immortality is a peacock's crown.

Marillah says, "You know Welles' mamma comes home at two AM and it's eleven-thirty. You really think you're gonna have this mess cleaned up by then?"

The voice that comes from Mika's robot-throat is low, bumpy, a muttered stream, as if her jaw has been wired shut. I can't decipher what the words are; they don't appear to be projected at me. She holds the man's left hand tighter, presses it to the lip of the tub, makes a quick slice with the needle.

"That's the rest of the T, right?" the woman on the toilet says.

"Can't a soul piss with some privacy in here?" Marillah says.

"She's a dyke," mutters Mika, her teeth still clenched, "with bad vibes."

"A dyke? Really?" Asks the trenchcoat woman with interest. "Hey, if you're a dyke, have you tried one of those funnels that makes you piss like a man?"

"Who's the ghost?" says Mika, looking up from her T at me.

"I think she's the dyke's friend," trenchcoat says, then smiles, "I *like* your jacket."

Marillah stands above her and says, "Are you gonna move aside for a minute?"

"I guess so," trenchcoat says, "We were having a private moment in here."

Marillah hands her bag to me and uses the toilet quickly, flushes. While she does this I turn my head to watch the man lying with a towel under his head, emitting noises like a sea lion: "mmm-mmmm, mmm-murrrrr-aaaaaaah."

The bronzed woman pours ink on a kitchen sponge, then presses it on his knuckles, fine black drips gliding down the porcelain of the tub and making spots on the man's denim thigh. The fingers of his free hand reach to pull aside her strips of pink. She bats him aside. "Not now, baby."

"Whose idea was it to get the tattoo?" I ask.

"She found this guy at Rick's," trenchcoat says, "and he's into her right away. He says he wants to have a good time, one he'll never forget. He says his girlfriend broke up with him and he wants to kill the pain, and she says she's on her way to a friend who can help and then he got to staring into her big eyes. They are soulful eyes, aren't they? When I first met her I was sayin' to myself *goddam*, I never met a woman with eyes as big as dinner plates. She's a real spitfire. She's given me spiritual counseling. The gift runs in her family. Under different conditions, I'm sure she'd tell you about it. She helped me out a lot when I lost my cat of twenty-one years, Sir Fleetfoot Fluffernutter. So this one, Devin, he says when he's lookin' into her eyes he knows he will believe whatever she says. *Well…*"

"Connor."

"I said Devin."

The woman in the white trenchcoat's mouth seems to expand to three times its original size, popping and crackling in the air like a heat mirage, and she sings a Blondie song: *"One way...or another... I'm gonna find ya...I'm gonna gitcha gitcha gitcha..."*

"Have you been here before? In this house?"

"First time. That boy Welles is really a lil' businessman. I mean he has something for *every*-one. I'm the designated driver." A fruity fume of alcohol rises off the trenchcoat-woman, and is followed by a blast of sourness, which I know comes from a dark pit inside of her, a repository of the powders or pills that bring her teeth to gnash:

Radio static, yet all frequencies filled. Who can tune in? Who needs to? Me. I am trying to remember everything she says, the pattern of pores on her face, the discoloration on her left loafer which might be a splotch of vomit or a drop of runny sour cream, as if I can retreat at a later date and like an ancient scribe add up this information on sheets of pressed goatskin and it will spell out the meaning of life. And why shouldn't it?

How much do I need to know? How much does anyone need to know?

Marillah and I move in the direction of the light at the end of the hall. Hip-hop is playing from a set of speakers that are so small they look like toy speakers for a dollhouse.

Welles is sprawled across the sofa with another boy in his late teens. I walk close enough to them to hear them analyzing the music, speaking soulfully about what the man rapping means.

"See here," Welles says, "this is the best part comin' up, where he's sayin' everything in his life has led up to this moment, this is his one chance to prove what his strength is. It's his chance to become a man. His dad thinks he's a failure, and his girlfriend, she want him to play it safe, but he can't play it safe, he has to make a bigger statement. He knows what his strength is. Nobody else does *yet*. So he can't blow it. Just listen, here it comes..."

At this moment, Kade hops in from the kitchen wearing a kimono covered in roses and a bandana over his nose.

"Shit, shit shit..." I didn't do it right! I can't let the smoke touch my skin!"

"Oh…fuck," Marillah says. "I'm talkin' to Welles, then it's time to get out of here."

"Git the fuck outta my mamma's bathrobe!"

"I can't let the smoke touch my skin! This is serious!"

"Tone it the fuck down, or I'm rippin' that bathrobe off your back and thrown' you out that window without the shoes on your feet."

Kade has a spatula in his hand, which he is waving in the air as if he is fanning himself.

He says, "No one breathe!" and returns to the kitchen.

"Critical mass," I whisper. The sound doesn't come out; only my lips, moving as if in prayer.

Marillah disappears down the hallway with Welles. She comes back in ten minutes, which feel like ten thousand. While they are gone, I lean at the edge of the sofa, watching a man nod into a pillow as a rapper tells a story about becoming a man, he knew he always had it in him, but even after he is a success, there are haters telling him he's not all that, and his girlfriend who left him because he wanted to be *more* is back, asking him if he'll buy her a car, a dress, if she can have his baby. The overhead light has been turned off; a metal desk lamp on the dining room table shines a focussed beam over heaps of envelopes—maybe gas and electric bills, maybe letters from cousins, or sisters, a church.

Kade emerges from the kitchen holding a bowl of foul brown chunks, which he tells me is a failed experiment with some of the pills he found today.

"Shit. The microwave has a devil face now. It's freaking me the fuck out. I'm putting this in the bathroom."

He brings his bowl to the chamber where I imagine a man is still having LOST SOUL scratched on his knuckles by a wannabe witch with basketball breasts.

In a shadow at the far end of the room and draped with mardi gras beads is a picture of Welles on a bicycle. Behind him, ancestors—in starched collars and ties and button-down sweaters— in suits, holding a diploma, a bouquet, a small statue that looks like it is whittled out of wood—holding a winning ribbon for a contest that seems so small compared to nuclear warheads and bad cops and tours in Iraq—ancestors who coalesce in these portals; who can only coalesce in gradients of black and white, summoned from a world before the new people.

Can you hear the pistons, birdsong? Can you hear the radios, the horns, the guns, the voting booths and hammers? Can you feel the brush of tall reeds swaying against your leg? Do you smell the pomade and aftershave and griddle oil and rosewater and cancer? Do you feel the shudder of heavy bodies on sheets and the inward slide, the devouring starburst of cock impacting cunt—in the world before these new people?

Marillah walks me to the trolley stop. Her mind is faraway now, calculating volumes of life to be lived for the next twelve hours, as if the next twelve hours are a room she is ready to paint and decorate and fill with objects of art.

First she has to close the door, turn the lock. Her eyes don't see me as she lifts her arm in the air, a wave that is meant to be casual. Her wave feels like a mission aborted lifetimes ago.

"See you around," she says, and the doors slide shut.

On all sides of me are intoxicated people, eyes focussed on laps, frantically texting phones, heads leaving oily stains on windowpanes— every soul turned circumspect, as if several generations of problems are weighing upon this assortment of humans at once, demanding to be solved. Or is the solution as simple as hydraulics; what can, in the next two hours, be put in or shot out? What can be done until there is no more energy to *do*, and the trance takes over—the life done after living this one?

Bertha Boulevard Meat Kids

Someone has thrown away a life. It is eleven at night on Bertha Boulevard and the bus stop sits eight feet from a sign that says "Where the Sidewalk Ends." It is cold enough to see breath and the boy is barely a boy anymore, his body stretched out to six feet and his face as long as a green bean. He wears a street boy's baggy pants and a hoodie and trenchcoat and backwards baseball cap over greasy brown hair. His combat boots have holes that cry like open mouths, and he's licking his lips, looking sideways at the punky girl and the dazed one with lines like gashes in his face and a stooped back and blonde hair. They are together, lean over the cardboard box they've hauled from the Goodwill Donation Center. Someone has given away a life in this box, an after-hours drop. Three souls are ready to see if the life was anything good.

We have time. It is late and the Fred Meyer is about to close and the only pedestrians are tweakers who punch street signs and fondle broken tables, and the bus comes once an hour, and sometimes not at all.

Before digging through the box, the tall one has to adjust his meat. I see him reach into his pants, an exaggerated wiggle of his hips. He's digging both hands in, knuckles covered in inked arrows and x's and a smiley face. His hands are in up to the wrist and go deeper.

He takes out a slab of beef that is three feet long, blood and bones and fat glowing crocus white in the light. His meat is shrink-wrapped in plastic, so intimate and clean. Now that his meat is exposed he wags it in the air, slapping it against his thigh. He giggles and cannot stop. His companions are bored but I take in his childish delight at what he has, will have to cook quickly. While he waves the meat in the air, the others rifle through the box, and shake their heads and move away.

Still clutching his meat, he struts over to the box, digs a long white wrist in a pile of beat-up electronics, hair scrunchies, an empty water bottle, light bulbs, paperwork.

He fishes out a picture frame of a smiling lesbian couple, then a framed picture of a cat posed in front of a Christmas tree.

"Who gets rid of this?" meat boy says.

On a daily basis people swerve around him as if he will steal their kidneys and he is asking why the cats, why the lesbians.

The busted stereo amp and the "Exotic Vanilla Scented Body Wash With Triclosan"—yeah, they are obvious, pose no mysteries and promise no transfiguration.

Who throws away a memory?

I think for a moment of rescuing the Christmas cat and the lesbians who may have long since vowed to destroy each other, but I have recently been evicted and know too well the work it takes to leave things behind without starting to amass them all over again.

When you are evicted you ask how much skin does a living being require? At what point does the skin grow thick and striated like a harness and one chokes?

I look at the three: Delirious meat boy, woman shaped like a tomato with raccoon eyes, the man with blonde dreadlocks, and stubble that entombs his youth like volcanic ash. I think about them going to a friend's kitchen, or a spot in the woods, and they make a fire and warm their fingerbones by the flames and they stab at the plastic-wrapped meat with pocketknives until it peels away, and with their fingers the meat is torn into pieces and held through plumes of smoke until their sleeves and hair and chins and lips and teeth smell like tallow and burning poplar and dripping blood.

What will they do with the extra meat?

It is November and the hemisphere is turned delicate with frost. The reeds bend, and trees spread across the horizon as if they have been cut like paper dolls.

If the buses are running, the travelers can make it two hundred blocks in an hour.

The New People move over the Earth, a supply that will not exhaust itself.

Do the New People understand the weight of paper dolls, and the sudden issue of flame?

How is Charles Atlas?

And under cover of night or the eerie blue glow of a thousand screens a thousand fingers lazily probe abdomens, shoulders, itemizing new moles, misshapen scars, unruly hairs, doing the monkey things while selecting plasma screens, rose-gold rings, horror movies to zap away a paycheck, an evening, a dangerous depression. Who is a supermodel now? How is Charles Atlas as he adjusts the volume control and looks up five possible degenerative nerve diseases that correspond to the tremor of his hand? The color of his urine is wrong. A website tells why fuzz is forming on his tongue, that his great-grandparents passed him an incurable melancholy. DNA is triggered, sanity never safe. There are diseases of the blood. Icons falter.

The Last American Virtue

He was eighteen and aimed to shoot up Southside High. He carried fourteen pipe bombs, a propane tank, a sawed-off shotgun, a .22 caliber in a duffel bag and a backup bag of ammo and walked the halls waiting for the right gamma rays to hit his skull but students told their teachers before the ruin bloomed. He got 8½ years.

He was seventeen and arrested in the parking lot of Malcolm High after a staff member saw him take a swig from the long glass bottle and don a ceremonial black trench. A search of his car produced a bolt-action rifle, 20 bombs and a note saying he was ready to hurt everyone at school except for three friends.

Natalie wrote in her diary of a need to fight back. Pipe bombs, then the gun: get sixty, get eighty, get them down, get them bleeding, then no more laughter, no more useless eyes. Then suicide in the food room. Ham and mustard, rue morgue red. "They're fucking heartless. Trust me, I know. They're the reason I started cutting myself and they're the reason I am going to end up shooting a school. I already have a plan."

Brooke, clean red hair and a jaw that knots like unbaked porcelain. Underseas thoughts float over a microphone, her gods are of Columbine: "They saw the strings that control the system, and they aren't fucking sheep."

Fame is the last American virtue, the final goal. Feel the holy fire of fame enter your body! Fame as an anti-hero! Fame as the lone shooter, the one who STOOD UP AGAINST…

Fame to enter a video game made flesh made video game all over again: Man-man-man, young man and old—all baby-snakes armed to the teeth, the transubstantiation of video-god to human-child and back again.

Vows:

I now pronounce you man and smartphone.

YOUR
TAX
DOLLARS
AT
WORK

Wealth in America
(Less than Zero)

In America the 1% hold 40% of the nation's wealth in 2017, up from 22% in 1980.

9.9 percent of Americans hold *all* the resources and property in the nation.

The rest of us rent.

70% of the nations on Planet Earth have a *smaller* income gap between the rich and poor than the United States.

In the early 1900s—a "gilded age" we associate with Carnegie, Rockefeller and Hearst—the richest 1% of Americans made 18% of all national income.

In 2018, the top 1% make 25%.

In 1952, corporate profits made up 33% of the nation's taxed revenue.

In 2017, despite record-breaking profits, corporations contributed less than 9% of their income to the working of the nation.

Amazon CEO Jeff Bezos makes $275 billion a day, or $3,182 a second. His warehouse employees make $28,000 a year, and have timed 6-minute bathroom breaks.

The wages of Walmart's full-time workers are so low that they receive $6.2 billion in food stamps, Medicaid, and subsidized housing.

In 2015, taxpayers spent *$152.8 billion* to support low-waged workers across the nation.

Among the 100 top-earning corporations in the US, nearly 40% paid no taxes *in at least one year* between 2008 and 2015.

What companies—from *Nike* to *McDonald's*—do is this:

They use loopholes to define their taxable income as zero—*or less*.

They get rebates. This is what they *received* from the IRS over an 8-year period:

AT&T ($38.1 billion), Wells Fargo ($31.4 billion), JP Morgan Chase ($22.2 billion), Verizon ($21.1 billion), IBM ($17.8 billion), General Electric ($15.4 billion), Exxon Mobil ($12.9 billion) Boeing ($11.9 billion) Procter & Gamble ($8.5 billion), Twenty-First Century Fox ($7.6 billion), Time Warner ($6.7 billion), Goldman Sachs ($5.5 billion).

One five-story office building in the Cayman Islands serves as the home address to more than 18,000 corporations who have moved their banking outside the US.

Do not ask what corporations can do for you; ask what you can do for your corporations.

Death and Taxes

IN DECEMBER 2017, CONGRESS PASSES A BILL THAT GIVES $1.5 TRILLION IN TAX BREAKS TO AMERICA'S WEALTHIEST CITIZENS. THE TAX BILL FAVORS TECH COMPANIES AND THE FINANCIAL SECTOR. 20% OF THIS SUM GOES TO THE 1%.

TO OFFSET A BUDGET DEFICIT OF $1.5 TRILLION, THE BILL OUTLINES FUNDING CUTS TO ENERGY AND HOUSING PROGRAMS, SOCIAL SECURITY, AND MEDICARE...

The bill also lifts the ceiling on tax-free inherited wealth, from $5 to $11 million.

Prompted by Medicaid cuts, the state of Louisiana sends 30,000 *eviction alerts* to elderly patients in its nursing homes.

Once this threat hits the national news, Louisiana lawmakers are compelled to re-balance their budget.

Instead of cutting funding for nursing homes, they write a proposal to cut public college assistance, eliminate the food stamp program, close parks and museums, and cut funding to a child welfare agency.

203 members of the Senate and House of Representatives are millionaires—66% in the Senate, 41% in the House—with 46 in the range of $10-$300 million.

Everything You Always Wanted to Know About Deregulation (But Were Afraid to Ask)

The *Glass-Steagall* legislation, part of the *1933 Banking Act*, limited the ability of commercial banks to make high-risk investments. Architects of the act wanted to prevent another disaster like the *Great Crash* of 1929, and the subsequent *Great Depression.*

In 1989, President George H. W. Bush repealed the bulk of Glass-Steagall. Bill Clinton did away with the rest of it.

Without such roadblocks, the economy would BOOM!

Banks could bet for and against the successes of their investments at the same time, then sell off the debt, making profits from every sale along the way—a practice which led to a construction bubble, an easy credit bubble, massive foreclosures, and widespread evictions.

Wealth was supposed to "trickle down."

It didn't, and the market crashed in 2008.

The 2008 TARP bank bailout reported as totaling *$700 billion* comes with fine print: America's most powerful banks who defaulted after engaging in money laundering, selling toxic mortgages, and a rainbow of other scams, were guaranteed *$29 trillion of taxpayer money* over *two decades* of payments.

Obama's Secretary of the Treasury, Tim Geithner, who previously worked for insurance giant AIG, passed $326 million of TARP funds to AIG executives.

Citibank, Chase, Goldman Sachs, Wells Fargo; a long list of culprits were handsomely rewarded for losing billions of their clients' money, *in addition* to making millions in predatory overdraft fees, and loans designed to default the poor.

Barack Obama's campaign received $44.3 million in 2008 from

the finance and real estate sector, up from the $36 million that the George W. Bush campaign received 4 years earlier.

The financial sector spent *$467 million* on the 2016 local and presidential campaigns, with 44.2% going to Democrats, and 55.4% to Republicans.

In 2018, the Trump administration revised the 2010 *Dodd-Frank Wall Street Reform Act,* insuring that banks too big to fail can operate with the same amount of oversight they had *before* the 2008 crash.

It kinda makes you want to eat a piece of *Mickey Rooney's Sinfully Rich Devil's Food Cake,* doesn't it?

Dahling, it makes me.

Exhilarating Grift

Politics...what an exhilarating grift! In our nation where public school teachers buy books, pencils, and school supplies for their students which the schools and their own families can't afford. Our nation where cancer clinics, psych wards, and nursing homes have to decide which patients to retire, kick to the curb on an hourly basis. Nation of the $8,000 emergency room check of the pulse, saline solution; a mouth-swab for flu. The curbs are getting too full and no one is saving for a coffin when the meth and pain pills and Netflix are our life rafts. O great tax bill which whispers sweet nothings of the ourobouros trickle-down; 500 pages of mangled and partially xxx-ed out legalese rushed through the Senate before the documents can be dissected in tepid public debate; o rewritten taxation of the nation designed to be the death knell of the middle class in a land where 70% of its citizens have less than $1,000 in savings.

Regard the breeze, the spray; a new wave of dumpster-diving and shoplifting sprees in the decade to come! The system is broken because the ones who bought it will find new toys in the developing world, which is not here, o land of the slave. America, land of rigid principles, where the masses are brainwashed to believe that mercy, a single mercy, however small, breaks the machine, and protest is crushed by armies dressed like beetles, rubber bullets. And if you keep marchin' in those streets they'll throw you in jail and fake your suicide. In the words of a great philosopher, *"I'm lovin' it!"*

In Front of the Justice Center

A prisoner's plastic baggie labeled "Property Envelope" sits on the ground, pocked with rain and the marks of feet impacting gravel. A palm-sized notebook lies next to it, candy red cover and pages turned to a mulch resembling egg whites beaten, fake volcano foam. Its pages are scattered, text is washed away. A lighter lies unattended in the pile. It must no longer work; an offering to the ghosts.

I get a coffee and pass by the pile again. Someone has stolen the baggie, kicked the notebook open, and scattered its hidden contents across the sidewalk...revealing several $100 bills of Monopoly money.

Indentured and Torn

US prisons are privatized and filled by quota. They contract out millions of men and women as labor to the following corporations: McDonalds, Whole Foods, Bayer, Chrysler, Victoria's Secret, Bank of America, Chevron, Motorola, Microsoft, Costco. ExxonMobil, Pfizer, Pepsi, Shell, Procter and Gamble, Starbucks, K-mart, Koch Industries, Merck, John Deere, Verizon, Walmart, Wendy's, UPS.

They earn on average earn less than $2 a day.

African-Americans and Latinx make up approximately 32% of the US population.

They make up 56% of the incarcerated population.

If African-Americans and Latinx were incarcerated at the same rates as whites, prison and jail populations would decline by 40%.

In the past 30 years, spending on prisons has gone up at *triple* the rate of spending on K-12 public education.

With 5% of the world's population and 25% of the world's prison population, the United States has the largest incarcerated population in the world.

Debt in America

80% of Americans live from paycheck to paycheck.

60% of Americans have less than $500 in their bank accounts.

39% have $0 in savings.

Medical debt is the #1 cause of bankruptcy in the US.

The personal debt of Americans is $13 trillion in 2018.

In 2018, the US National Debt is $21 trillion.

Congress approved a $717 billion defense budget for 2019.

America's annual defense spending is more than that of China, Russia, the UK, France, Japan, Saudi Arabia and India combined.

Debt is the American way of life.

Upgrades

The Pentagon has a budget of $717 billion dollars a year. Where does it go? A lot of it goes to planes and missiles.

An F-35A Joint Strike Fighter costs $100 million, more than twice the cost of the F-16 it replaces.

The $131.2 million carrier-borne F-35C Joint Strike Fighter replaces the $65 million F/A-18C Hornet.

The Marine Corps' F-35B costs $131.6 million each, more than twice the price of the $50 million AV-8B Harrier II and the F/A-18 Hornet.

The F-22 Raptor costs $250 million, replacing the $65 million F-15 Eagle.

The $80 million F-15E Strike Eagle replaces the $65 million F-111 Aardvark.

The $16.9 million MQ-9A Reaper drone replaces the $4.03 million General Atomics MQ1-Predator drone.

The Reaper flies longer missions with increased payload! It can carry up to 4 Hellfire missiles in addition to multiple Paveway-II laser-guided bombs.

A US Air Force General sez: "We've moved from using UAVs primarily in intelligence, surveillance, and reconnaissance roles before Operation Iraqi Freedom, to a true hunter-killer role with the *Reaper.*"

Still / Born

As far as human evolution goes, the line between stillborn and still-born is so very fine.

Only the Stones Remain

The US has spent $7 trillion in the "War on Terror" since 2001—deploying special ops in 76 countries—as far as the Phillipines, Yemen, and Niger—to obtain access to the richest fields of oil the planet has to offer.

Some say the ultimate goal is to surround and conquer Iran.

Some say the ultimate goal is to send a message to Russia and China.

Some say these wars and the extraction of fossil fuels are an attempt to hasten Armageddon.

Some say that once an agency like the Pentagon is granted power to dominate a nation's taxpayer money, they will not give up this power.

In 2016, the world's 100 largest defense contractors made profits of *$374.8 billion* for the sales of planes, ships, missiles, guns, radar, guidance and surveillance systems.

Who's your daddy?

Ketchup

Yesterday a homeless man told me that one of the most imbecilic effects of Reaganomics was the classification of ketchup as a vegetable.

Housing in America

In America, empty homes outnumber the homeless 6 to 1.

18 million vacant homes sit across the nation. The amount of empty dwellings that were bank-owned soared 67% in 2015.

Since the financial crisis of 2008, 9 million homes have been foreclosed. Banks sit on these homes for years without keeping them up to code. Cities have attempted to fine the banks for negligence and force homes onto the market—to no avail.

The lowest average price for a 1-bedroom apartment in America is $470 in Wichita, Kansas. The highest is $3,800 in San Francisco.

The average rental agency requires a prospective tenant have a monthly salary *3 times higher* than the stated rent, and a credit score of at least 620.

1 in every 5 Americans has no credit history. 51% of Americans have subprime scores, below 620.

Those with felony records, bad credit, or poor work history are banished from renting an apartment or buying a house.

They are left to trailer parks and residential motels for the remainder of their earthly existence.

Health in America

30 million Americans are without medical insurance. The cost of x-rays for the uninsured is between $400-1000.

The average cost of a birth in America is between $15,000-$32,000.

The average cost of a Cesarean section is $50,000.

The average cost of a death in America is $10,000.

The average cost of hospice end-of-life care is $622 a day.

In 1943, a birth in the US cost $29.50.

The Movers and the Shakers

While presidents shape the 'flavor' and zeitgeist of a nation, you get that they are puppets, right? Howdy Doody, Lady Elaine, Big Bird; the sheer unfolding of the past fifty years of history especially should ram it down our throats that presidents are not godlike-figures steering their nations with a divine right, like kings, like Kubrick on the set: They are agents of change, a change which is almost exclusively for profit, and the more *philanthropic* candidates who manage to push their way into office must inevitably choose lesser evils lest they be fired for incompetency.

If we want to know what forces are really in charge, who steers the buffoons we see paraded on media montages engineered to the specs of the highest bidders—we must follow money trails, read whistleblowers, wikileaks. The "real news" has to do with economics and dwindling resources, rather than reality tee-vee.

When I was fourteen years old I was on a school field trip, where I and a number of students ended up in a shopping mall. A psychic fair was underway. Four tables were occupied by a motley crew of tarot-readers and palmists.

This was a rare opportunity away from the watchful eyes of my family. Infused with a burst of confidence, I strutted up to a guy in a Hawaiian shirt, an oily fro, and a walrus moustache that reminded me of the movie critic Gene Shalit. I was tarted out: my hair dyed white, my face-paint a seductive olive green, my lips a pale neon like the color of a Minnie Mouse shoe buried in snow.

This guy saw through my skinniness, my weirdness, and instead of something beautiful, he saw something remote and frightening

199

to him. He seemed hostile to me, as he told me the Tarot dictated this: I wanted to be famous, I wanted to be adored, but instead I was possessed of a different type of mind. Instead of being celebrated, I would *lurk behind the scenes controlling things.*

Some might have taken this as a compliment. After all, controlling things behind the scenes, doesn't that sound more powerful than being a celebrity or politician marched around to endless appointments, kissing babies, repeating empty words?

Or was he being sexist? Did he think I wanted a man's power which I could never get with my mouth that moves in a crooked way, my walk that at that time lacked grace, my clothes that reeked of onions and spit and menstrual blood?

As I've watched politics over the past few years I think about the ones who gain media coverage and glory versus the ones who acquire power and recognize that they can gain more assets by hiding their faces, by hiring proxy faces, employing muscle, pulling strings.

When we look at the candidates running for president and we get into heated debates about who lands in office and how the country will become unrecognizable after they do—I wonder to myself: Who is really pulling the strings as these faces are broadcast from the carnival floor?

The Money Trail

The defense industry has spent more than $1 billion since 2009 on *perks* to secure the loyalty of members of Congress, employing between 700-1,000 lobbyists a year.

Congressional reps move through the "revolving door"—from the Pentagon to posts at weapons companies, and back again.

The US nuclear arsenal has 4,600 nuclear warheads in its active stockpile.

A single nuclear-armed submarine carries the TNT equivalent of *7 World War II's*.

In 2017, the US supplied $3.67 million in military aid to Afghanistan, $808 million to Iraq, $3.1 billion to Israel, $319.7 million to Pakistan, $367.6 million to Jordan, $1.31 billion to Egypt, $313.5 million to Syria, $203.9 million to Columbia, and $85.6 million to Mexico.

The US government is the biggest arms dealer in the world.

The top buyers are Turkey, South Korea, Taiwan, India, Singapore, Iraq, Egypt, Poland, Japan, Romania, Bahrain, the UK, the United Arab Emirates, Greece, and Singapore.

2010 was a *record year* in arms sales: The Obama Administration made $102 billion, driven by a $60 billion package to Saudi Arabia.

The US kill list is called the "Disposition Matrix." The Obama cabinet discussed past and future hits at weekly meetings dubbed "Terror Tuesdays."

Facial recognition technology allows drone-operated Hellfire missiles to target and incinerate dozens in a single strike.

Only 2% of drone strikes hit their stated targets.

Since 2001, $4.7 billion has been spent in Afghanistan.

In 2017, the Trump administration dropped an average of 121 bombs a day on Afghanistan.

An average air strike is priced at $2.5 million and drops 2 bombs.

Having invested in the destabilization of Afghanistan for the past 40 years, the US—in concert with Russia—has bombed Afghanistan into the stone age.

Watercolor Paintings

Watercolor paintings of rowboats and pencil portraits made by 'suspects' at Guantanamo are destroyed, often in front of the men, to make them understand that this is not a place to thrive.

Sticky Fingers

According to the UN, it would cost $30 billion to resolve world hunger. This is 4% of 2019's $717 billion defense budget. The US could resolve world hunger *23 times over.*

George W. Bush's military averaged 24 bombs a day, 8,750 a year.

Obama's military dropped 34 bombs per day, 12,500 in a year.

Trump's military dropped 44,096 in 2017, one every 12 minutes.

At least 8 wedding parties have been droned since 2001.

There were 57 drone strikes under Bush, 540 drone strikes under Obama, 107,107 airdropped missiles and bombs in Iraq and Syria by US and Coalition forces since 2014.

The Obama administration dropped 26,171 bombs in 2016. 23,000 were dropped in Iraq and Syria in 2017.

In 2018, The Trump administration dropped 2,911 bombs in Afghanistan for *Operation Freedom's Sentinel.*

There were 161 drone strikes in Yemen and Syria in Trump's first year of office.

According to Air Force Central Command, manned and remotely-piloted aircraft dropped nearly 600 weapons in the month of May 2018.

In 2018, more bombs were dropped in two months than in the entirety of 2015.

In 2018, US aircraft flew 726 sorties in Afghanistan in one month, with 73 of those sorties including "at least one weapon release."

In Thetford Township, Michigan (pop. 6703) a police department of *2* received 4,000 pieces of surplus military equipment valued at $2.7 million, including parachutes and mine detectors.

When the US government says it does not have the money to give every citizen clean air and water, free college education and healthcare, and food if they are hungry…

They're lying.

Paradigm Shift

We live in a world where fish have toxic levels of our toilet-flushed detergents and antidepressants. Are our fish cleaner and saner than we are?

Is it Hot in Here, or is it Just Me?

Americans consume 35% of the world's gasoline.

In 2017, Americans used 143 billion gallons of gasoline, which equals 391 million gallons a day. The US airline industry used 173 million gallons of gasoline.

The jet fuel expended on a transatlantic plane ride melts one square meter of arctic ice.

The average US family melts a football field of arctic ice every 30 years with their food and energy consumption.

A big "energy goal" of the Obama administration was to turn the US from one of the world's largest importers to one of the largest exporters of gasoline. This could only be possible with fracking.

Oil companies shoot up the Earth: They inject high-pressure jets of water mixed with industrial solvents into wells to bust rock, release pockets of oil. Exxonmobil has written loopholes into US legislation to keep the magic ingredients of their frack fluid secret.

Frack-wastewater kills pets, fish and people, comes out of the tap a muddy brown. It contains lethal amounts of arsenic, benzene, tolulene, lead.

29 US well-sites had earthquakes induced by fracking. 36 well-sites had quakes induced by post-fracking wastewater disposal.

Ice caps melt. Jet streams falter. It wasn't supposed to happen this fast.

US wildfires burn 4 times the range they burned in the 1970s.

In 2018, fires consumed 8.6 million acres across 14 states.

There are more floods and hurricanes in the Gulf region, more toxic algae blooms, more crops that fail in increasingly volatile weather.

The current rate of ocean warming equals 4 atomic bombs dropped per second.

Based on current models of warming, if humanity doesn't lower CO2 production, Earth's mean temperature will rise 8°F by 2100, a temperature that no longer supports mammalian life.

More is better.

McMuffin Nation

We tell you what you want and congratulate you on having "so much choice."

Voting in America

US eligible voter turnout has hovered between 50-60% for over a century.

11% percent of the US adult population lacks a photo ID, which disqualifies them from voting in their states.

In 2008, Republican senator John McCain stated that ACORN, an organization that focuses on registering black voters, "is on the verge of maybe perpetrating one of the greatest frauds in voter history in this country, maybe destroying the fabric of democracy."

Crosscheck is an organization dedicated to purge voters from the rolls in 30 Republican-controlled states. In Michigan, where Donald Trump won the presidential race by 13,000 votes, Crosscheck purged 449,922 voters from the polls. In North Carolina, where the margin was around 177,000, Crosscheck purged 589,393.

In 2013, the Supreme Court approved revisions to the Voting Rights Act of 1965, making it easier for states to eliminate polling places. In a nation whose population increased by 150 million in 50 years, polling centers decreased. Between 2013 and 2016, 898 polling centers ceased to be, with the majority in African-American and Latinx neighborhoods.

2010s Citizen's United vs. the FEC: The Supreme Court rules that political spending is a form of protected speech under the First Amendment. Candidates for public office can receive *unlimited* financial backing. Hundreds of millions from special-interest groups and the corporate sector flood Republican coffers in bids to win the House, the Senate, and the presidency.

The Mercer family, tech billionaires and right-wing investors in Breitbart News, donated heavily to the Trump campaign, convinced that American voters would only support a candidate from outside the D.C. establishment. Their stated goal—to "save America from becoming like socialist Europe."

Leaked memos show the Democratic party promoted the presidential bids of Republicans Ted Cruz, Donald Trump, and Ben Carson, men with low political credibility and far-right views as 'pied piper candidates,' to make Clinton *look better in comparison*.

At the urging of both parties, networks commenced serious coverage of Trump until he gained popularity over *dynastic* contender Jeb Bush, with a blackout on Democratic contender Bernie Sanders. Liberal affiliates covered the Trump campaign with a combination of incredulity and mockery, which emboldened Trump supporters at the polls.

Superdelegates are unelected representatives of a political party who get their positions by having held office, or through financial contributions to the party. During the 2016 Democratic National Convention, superdelegates from West Virginia, Michigan, Rhode Island, Indiana, Montana and Wyoming rejected the publicly-elected wins of Sanders in their states, nominating Clinton.

In 2012, the Koch Brothers, representing Big Oil, spent $400 million on local and presidential campaigns in support of continued drilling and "small government." In 2016, they used a budget of $889 million to support candidates who are pro-fracking and deny climate change.

2016: Rebekah Mercer held a high-level position on the Trump transition team, handpicking Steve Bannon, John Bolton, and a monster-mash of resurrected Think Tank darlings from the far-right to shape policy.

2018: Led by Minority Leader Chuck Schumer, one of the only Dems documented to haven taken Koch Bros. $$$, Senate Democrats approved a deal with Republican Majority Leader Mitch McConnell to fast-track *lifetime appointments* of 26 Trump-pick judges who are vocally against rights for women and people of color, and for harsher and longer jail terms.

It would have taken *1* dissenting voice to slow, if not stop all 26 appointments.

One of the appointments was not able to successfully pass the *Bar Exam*.

In 2019, *1* in every *7* circuit court judges will have been vetted by the far-right.

Bills to restrict public assembly (**protest**) are headed to senate in several states, having already passed in the Dakotas, Oklahoma, and Tennessee.

In this short century, America has already seen two Republican presidents who have *not* won the popular vote, and have been installed by the Electoral College.

Hard Laugh

Welcome to the hard laugh, the hard cry, the slide-over tumble-down lean-in feel-up canned-laughter-look-inside. Rest here, deposit your gummy cheek on this pillow of doom! You confessed a great deal when you fell asleep. Yes, we gained. You were asleep, and that is when we found you. We inspected the switches, checked references. We rearranged the set of flesh on your bones. You are all bones, exodus bones! We met an entire cast of characters you used like clothing, like kitchen appliances. We had you surrounded, so much so we were losing interest, selling the patents to your hands. Yet you eluded us, by becoming stone! We'll give you hunger; or the compelling guise of back-seat heat-seek. You are primed. Look at what a night's sleep has done for us! The dawn of civilization never looked so vital.

Guns n' Poses

9 gun-rights political action committees have donated $5,624,770 in the past year to politicians to enable greater sales of their products.

During Obama's two terms the arms and ammo industry saw an 81% increase in jobs.

In 2005, gun retailers reported 8 million background checks to the FBI. This number rose to 25 million in 2017.

During the 2016 presidential campaign, gun purchases reached a record high. Collectors feared harsh restrictions on gun sales that might come with a Clinton Presidency.

Doomsday preppers bulked up their arsenals. Keyboard warriors went insensate, nearly drowning in drool at the prospect of a civil war, which both the right and left discussed as a consequence of the 'wrong candidate' ascending to power.

In 2018, Shares of Outdoor Brands (formerly Smith and Wesson) have fallen 30%. Remington files for bankruptcy.

Background checks have fallen by 25%. Retailers call it the *Trump Slump*.

In America, gun sales traditionally take a sharp dive under Republican rule.

Democratic presidents are useful tools for the INDUSTRY to perpetuate the enemy myth:

A HOSTILE TAKEOVER BY ELITES

SNOWFLAKES WHO WANT TO REPLACE GRANDMA'S MEDS WITH COLD YOGA

OUTLAW COMEDY/RED LIPSTICK/GOD

THEY WILL STERILIZE THE WHITES

AND...

GIVE EVERY BABY A DICK, THREE CLITS,

AND A LOVE OF ORGANIC LEMONS.

1955 / 2018

This is the sign that marks the place where Emmett Till's lynched body was dragged from the water. The year is 2018 and it is riddled with fresh bullet holes.

His skull was crushed, his ear was torn. He was identified by a ring.

The men who lynched him were put on trial for 67 minutes and set free.

One year ago the woman who accused a fourteen-year-old child of whistling at her confessed on her deathbed that she made it up.

Simply being near a well-dressed black youth in a grocery store made her uncomfortable.

She does not get her name here.

Race in America

1 in every 9 black children has a parent in prison.

1 in 3 black children live beneath the poverty line.

African-American property-holders suffered the greatest losses after the market crash of 2008.

In 2017, the FBI labeled *Black Lives Matter* as "black identity extremists"—violent threats to the state.

59% of mass shooters in the past 40 years have been white.

The imprisonment rate of blacks for drug charges is 6 times that of whites.

Black youths between the ages of 15–34 are 9-16 times more likely to be killed by police than whites.

In 2017, 22-yr-old Stephon Clark was shot at *20 times* for having a cellphone in his hand.

In 2006, Atlanta police erroneously made a drug raid on the home of Kathryn Johnston, a 92-year-old African-American woman. They fired upon entering and Johnston was immediately killed. Finding no drugs, police planted marijuana in her home and submitted cocaine in court as evidence of what they purchased from the address. 3 officers were given sentences of 5-10 years.

Donald Trump launched his presidential campaign with a speech that promised to "clean up" American cities from the threat of Mexican "rapists."

In May 2018, 10,773 Mexican and Central American children were in US detention facilities. ICE has "lost track" of 1500 of them.

The private prison system charges a head fee of $133 for undocumented adults, and up to $750 a child.

Since the election of Trump, racist comments on Twitter increased 67%.

In 2017, a 22 yr-old white supremacist entered the Mother Emanuel AME Church and killed 8 parishioners and the pastor during a prayer meeting. The killer used a Glock, a gun that requires 6 pounds of force to pull the trigger. One of his victims, an elderly wheelchair-bound woman, was shot 11 times.

5 indigenous Standing Rock activists who have mobilized their tribes against Big Oil have been found mysteriously dead in the past 2 years.

Rock Around the Clock

THE FINE AND TUNING-FORK PRECISE BALANCE OF
LIFE AS WE KNOW IT THAT TOOK BILLIONS OF YEARS
TO EVOLVE ON THIS PLANET HAS BEEN WIPED OUT
BETWEEN THE TIME BILL HALEY'S "Rock Around the Clock"
was released and now. Why I wear pairs of SHOES that are older
than the initiation of our current extinction event!

Plastics Make It Possible

Of the 8.3 billion metric tons that have been produced, 6.3 billion metric tons of plastic have become waste. 9% of all plastic ever made has been recycled.

Half of all plastic manufactured is trash in less than a year.

8 million tons of plastic enter the oceans each year.

There are 5 patches of plastic in the oceans around the world called *gyres*. The one between California and Hawaii is the size of the state of Texas.

Every minute, a garbage truck of plastic is dumped into an ocean.

The risk of coral death rises from 4% to 89% after it contacts plastic.

If plastics disposal continues at this rate, there will be more plastic in the oceans than fish in the year 2050.

Playing With Fire

When playing with fire don't be surprised when you wake up with half your hair singed off and the new nickname of Stumpy. When this happens a second time and you find yourself as a skull resting on top of one lung and a charming facsimile of a kidney doing wheelies on a motorized scooter headlong into a volcano, well then it's time to admit you have some serious problems with normalizing pain/and or pattern recognition/and or an epic death wish to rival the gypsy moth.

Death in America

Every ten hours a West Virginian dies of opioids.

According to the CDC, 64,070 Americans died from drug overdoses in 2016, a 21% increase over the year before.

15,466 deaths were from heroin overdoses. 20,145 were from fentanyl and synthetic opioids.

The highest numbers of deaths were in West Virginia, New Hampshire, Pennsylvania, and Kentucky.

Suicide rates have increased 24% in the past 20 years.

Every day, 22 veterans commit suicide.

In 2016, the states with the highest rates of suicide were Montana, Wyoming, Utah, New Mexico, and North Dakota.

Between 2001 to 2010, the risk of death in the US was 76% greater for infants, and 57% greater for children ages 1-19.

American youths between the ages of 15 and 19 are *82 times* more likely to die from gun-related homicide than those in other nations.

Bulletproof backpacks for children are available for purchase with price points between $90 and $400.

In 2018, 10,000 endangered species-themed condoms were handed out on Earth Day.

Finger-Licking Good

In Wisconsin, a juggalo-wife cooks her finger to feed her husband as the ultimate act of love.

Diet in America

The average American consumes 150-170 lbs. of refined sugar a year.

The livestock industry is responsible for 18% of global greenhouse gas emissions.

Cows are responsible for 9% of all CO2 emissions on the planet. Their farts and manure emit one-third of the airborne methane on the planet. Methane raises global temperatures faster than CO2.

Commercial fishing has brought whales and dolphins to the verge of extinction. At the current rate of "harvesting," orcas and dolphins on the West Coast will be extinct in 15 years.

An Orca who researchers call J-35 carried her dead newborn calf on her nose for 17 days of grieving. When her energy flagged, members of her pod carried the dead calf for her. Reading about her makes me cry.

In July 2018 fertilizer run-off from sugar crops and cow feces caused an epidemic of cynanobacteria off the Florida coast, killing 5 million lbs. of ocean life.

Americans consume 270.7 lbs. of meat per person a year.

Americans eat more meat per person than in almost any other country on the planet, except Luxembourg.

The New Normal

This is a dead loggerhead turtle. She is on her back. Her mouth is open. Look at all of those wrinkles! Her eyes no longer see.

This is a dead manatee. He is on his side. He reached this rocky shore and was no longer able to live after quantities of poison swallowed. The red tide is filled with a neurotoxin that keeps his kind from taking in air. His face is a cross between a pit bull and your father.

This is a dead dolphin. Why do dead dolphins always look like babies? This is why they aren't in the news.

Here are four dead sharks.

This silver ribbon is made of three-hundred-thousand fish, belly-up, rotting. A team of people rake them into piles and these go to dumpsters.

"The water was white with dead fish," says a volunteer.

Veterinarians feed a brown pelican with a plastic tube.

A pile of dead turtles is leaking black blood. They must be stored for later.

The air conditioning is on high.

Cherry-flavored Synthahorse

One thing about the class divide is that the growing gap doesn't just isolate the poor in geographic locations, it also isolates them in *time*. The poor will be forced to not just give up any healthcare more complicated than a box of bandaids, but also their access to evolving technology.

I get a vision in my head of an entire class of people who live in areas where the only food nearby is canned cheese and *Lorna Doone* cookies at a gas station and they can't afford to travel more than twenty miles from where there were born, and they will be stuck in the most perverse version of 1988, or 1994, with little perks like video games and virtual reality goggles that will be made just cheap enough to suck out the bulk of your income after taxes.

Due to this one remaining lifeline of virtual reality, you can feel like you aren't stuck in an eternal 1988 or a 1994...until hunger forces you to remove the goggles for a midnight snack of cherry-flavored synthahorse.

Rx:

feudalism with optimum mouthfeel

Labor in America

The average productivity of an American worker has increased 400% since 1950. An American in 2018 has to work *4 times* the amount of a worker in 1950 to afford basic amenities.

40% of US employees work more than 50 hrs per week.

20% work more than 60 hrs per week.

The US poverty line for a single person under age 65 is $12,486.

40.6 million Americans lived in poverty in 2016.

11 million migrants and undocumented immigrants make up 5% of the nation's workforce.

The US is the only country in the industrialized world without paid parental leave.

The Lyft rideshare company sent out a press release celebrating a driver in Chicago who picked up fares while in labor.

McRaperson

When a nation ends up being run by corporations, you see all of the crappy things happen to civil rights, labor rights, and the environment that you'd expect as an employee of Exxon, Walmart, or the Hormel Ham slaughterhouse. You get unsafe working conditions, weird viruses that can only come from cannibalism, exposure to irradiated water and sex with syphilitic sheep. You get employees trying to steal electronics and painkillers because there isn't a living wage. Your co-workers brawl over barely measurable rewards like who gets to work double-overtime and who doesn't have to work on the harelip-methhead's shift. You find ways to justify losing fingers because at least it is steady pay, and then you discover that the company has taken away your pension, gone bankrupt, and owes money to people you've never even heard of. So you're laid off…and as you leave work for the very last time with a roll of stolen toilet paper tucked under your bra you're hit by your boss's Mustang convertible, which his son is taking for a joyride. There's a ball-gagged hooker in the trunk but the cops look the other way. Despite the broken spine and brain damage that guarantees an IQ of negative-two for your remaining days, your body is kept on life support so that your boyfriend, your mother, and eggs fertilized in top secret laboratories and yet to be extracted from your brain-dead amniotic sac are legally bound to a level of medical debt that once required computers the size of tanks to calculate. At least you won't have to watch the Compulsory Safety Videos anymore while eating takeout Pizza Hut with the woman obsessed with Tweety Bird kitchen magnets and that guy in Costco fake-Adidas shoes whom everyone calls Rapey McRaperson. If you could still think about things in a contiguous stream of coherent electrical impulses, you'd look back at all of the job interviews you've had where prospective employers asked you if you were a "team player"…and you would realize, once and for all, that being brain-dead makes you the most valuable player on the team!

Cancer Alley

1969-2019...

See Louisiana's Cancer Alley, where 136 petrochemical plants dominate the landscape like eerie miniature cities, futuristic and bland, belching clouds of rotten egg and clots of white smoke 24-7. At night they give off light the color of urine from a dying kidney. Scientists have concluded that the residents of this strip of land between Baton Rouge and New Orleans have a 100% chance of getting cancer in their lifetimes.

2018: Scott Pruitt, a lawyer with no scientific background, is appointed by the Trump administration to head the Environmental Protection Agency, which oversees the safety of air, water, agriculture, and food production in the nation. His first week on the job he has a $25,000 soundproof phone booth installed in his office, and spends an additional $9,000 to scan his office for surveillance equipment.

The day after the Trump inauguration, all wording associated with climate change, and studies that indicate the *scientific existence* of climate change are banned from being discussed by the agency.

The result? Corporations whose practices and products contribute to global warming are no longer liable to be fined—i.e. have their *growth slowed* by the EPA.

Under Pruitt's tenure, the EPA lifts regulations on oil extraction, coal use, pesticide use, the use of aerosols and industrial solvents, and endangered species protections.

He appoints a banker who has been banned from the financial industry (and to whom he owes several thousands in loans) to head the department that oversees cleanup of the most toxic land in the nation—*Superfund Sites*, where industrial waste has killed millions, via asthma, cancer, and birth defects. They lift "priority status" from 27 Superfund sites, saving the corporations who created the waste *billions*.

50 million Americans live within 3 miles of a Superfund site.

See underground acid pools, a radioactive lake that has been burning since the '80s, mercury landslides, smelting ash, PBBs, DDT, thyroid disease at age 5, birds fall mid-flight, girls sprout breasts at age 7.

As an encore, Pruitt opens millions of acres of national parks and monuments to oil and gas exploration.

On charges of corruption, Pruitt is fired in July, 2018. The Trump administration appoints his successor, a lawyer who worked as a lobbyist for a coal company.

Hundreds of environmental protections that people struggled for over a century to put in place are lifted in one year.

America is going to get uglier, fast…

But oh, sweet reprieve!

Science may not be allowed to prevent our illness, but it is required to make us drugs for after we get sick.

The most lucrative industry in America is not Big Oil. It is not in Silicon Valley. It is *Big Pharma*.

Americans spend $446 billion a year on prescription medications, more than twice what they spent in 2002.

We take drugs to *be* less sick, *feel* less sick, *ignore* the sickness that surrounds us.

We take drugs because we are shown what will happen to us if we doth protest the **Sickness Above.**

The Lizard King

You could give your life a thousand times over and it wouldn't stop the tidal wave approaching, the darkness encroaching, the smell of cigarettes and offal that rise from every crack; regard the monk who set himself on fire, he sold magazines but didn't stop the arms trade; and the vats of napalm grew fatter, and extinction is silent like the faraway meteor shower—light years, gift wrap of death. A human being can get used to anything, poker chips and meat chips and love on a screen. The Lizard King sings a song of self: Try it! They can't wait to spit on your grave. Trust is expensive. We've seen this show before. Magic tricks fade.

Background Noise

The 1981 *Military Cooperation with Civilian Law Enforcement Agencies Act* allows the U.S. armed forces and private security companies to work with domestic law enforcement to target and subdue "opposition."

Police have access to full body armor, tactical armored vehicles, machine guns, surplus aircraft, water cannons, sound cannons, heat rays, bayonets, grenade launchers, and drones.

MOVE was a Philadelphia-based black liberation group founded by John Africa in 1972. In 1985, a police helicopter dropped a bomb on the urban commune, causing a fire which killed 11 MOVE members, including 5 children. The fire spread through the neighborhood and destroyed 65 homes.

In 1993, the FBI used sound cannons, spotlights, and prolonged use of tear gas in a raid of the Branch Davidian religious compound in Waco, Texas, despite the group's leader, David Koresh, having already surrendered. The compound caught on fire and 79 people died.

The 2001 *Patriot Act* gives law enforcement permission to search a home without the occupant's consent. Americans can be imprisoned without trial if they fall under suspicion of seditious activity.

The 2012 *National Defense Authorization Act* gives the power to inter indefinitely.

PRISM is a program under which the *National Security Agency* collects digital and phone communications of every US citizen. The NSA works in concert with Google, Amazon, and AT&T.

The NSA uses malware to hack power grids, hospitals, banks, and the offices of governments around the globe. Exposure of NSA policy has brought the US to demand Edward Snowden's arrest on counts of espionage.

Since 2010, the Pentagon's *Defense Advanced Research Projects Agency* has spent $28 billion on robotic soldiers and drones, with the goal of achieving a 50% robotic army by 2025.

Fucking You Into Virginity

Saying you're going to bring peace with guns is like fucking someone into being a virgin.

Rent-a-Kills

The US not only has contracts with private sector firms to manage prison facilities for adults and "unstable" teens; it hires mercenaries to protect its employees and corporate donors. The use of hit-man help has been happening for a long time. It is not NEWS, and guess what? It rarely makes the news!

During the Standing Rock demonstration, a woman delivering water to protestors had her arm annihilated by a grenade. It was later amputated. Tribal elders were targeted by grenades, rubber bullets, tear gas, and water cannons in 20-degree cold.

The security service responsible for this is G4S. They are UK-based with operations in over 100 countries. They are the largest private security firm in the world.

G4S run prisons, transport cash, provide guards and private militia. Many countries have contracted them to take over police functions.

In Palestine, G4S services checkpoints, prisons, and detention centers. They act as occupation forces and guard settlements.

In Charlotte, North Carolina, G4S were hired to back up police in response to what the police call "increased racial tensions"—after officers murdered Keith Scott, an African-American who happened to live next door to a man with an outstanding arrest warrant.

G4S operates in North America, Latin America, Africa, Europe, the Middle East, and Asia. Their clients include Exxon, Philip Morris, and the Pentagon.

G4S is the go-to firm for crushing resistance.

Skin Deep

Eleven or so years ago I got scabies from a one-night stand and I ended up looking at endless online skin-rash forums for a number of red-eye nights. My god, these forums were like little fiefdoms for some people. YES, YOU CAN be King or Queen of a scabies chat forum for your ENTIRE LIFETIME, if you wish. People with handles like Razorgrrl53 and BigPapaBear would be moderators for the hundreds of sad-sack souls who, in desperation, would smear peanut butter, motor oil and toothpaste on their skin to stop the infernal itching.

Once you have patches of red, scaly flesh…once you have welts marching like advancing armies across your torso, with NO END IN SIGHT…(*What will be left unscathed, a single earlobe?*)…oh, you'd better believe a person panics.

Like Lady Macbeth cursed, "Out, damned spot!" and she scrubbed and she scrubbed but she still saw the blood on her hands from a murder long committed.

My skin was on fire. I had sleepless nights. My foray into scabies chat rooms went sideways. I found myself swept up on a tide of human desperation…

There are chat rooms for people who believe they have intestinal worms. They take pictures of their stools, replete with gooey-looking worms, or maybe these are strands of spaghetti, or maybe spinach, or partially-masticated corn, or…to be honest, I didn't *know* what I was seeing…maybe they *were* worms!

I read an article about Joni Mitchell and her Morgellon's disease. She feels insects creep *under* her skin. Between her blood and her epidermis is an alien dimension.

I read thousands of lonely-onlies chronicling all-night patrols against bedbugs and lanolin and radar and mind-invasion in a mirror-hall of digital supplication.

They perform turd autopsies on garbage bags. They use scalpels to pry "black specks" from their palms. They need to know what lives on their inner thighs, making vibrations and hatching eggs. They fear they will never again be fit for public consumption.

We are pod people! Mites and bites and parasites are real! In our technologically-advanced society, people *still* suffer from tapeworms, and in one case, bot-fly larvae extracted from their flesh. The Zika virus brings entire nations to fear reproduction, fear the birthing of babies with shrunken heads.

A human being hosts billions of microorganisms! It is only a matter of time before something gets in; the *effective* thing...

However there are vigilantes of the underskin who have disorders beyond diagnosis. They have moved on from biology and into stranger terrain...

We've all heard of memes. I don't mean pre-fab images of Willie Wonka or Kermit the Frog sipping tea and saying "I'm NOT with her." I mean ideas so big that instead of going, "We the people have thought of this idea," the idea is *larger* than us, uses the people.

The idea grows like a virus. It shapes *us* to keep *it* alive. Even the people who think they are in control of the idea are no longer in control.

Nike and Apple and Westinghouse! ExxonMobil and DOW! The holy spirit of data is fused with a physical supply-chain of material resources and labor. Nestle and Saab and Citibank are mighty as superheroes, as unforgettable as Phil Collins songs—and made of numbers and codes.

These entities have legal rights, dance above liability. They use vast swathes of human meat as their servants, their sculpting paste. They find fertile nations and devour them. They make the plantation owners of the nineteenth century look like Bo-Peep.

This website promotes the use of cookies. Every box of condoms and tentacle-porn you've bought online goes on your Permanent Record. The Entities Among Us use two brains: Technology and Law, and two fists: Beaten Men and Bombs.

They smash the sovereignty of nations, of species, of land, the air we breathe.

What is in a meme? *Class Mobility. The American Dream. Pull Yourself Up By Your Bootstraps.*

Do market forces reflect our natural desires, as Adam Smith suggested, or are we members of a cargo cult, desperately hoping to lure gods to earth, gods whose spectral fingerprints magnetise our deodorant and chewing gum, and through the use of these products we become holy?

Shimmering above us and just beyond our grasp are Banks Too Big To Fail, Gun Lobbies, Oil Brokers, Plastics Czars, Nations whose GDP is made of heroin and cocaine. Our Trusted Household Brands Pay No Taxes and Have Offshore Accounts, mighty providers of metals and peaches and cellphones and mood elevators that make teenagers roll like worms, and yet heads do not roll.

They make a wager on your death called life insurance, and drive you to it.

Are your carrying explosive agents in your luggage? Or your touch?

My skin is on fire. Invaded-nation men with families to feed and greed-to-be-machine haul monkey hides and rhino horns and woman-meat and child-eyes and palm oil and wood to make clarinets and condos; this forest is sold for a digital watch and a pair of snakeskin boots; go on OK Cupid; these passcodes and immortal tits, diamonds and copper wire, unused fighter jets and spent napalm, jails and vaseline, fears and futures and derivatives, and the storage cells of every online like.

There is a website where you can order a pre-made tinfoil cap to block beams of electromagnetic mind-control.

Once I sat at the bedside of a dying woman who believed doctors had performed malicious operations on her anus.

We feel monsters, but we can't cut deep enough. They *live* behind the ones with names.

What does violation mean in a post-industrial state?

"My god…the scabies have entered my ass-crack!"

I let it get bad—to the point where I couldn't eat or sleep. The online forums suggested I slather myself in margarine, borax, Dawn detergent, turpentine, and dog dewormer, vows writ by scribes who would, if they had to, wear these substances 24-7, because there is no cure like vigilance.

I could not end up like this.

By the time I went to Planned Parenthood, the welts had overtaken every part of my body except my head. When I lifted up my shirt, the doctor (wearing a lab coat and everything) recoiled on her swivel-chair.

She gave me a prescription for a hundred-dollar medicine and I paid for the appointment, then spent the rest of the day in a free clinic for low-income youth, watching a woman in bubblegum-pink lipstick and Angel jeans rush back and forth to the non-gendered bathroom, her lips crusted with a never-ending sluice of cocaine.

I was given a tube of permethrin cream at no cost—permethrin, a toxic and very effective chemical with a slightly mentholated scent that I smeared all over my body, through my hair, wore like a sacred ointment (even while ordering drinks from the waiter who gave scabies to me) for twenty-four hours.

Where is the parasite?

Is it a who? A what? A they? Is it like mad cow? A prion, beyond life? Is it a void that yawns? Whose passing we sense in waves, like death, like deadlines, like hate?

What is a parasite? Well it depends...on whether you have the eyesight of a microscope or the hindsight of a historian.

Man on the Street

"A peaceful person running for president? It would be like auditioning to be the lead singer of AC/DC and thinking you're going to get up there and sing folk songs."

Vet Tale

We are a hair's breadth away from the Roman Coliseum, napalm death, a famous plague no one lives to write about. Flesh is poetry; neurons lie.

Once I was a writing tutor for a teenaged girl whose father was a Vietnam vet who recanted, heavily, when he returned to the States. He went on speaking tours around the nation and became well-known as an anti-war activist. He told me that one day he was giving a speech in a church in a small Montana town, and when he went out to the parking lot, a shadow emerged, a shadow in army fatigues.

The man in the shadows spoke softly, saying that he was sent to kill the anti-war vet, but he would not, because they were in the same platoon, and the would-be assassin knew of the soldier's bravery.

"I thought I would let you know," the shadow said, and disappeared.

Twenty years later, the vet was in an SUV telling me this tale.

"We did things to people we didn't think ourselves capable of before we shipped overseas. All of the civilized things you see here..." He waved his hand at the traffic lights, the billboards, the flowers sold by a corner vendor: "are illusions, the finest spray over a bloodthirst...each of us contains. I watched soldiers crush people with tanks. Bodies falling like ragdolls. We burned entire villages. I saw children's flesh melt. I can close my eyes and see these things playing like a never-ending movie."

It was four-thirty PM, and I had earned thirteen dollars an hour and a reminder of human barbarism.

"Civilization is a thin veneer," he said, and he said it many times.

Iraq, 2003

The U.S. detention center in Abu Ghraib, Iraq, 2003: No trials are conducted to determine the innocence or guilt of the men incarcerated. Prisoners are stripped, forced to perform sexual acts, piled naked into human pyramids, hung by their wrists, have their heads soaked in urine, are maimed by attack dogs, walked on leashes, deafened with electronic devices, repeatedly given electrical shocks, raped with broomsticks, forced to masturbate at gunpoint, brutally beaten, used for target practice, burned, frozen, and photographed during all of these acts, with their torturers giving the "thumb's up," including over a body packed in ice of a man they have murdered. None of the U.S. soldiers responsible for this torture serve more than four years' prison time.

Try This Shit

You hit forty and everyone around you is either psychologically or physically dying in ways that can no longer be covered up with underground fashion or enigmatic smiles. When people say "fuck you" they mean it with an unrepentant rage and when people say "I want to die now" it is a biological request rather than an experiment in literary ennui. Almost everyone is a child throwing a tantrum and yet living another day, participating in the great human pantomime.

People lash out. They do deadly things; they wake up anyway, they ask for more love, they ask to be held, and you try to tell yourself: "I can fix none of this" yet feel it in a way that isn't the same as being heartless.

You find yourself surrounded by a crumbling world you knew you could never really fix; it would be like thinking a poem or the flight of a yellow balloon can cure the savagery of the human genome, and that would make things pretty dull anyway, wouldn't it? If the monsters we love were lobotomized, where would the romance go?

When I was twenty-two I was writing short stories based on my dreams and nightmares. I remember one about a party where people were saying, "Have you tried this shit?" but in fact it was a drug that came in a sealed glass vial and it was a compound extracted from human fecal matter that imparted a sublime high.

One day I went to a garage sale and bought a purple chair and I walked into a cafe with this purple chair and a skinny man in his mid-thirties with shorn hair and a nervous look started telling me he was a Gulf War veteran. He said he had seen things the government was covering up.

He said he was a hunted man, and had been moving around.

He had rolls of film he stored in a security deposit box, of people tortured and dismembered, and the use of weapons that no one knew the US government had. He said he was going out on a limb by telling me, but he could tell I was on his side.

He shook. He was eaten alive by nerves. For all I know at least half of what he said was true. The longer he went on, as I sipped my coffee, I felt that we were an *army of two* against the world, against the duplicity, the abject greed, the spider-nest drive to capture all free life in a web and convert it to food and lucre to support the next day's conquests.

I told him I was a writer and that my writing was going to show what monsters people were. I told him that like him, I wanted to expose hypocrisy, and that I didn't want to repeat my life in the world as it was, ad infinitum.

No, I would *not* change the human genome! I would not lessen the savagery of the species; but I had an ego, I had the desire to change something. I was young enough to believe many things even while holding the invisible tablets of cynicism, commandments that kept me looking at the depravity, the rapid on-off love-you hate-you that every mind flickers through over the course of a day.

"Amnesia," I would say. "Greed and amnesia." I would intone these words like prayers.

And when you hit forty you see others who intone these words like prayers, and some of them have outrage, and some of them have broken feet, and collapsed lungs, and some of them are still in their twenties and act like soldiers in faded black fatigues, shuffling in and out of buildings after baking bread and cleaning floors and fixing bikes or cars or trimming hedges and they will tell you that it is always time to die and yet they do not want to die, and they will tell you that America is over, and they will tell you they are not going to vote.

Do you know how many people are not going to vote? MILLIONS! It is those getting the most fucked-over who are not going to vote in the next election because they have ceased to believe that what happens on top can be fixed, or could ever be fixed, and that a slow fuck versus a fast fuck doesn't matter in the end.

The rainy season is here and I wonder where I will be in five years, ten years. I am a traveler. I say this in my soul.

You can call my soul naïve. Say that because I still want to live and swallow the clouds and the blueness of the sky and feel the warmth of tropical waters on my feet, and hear people speak other languages that are not American Decay, American Futility, that I am naïve. But let me whisper to you once again:

I want to see as much as I can before I die. I will tease the world to show me something; prove me wrong, show me *something* I have never seen before, something that isn't just a drug made of shit in a glass vial that imparts the most sublime dreams and flurries of forgetting.

THE
GREAT
DIVIDE

The Kingdom of Zion

He circles the block and angrily chants: "The kingdom of Zion is for white people, the kingdom of Zion is for white people!" and his legs and fingers move with a musical cadence and his leather jacket and slacks fit him so sublime like the night itself, like squid-flesh; and he clearly doesn't like white people and I can't blame him but I also wonder how long it will take for his rage to burn out or if he'll tire of the setting as this part of downtown is filled mainly with wraiths who look like casting rejects from a movie about the life of Thor with Thor's handmaids played by Jerry Garcia's undead harem; and perhaps the chanting man will find a more appreciative audience closer to Burnside…I wonder if he is taking a brief vacation from a medication; for all I know he could be a brilliant architect or physicist or chef and I haven't got the courage to ask what he means because his anger is so fresh it leaps across the sidewalk like a taser-stream; and I ask myself what separates this man from any other American, he is out here rapping what he means while everyone else hides in bunkers and types, teeth gnashing, eyes like over-easy eggs.

Same Page

Guns don't kill; men kill: Oh, wait, not all men kill? Okay, only crazy men kill. Wait, not all mentally ill people are murderous? Not all men who kill are straight coz this latest mass-murderer actually dated dudes at this gay club? Not all guns kill people, just hundreds of people in mass murders every month, in shopping malls, schools, and office parks, acts that must have been committed by crazy people or religious freaks so that makes guns okay? Some are just bought and sold as fetishes of sex and fear and the Old West and Foreign War and the things that stop Black People and Reptile Aliens and the Cops are going to take EVERYTHING AWAY but our guns, have you figured it out yet? And the gun shows overfloweth like new churches with the sleek steel symbols of FREEDOM, so are we all on the same page? No.

Dirty Water

Woman, you are supposed to die. Didn't we tell you by now? If you can't be quiet we need to slice you. It won't take much because we started early. When you were in the crib we started sticking pins in your neck, your hands, your thighs. We blindfolded you, bound your feet, made you bottle blonde, plucked your pubes, told you not a peep when we are in the room. Woman, you're listening! Don't tell us our mamas raised us to be better, you will never. Is she dead yet? I saw movement! The only good woman makes her voice like candy. When stuck like a pig, she squeals. Remote control, like a dead one. Late movie, make it hurt. Take her eyes, pull out her pink. She's inside-out. It's not enough. Break every mirror, break every eye, break every bone so she knows we mean it. Let this be our little secret. She's dead but will live another sixty years. Where the fuck are the car keys?

Misty

"I don't care if you have three dicks and a twat in the middle of your forehead. You're still entering a corrupt system." —An Innocent Bystander reacts to the news that two transgendered people named *Misty* have won primaries for congressional seats.

Tunnel Vision

TUNNEL VISION: Do not teach the slaves to read. Oil, water, silicon are locked down. News does not exist and never has. Power of the few secluded from the many: The many are lubrication, are juice, contained within a lasso of law, codes you must be born and prepped for a lifetime to decipher.

LIFE-STUFFS: The masses live in a continuous state of distrust. Drones to artificially pollinate genetically-engineered foodstuffs are in mass production.

HIGH: "Upload yourself to the Cloud" say the ads, but they do not mean the Himalayas. Virtual life has been delivered to a species who feeds from the screen-teat in rental coffins, pushbuttoned infrared diagrams of celebrity ass. Deathbed leaks keep us humble. Pop quiz. Showtime.

BETTER NOW: The past snaps awake, shows up with an accusatory finger. We tremble for two seconds, but the past is a buffoon, has lost all but two of its teeth. It needs drugs to leave the front door, and is easily forgotten.

SAFE: I wear insecticide instead of perfume.

Fake News #1

In 2018, 5 corporations control 90% of the US internet, cable television, and printed news publications: Time Warner, Disney, Murdoch's News Corporation, Bertelsmann of Germany, and Viacom.

30 years ago, 90% of media was held by 50 unique companies.

Media has been bought by the highest bidder; of these there is no shortage. Corporations have poured billions into super-pacs and anonymous donor shells, lobbying for businesses to have the same legal rights as individuals, for the breaking of labor unions, and the promotion of an anti-government narrative that implies laws are controlled by illegitimate figures—*fuckboys, immigrants, and undersexed dykes*—out to ruin the common man.

Resentment and greed are legitimized in political discourse: The public is soured on labor unions, environmental preservation, public education, and journalism as an institution.

Citizens on both the left and right are alert for "fake news." Many have ceased investigating global news altogether, opting instead to follow pundits—entertainers who preside over niche forums, offering daily soundbites on who is for and against the *team*—false flags, lizard people, a Satanist pizza parlor run by Hillary Clinton where she presides over a child sex-slave ring, an obsession with a mythical videotape where Russian call girls are hired to urinate on Donald Trump.

Election 2016: Every night Americans get a 20-minute dose of Trump first, Clinton second—and occasionally a 1-minute clip of "wild card" Sanders, whose message of universal healthcare and labor reform is deemed "unrealistic" by mainstream media, despite his appearances attracting more supporters than the *other two candidates combined.*

Broadcast Media elects Trump well before the Electoral College and those pesky *people* do.

All is sensation. Welcome to the Cartoon.

Fake News #2

2005: After pressure from religious groups. the state of Kansas changes its public elementary school science curriculum to include textbooks that state that the evidence-based theory of evolution is a "theory in crisis"—and that an Earth magically conjured by a supernatural entity is a "viable alternative."

2017: The Michigan state government decides to remove the word "democracy" from all elementary school textbooks.

They also vote to expunge the history of 20th-century civil rights movements—including references to Native Americans, African-Americans, Latinx, people with disabilities, and the gay and trans community. This history is replaced with a statement that says "expansion of civil rights for some groups" is "an infringement of rights and freedoms" for others.

2 in every 4 Americans believe the sun revolves around the earth.

1 in 10 American science teachers say that humans play no role in climate change.

A growing minority of Americans believes the moon landing was faked.

A vocal minority believe that Barack Obama was an Arab double agent, *and* the Judeo-Christian Antichrist.

The US population is 26% evangelical.

77% of U.S. evangelicals believe that we are living in the *End Times,* the last period before Christ returns to Earth to judge the masses.

In 1971, Ronald Reagan said: "For the first time ever, everything is in place for the battle of Armageddon and the second coming of Christ."

Youtube talk show hosts speak of aliens in the White House, the falling of the Twin Towers being an "inside job," that the Sandy Hook shooter and 22 dead elementary school children are "crisis actors" hired to sway legislation on gun control...while hocking dietary supplements, toothpaste, bulletproof vests, "brain pills," and dating apps.

The Best Flavor

If we must have mind control—what is the best *flavor* of mind control?

Whodunnit?

One last thing about political infighting: I overhear way too many arguments where one group that labels themselves as socially/ politically progressive puts down everyone else who is essentially on their side, meaning NOT THE ONE PERCENT. I hear, "The pink pussy hats are a psy-op," and "All Democrats are dupes being played by Neo-Con Think Tanks," and "Black Lives Matter will never enter a peaceful debate," and "Antifa is just too angry and wants to smash things," and "Me Too is made of man-haters funded by the Democratic Party and don't realize how puritanical they are by forcing the Media Eye onto tabloid accusations instead of talking about the Prison System and the way Status Quo corporate-owned governments across the planet are starving out the loyal consumers they no longer need, one long cull during environmental meltdown, and they would like to return us to a society where men and women must wear Scarlet Letters in the Streets," and "I wish a violent death on everyone who voted for (insert names here)" and "Protest does nothing; you must *BUY NOTHING* and *GO OFF THE GRID*," and "We can never trust anyone who makes over 30,000 dollars a year," and "Third Wave feminists are like rabid dogs and would love to start a totalitarian Valerie Solanas-type regime," and "Second Wave feminists think buying reusable bamboo-fiber pantyliners and giving 5 bucks to the Southern Poverty Law Center is enough," and "We are all being played," yes, I agree we are all being played, but this constant dismissal of the other millions who are being played gets us NO FUCKING WHERE.

2016-2018

2016-2018: a period of time in which we started to see the final membrane-thin flaps of consensus reality break down, and we looked askance at our best friends, family members, and co-workers as they suggested that microwaveable mac-and-cheese, pink hairbrushes, inflatable frogs, and dildos should run for president.

The Most Terrible Job To Have

I had a phone call with my mother yesterday, our first one after the election, and of course I was curious to know how she voted, but also pretty certain what the response would be, because I know the lady so well. I should preface this by saying that my mother has over the course of her entire lifetime believed that her phones has been tapped by Soviet spies and a organization that has at times been loosely called the "Syracuse Mafia"—but these days, who does she think is tapping the phone? Who, in 2016, is working to tabulate the information?

"Who got your vote?"

"Well…I don't want to say on the phone," she said in a sheepish voice.

"It's okay, you can tell me. Was it Trump?"

"I don't want to say any names, honey."

"Were you with Her?"

"I'm not sure I should really say."

"Can we do it with a guessing game of yes or no?"

"Well honey, let me put it this way: I thought about your grandparents and how they would want me to vote. You know the two of them were lifelong Republicans, and loved Ronald Reagan and were very upset about the scandal with the Clintons. They felt so sorry for Monica Lewinsky."

I didn't bother to say that at the time I suspect that Monica Lewinsky was probably enjoying herself. She did, after all, keep the dress!

"You know honey, I could have gone either way. I mean, I could have tossed a coin and voted for either of them. I don't have anything against Donald or Hillary. I really feel sorry for both of them right now. Being the president of the United States is the most terrible job to have, and they were both fighting to get it. And that poor Hillary has health problems and you know that Donald, they say he has low blood pressure, though it is hard to believe with all of the screaming that he does! And of course I don't like all the things he says about women. You'd think that at his age, he wouldn't be having so many affairs with women anymore."

My mother has never had cable tee-vee and doesn't own a computer. She hasn't dated a man or kept close friends since 1973. She lived with my grandparents until they died, in 1998, and 2006.

I say all of this as a preamble, as a way to describe the couch the cushions of her thoughts rest on: She is isolated. She is an innocent. She watches *My Three Sons* every day on a network of all '50s-through '70s broadcasts called "Me TV." (They play Gilligans Island on there too, if you must know.)

All of this is a character sketch of a human being who, since day one, has believed in God, says her prayers every night, and has never once doubted the veracity of ANY piece of information she has heard on television.

"I am a registered Republican, honey," she said.

"Were you always a registered Republican?"

"Yes, I have been since the early sixties, since I was able to vote. The only time I wasn't a Republican was when I went to the Convent School, and you know it was an all girls' school with nuns, so it was hard to find boys to take to dances. We had to be inventive. I had two friends who told me about a group of Young Democrats they belonged to, to find boys. Most of the boys in the city were Democrats. Syracuse has always been a city high in politics, and Democrats are very popular here. You remember when the Clintons were visiting that restaurant on Erie Boulevard so much in the nineties? They had all kinds of meetings with big Democrats in the city."

"You mean you were in this Teenaged Democrats club just to find dates for school dances?"

"Well yes, honey. And a lot of these boys were good-looking and came from good families, so there was a nice selection, very respectful."

She is an innocent, one of an older generation of innocents, and they made sure to vote. I knew that she would vote the way she did because ultimately, she will vote for whichever candidate promises the most "protection"—whatever protection is.

To my mother, Foreign Policy is like an obscure form of math, and National Security is sold like a bag of maxi pads, explained with about the same level of detail: "Absorbs more liquid! Stays fresh longer! NEW, extra protection—with wings!"

I love my mother, deeply. I don't think she is an idiot, however she is like a lot of people who don't do research, who do not consult the news on more than one channel of tee-vee, or one website. She learns everything from the glowing box in the corner of the living room.

There are people of both parties who have no idea of what the branches of the government are, or even where Italy is, or what gravity is—but they vote!

There are people who don't know what an electoral college is, and they have not heard about how 868 polling places were closed this year, before a major election, in what seems like a concerted obstructionist move to keep Latinx and African-American voting districts with limited time in long lines, and stranded. Out of 50 states, only 7 have mail-in ballots.

In the Age of Information, we, as human beings, continue to live with tunnel vision.

We are a nation of flowers blooming to private suns. We seem to move like clockwork, each of us operating with a designated enemy, whether it is Liberals, Lefties, Rednecks, Elites, Neo-Nazis, Sex Freaks, Putin Puppets, or Those Who Do Not Understand The Value of Order.

Security! Order! Us against Them! And What To Place Here Next…if we are, as a nation, reduced to Ground Zero?

We have so many names, so many enemies, and so many Dream States—and we want to do the 320-Million Right Things.

ELECTION WEEK, AND TAKING IT TO THE STREETS

An American Soap Opera in Four Parts, As Seen From Inside The Portland Bubble (November 2016)

Converging upon Portland's city center for the past four days were people from too many walks of life—*too many* for the police—by which I mean elderly hippies who marched in the Civil Rights movement, teens so young that they don't remember what occurred before Obama took office, veterans in wheelchairs, cooks and cab drivers, Black Lives Matter activists, Black Bloc activists with bodies obscured-yet-visible, their mouths behind bandanas, the women in camo pants and tank tops, the men pale, thin, moving like burned cigarettes in utility jackets and combat boots.

I watched a drunk skater-dude in a Guatemalan poncho and college kids in chopper tees stumble backwards from flash grenades. I watched ladies with therapy pets who resembled their therapy pets advance and retreat behind the doorframes of closed cafés.

I watched hardcore punks with hair a rainbow of colors careen in figure eights, their bicycles serving as steeds did in revolutions long ago. I watched priests and poets and soccer moms, Latinas in short-shorts and proud bared thighs. I watched drag queens prance with pride—and coursing around me like a ghostly river were lesbians, striding hand in hand, glowing with the kind of youth that makes me think of doll parts.

There was SO MUCH YOUTH on the streets, and you know how those over thirty usually view youth:

"This marching is all for show! They're just having a big party. Statistics show that they didn't even bother to vote! They can't wait to jump on cars and smash things!"

Shall I even begin to address why so many young people didn't bother to vote, yet they bothered to march?

Can you blame them?

The kids, and many of their parents, are *done*. This country is in a deep economic depression, and the term *recession* is a cosmetic airbrushing of the severity of its poverty. In red states and blue states, the poor and middle classes are done with the system, but the system won't go away. The 1% against the 99% is a machine set in place in ways it has never been before, because the world's technology is at its disposal—cutting-edge, and highly-addictive technology!

But the plot only thickens! Our species has achieved a feat of cognitive dissonance *par excellence* with mass extinctions, weekly major oil spills, robotic jihads, and a level of normalized paranoia that makes Wile E. Coyote on the old Roadrunner cartoons look sedate.

In America, we have permanently passed the point where we can pretend voting is enough. Voting was never enough to hold our elected officials accountable to their promises.

This election has shown overwhelmingly that the "disillusioned" vote is one that must be captured to secure a win.

Our nation is a cracked mirror. You stare into the glass, hoping to find solace, but you are delivered more cracks.

November 6th, two days before the election...

The gay man and the drunk man stood in my living room and the drunk man asked the gay man who he was voting for.

The gay man said, "Trump," which made the drunk man tumble backwards in disbelief. He braced himself on the arm of a chair.

"No, who are you really voting for?"

The gay man carefully clasped his hands in his lap and gave a bashful yet determined smile. He repeated: "Trump."

"You're not serious!" The drunk man said. *"Trump?"*

"Yes." Again that bashful yet determined smile. Like a slot machine, he repeated: *"Trump."*

Randomly travel to any epoch of human history and you will find people collecting nuts, daggers, dried fruit…prayer beads and gas masks… in preparation for imminent apocalypse. I know many who speak of buying property in the middle of nowhere, going underground, getting passports, having "getaway plans" for when a civil war starts after this election.

"Things will get back to normal," pundits and popes say, "things always do."

November 9th, the day after the election...

Downtown Portland was a mournful stage today. People moved slowly, many seeming on the verge of tears, many with dazed expressions on their faces as if they simply could not believe that surreality supplanted reality last night with an airlock sense of efficiency.

Never in my life have I seen so many people clutching cellphones, not even bothering to look up as they crossed streets, got in and out of cars, ordered food, formed lines, oblivious to the mechanisms of leafblowers and cranes, oblivious to the sun as it burst through clouds and then sank in the west, riot helicopters commencing their arcs over Pioneer Square, commuters folding themselves into buses and trains, hungover from a night of drinking and the friction within their families, their marriages, their heads.

Never in my life have I seen people peer so intently into the glowing layers of Media, as if their phones might deliver unfolding scenes of disaster, or truth, or reassurance, or a different outcome, like a magic eight-ball shaken and through the dense blue liquid, a message emerges: TRY AGAIN.

Not only is there sadness in the air; there is fear, and the howls of those who feel glee in a candidate endorsed by the KKK and the American Nazi Party being elected on the 78th anniversary of Kristallnacht. Friends report the wagging of Confederate flags, men yelling from the windows of their trucks at women, and calling men "fags" with abandon. Rage is running high, and I don't believe that we as a nation are going back to slumber.

The only person I passed this afternoon who seemed to be happy was a homeless old man who felt a deep imperative to serenade me with a Phil Collins song: "I can feel it coooomin' in the air tonight..." his front teeth missing, his dreadlocks wild.

The eve of November 9th, downtown...

I emerge from a march that makes me feel like a crying ghost. Seeing hundreds of people, mostly in their teens and twenties cry, "Not our president!" is intense, rouses a rare and intrusive sense of Reality in my blood.

WHAT? Wake up? Something is Real? The continuum is... interrupted?

"Hey-hey! Ho-ho! Donald Trump has got to go!"
"My body, my choice!"
"Fuck Trump! Fuck 'im in the ass!"
A sign says:
THEY TRIED TO BURY US. THEY DIDN'T KNOW WE WERE SEEDS.

Women march with bare breasts. People at bus stops join the march. A homeless dude chants, *"Drop your wah-lets!"* with a chuckle.

A woman mostly obscured under layers of coats and a sleeping bag dozes through the whole thing.

A marcher in a mask tries to set trash cans on fire and another marcher stomps on a burning shopping bag.

An hour later my boyfriend and I are at a Plaid Pantry minimart where he is buying a carton of cigarettes.

I see through the window the clerk's skinny frame, his animated pacing.

The clerk is gay, not in a subdued way. He is also a florist. He often breaks into song. He is wracked with so many forms of inner pain that it seems his veins have worked their way *outside* of his body. With almond eyes, shorn hair, and a tweed cap, he assumes the Eternal Stage:

"You don't look like you're taking current events too badly."

"What do you mean?" I ask.

"You look like you're feeling okay."

"I may not be expressing it in an obvious way, but no, I don't think things are okay.

I wonder if, over the course of the day, this man has seen hundreds of crying faces, left-wing customers and loved ones expressing grief, some on suicide watches, no longer able to eat or go to work. I have absorbed the grief of many of these people in the past few days...

But me? Was the clerk assuming that because I was not in tears, I was *for* a GOP Future, replete with Creationist Placemats, Chastity Belts, Race Wars, and Oceans turned to Martian Canals?

"I never know with some customers. People you'd never expect come out for Trump!"

And this is where he gets *started*.

"I have a piece of advice for you after living on this Earth for forty-six years…

"I lived through Reagan-Bush Dynasty. I lived through the *grisly* Portland of thirty years ago, when skinheads stomped through the downtown blocks and they would think nothing of breaking a *homo's* back with a tire iron. I lived through muggings and assaults and the passing of Proposition 8, which in 2008 outlawed gay unions in California, where I was living with my partner.

"Just this year I visited North Dakota…I was in the *beating heart* of Red State America, and I can tell you *this:*

"People ask, oh *how* did Trump happen? Because this bubble of liberalism we live in is so small that the rest of the nation can't take it seriously. Outside of every city is the *real* America, *Red Rage Nation*. To pretend otherwise is to prolong a lie that keeps your life brittle and small.

"People all over the country are waking up to the idea that these two parties we keep electing are self-serving oligarchies made of shit, so when people say 'How did we let Trump happen?' I'm thinking, *honey, it isn't a surprise.*

"But grief is NOT the answer. I just had my lowest point a year ago standing at the edge of the St. John's Bridge, ready to throw myself off, but I yanked myself back from that brink because that is what a person has to *do.* This is what we have to do right now. We've got to get right on our feet again and make the future we want to live in."

We nod, and he goes on.

"As a survivor, I speak with a burning desire when I say honey, you can't survive by crying and pointing fingers. It doesn't *work* that way. Trump may be the best thing that's ever happened to us, waking us up to the necessity of revolution. This is our *time* to make powerful art, bring all of our splintered little subcultures together. *Trump*…is our return to the underground."

His hands mime knitting needles in the air:

"I feel like Norma Rae, ready to make hundreds of little mittens for the hands of every person who stands in the streets throwing bottle rockets!

"Off with you! Blow it up, little Billy! Because THIS...HAS...TO HAPPEN.
"Mark my words: In opposition we are stronger. In opposition we have the most meaning...allright?"

For those born high and born low, Trump was a means to an end. He was elected as the ultimate act of vandalism.

November 10th, an eerily warm fog, and flying crows...

My visions of this night start with an eerily warm fog, and end with flying crows.

The night is too warm for the first week of November. For the past week, a rosebush has been blooming outside my door. The fog on this night has a strange quality, as if, instead of moisture, it is composed of the candy-scented chemicals pumped from a dance club's smoke machine.

6 PM...

Protests have been going in Pioneer Square since 2. Marches organized by separate groups plan to converge in Holladay Park, by the Lloyd Center shopping mall. I watch coverage on a live video feed set up by one of the most conservative stations in the city, and while the newscasters harp on the usage of spray paint and the kicking of windows, even interviewing the manager of a car dealership about how cars coated in spray paint cost twenty-thousand dollars in insurance each to clean—something hits me more-than-this:

The people.

Their sheer numbers startle the eyeball, the mind. I see thousands of people on the move between the hours of 6 to 7. Their numbers are growing. This is *on*. To see waves of people on foot occupy streets that are usually filled with traffic jams—is electrifying.

I guzzle tea. I dress in black. I race out the door, knowing I have to be there. Through the fog, the moon rises and looms strange, like the eye of a cat, a melting scoop of ice cream.

I catch a bus downtown, then ride a train across the river to meet them. I chase branches of the protest, and this is what I see:

The crowd is a mix of people with different goals. The revolution can only be partially organized. Chaos is ever-present. Next to people with rainbow flags and candy, people in Halloween masks dance with baseball bats. Men in clown makeup stagger wildly.

High school freshmen are dressed to the nines in what they feel is "military" and hippie gear. Kids in hot pants and baseball jerseys who just flew out of movies and the mall's food court join the march, energized like bouncing balls, eager to be part of something exciting.

People of all ages hold cell phones above their heads. Everyone simultaneously appears to be a journalist and a cast member in a film.

The marchers stop traffic at intersections. Drivers honk and yell. Tensions run high. Some marchers chant *"Let's get row-dy!"* and others respond with their own chant: *"Peace-ful pro-test!"*

Mixed in the crowd are men and women who are trying to escalate the scene to violence, and they climb posts, set off firecrackers.

When the march reaches Holladay Park, a man with a baseball bat beats an electrical box until the lights go out. The crowd responds by putting their phones on "light" settings, raising them in the air like lighters at an old-fashioned rock concert.

A man screams, ***"Are you gonna let Nazi Germany come to the United States? You gotta put some skin on the line and speak their language because that's all these nuts can understand!"***

A woman on the other side of the crowd starts her own speech, which is met with a resounding cheer:

"It's not about destruction; it's about power to the fuckin' people!"

"Whose streets? **Our streets!***"*

A night before, the crowd successfully blocked the I-5 freeway entrance, walking, breathing, dancing and singing where streams of gas-guzzling cars have dominated for decades.

Tonight the protesters attempt to retake the freeway, but a solid line of 20-30 police in riot gear, backed up with sound canons, sting guns, pepper spray, and tear gas block the people's entry to the freeway, a freeway that they and their parents' and grandparents' taxes paid for.

"Whose streets?" they chant.

"Our streets!"

The crowd is restless. While some peel off and linger on this side of the bridge, at least a thousand make a turn to re-enter downtown to reconvene in Pioneer Square.

Along the way, lovers of chaos kick in windows, spray paint FUCK TRUMP on random walls. Organizers with bullhorns attempt to talk them down:

"This is *not* how to make change…*Peace-ful pro-test!*"

A couple men and women with lighters and road flares try to set recycling bins and random scraps of paper on fire.

"Don't mess with the fuckin' trees, man!" a woman cries, a voice of reason. But in this crowd of thousands, there are thousands of reasons.

I talk to teenagers, teachers, a guy in a trenchcoat bragging about his collection of knives.

I talk to a man in a cape that says BERNIE BRO, and an assortment of people feeling edgy, unable to smile about their run-ins with the cops, their suspicion of informers and plants in the crowd.

I speak to one of the organizers, then to a stout woman in her sixties leaning on a cane.

Poking above the collar of her mackintosh, in a way I don't notice at first, is a starched minster's collar. She is with a number of Epicoscpal leaders uniting for a peace conference to discuss how their religion can publicly combat the values of a Trump Presidency.

9 PM, and beyond…

Broadcasts go out across the country and across the oceans, showing Portland as a "leading city" of the American Anti-Trump protests. Many of these broadcasts stress that the outcome of the protests is vandalism and violence, but on the ground, it doesn't look this way.

To be honest, I don't view a dozen, or even three dozen broken windows as violence. Broken windows and burned trash cans are vandalism, but violence, in my opinion, is what human bodies do to human bodies and other living things—not property. Violence is the experiment in 2014, when the Portland Police's use of a sound cannon caused sickness and hearing damage to Black Lives Matter protesters, and also caused flocks of birds to fall dead from trees.

Reporters mention the broken glass and the fireworks people set off, but the reality I saw over the course of the evening is that even the most ominous-looking protestors had a sense of etiquette, and told cars of confused people to roll up their windows.

Police descend...

Around 11 PM, masked marchers direct traffic during one of the police's attempts to close roads around the protest. A masked woman in knee-high stockings and black cotton calms a car of confused blondes who look like they have just come from a bar, while her consort, a masked man who looks like he came right out of Mad Max Beyond Thunderdome, warns pedestrians that "The pigs are about to unleash the pepper spray, so if you want to avoid that, you better get out soon."

I watch one guy who looks like Hulk Hogan get so mad at a protester that he leaps out of his car to start a brawl.

Between the hours of 11 PM to midnight, cops close in on the remaining protestors, setting off flash grenades, using rubber bullets and pepper spray.

Paddywagons and an ever-present stream of cops stand by, some of them taking phone selfies before they close in on the crowd. Claims that this is an "unlawful assembly," which the police bullhorns repeat, are ignored until the police's flash grenades go off.

The thousands who occupied the streets have by this point dwindled to hundreds—sliding in and out of the intersections blocked by armored vans, a motley and exhausted mix of what I can only call audience-members and concerned citizens, along with the gawkers and goons you would find at a football game.

The police and remaining protesters move back and forth between a four-block radius of the city center like a tug of war for three hours. Some of the protestors climb up the side of a rain shelter as if it is a tree. They dangle from a light pole, ragdolls in black, try to stay off the ground and away from the reach of beetle-bellied police, but they are cornered.

Onlookers film with a sense of mirth until the cops unleash a rapid fire of flash grenades around 1 AM, and make mass arrests.

1 AM, the morning of November 11th...

The fog, it is beautiful. The trees are lit with Christmas garlands. Even the traffic lights glow like beacons of Oz, Turkish Delights, Tonka trucks in a Sears catalog, in this fog.

Every time a flash grenade goes off, murders of crows are jolted out of trees and move further away from the action.

I follow the crows under yellow maple leaves, the skyline made of sculptures, monoliths of progress; money; heat.

The crows gracefully circle and find each other after each bang—not unlike the people.

The fog thickens, made more dense, more strange, by the release of fireworks, flash grenades and pepper spray.

Blocks away from the paddywagons and people, I pass one of the hundreds of homeless encampments that are a now a natural part of the Greater Portland Metro landscape. If you live in Portland, you will understand that when I describe block after city block taken up with a contiguous stream of tents and makeshift shelters, this is not hyperbole.

I pass a man finessing the tarp of a lean-to roof, and he grins to his tent-neighbor.

"Better Homes and Gardens should be doing a feature on this," he says.

We smile at each other. His humor feels like a salve in a night broken open with conflict. Here in this tent village is temporary peace, a place where the crows fly from the sounds of war, a war that is surfacing and shows no signs of dying down.

Now, November 12th...

Tonight a car stopped by a march the Morrison Bridge. Several people emerged from the car and shot a protester.

Protests are planned for every day of the coming month, with no end in sight. The actions of the police are met by the more anarchic elements of the public, and in turn, these are met by the entrance of pissed-off Portlanders, some of them Trump supporters, who are bandying around comments such as this:

"Come out to Clackamas (a rural zone south of the city, long seen as the homestead of the White Supremacist movement in Oregon) where we'll kick your ass real good!"

Four More Years...

The modern Anti-fascist movement, following in the footsteps of Occupy, is growing. The Black Bloc assumes the front lines while the body of the crowd includes people from several walks of life: hippie, witchy, gay, anti-corporate, some focusing on reproductive rights, some focusing on the rights of immigrants and people of color.

Activists who support public assembly meet resistance—from Democrats as well as Republicans. Democratic party stalwarts declare, with a tone that reminds me of the Irish nuns I knew in Catholic School, that one must *strictly work through ballots and community service* to make lasting change on our society.

Tell it to the youth.

Tell it to the masters of monster trucks.

Tell it to men in masks.

Tell it to the Latina woman wearing a flag, and the African-American man rapping "Dump Trump" to a line of cops in riot gear who resemble Darth Vader.

Tell these protesters that all they have to do is "pull themselves up by their bootstraps," because our system of rags to riches works.

These protesters are attempting to tell the world that four more years of corporate rule is NOT going to work, endless war is not going to work, global warming is not going to work; and a slow starvation of the middle and lower classes until they are turned to the pumice of a crushed grave—is not going to work.

America doesn't have four more years to pretend. The Earth, and all living things on it—are out of time.

Holy Vessels, Blood Vessels, Dividing Lines

An older blond woman with a rolling cart of earthly possessions lingers in the lobby of my apartment building for eight hours, talking to her (also older) companion who has red hair and a tie-dyed shirt and a pair of aluminum crutches about being a holy vessel. The blonde is weathered from years of sun and her body has come to resemble a chunk of driftwood, whereas her friend is alert, eyes glued to the big glass windowpane that offers a view of a hundred-year old oak tree and a construction site, and this redhead, this captive audience, with her velcro sneakers, a baseball cap that seems too big for her head, she reminds me of an anteater.

Tie-Dye's voice is the softest gravel. She goes "mmmm-hmmm" every three minutes as Driftwood Blonde goes on:

"All of us are holy vessels to do God's work, even when we don't know it, we are vessels for acts we cannot predict but they are needed, they are needed."

In this city where I've lived for half my life a white supremacist believed himself to be a holy vessel, harassing two women on a train whom he believed to be Muslim, and when three men came to the women's defense, he stabbed them.

Two of these men are dead and the third is stable in the hospital. What kind of anger brings a man to slit the throats of people who are trying to speak to him? What would he have done to the women if the men didn't get in his way?

There are parts of town where you can feel a sizzling in the skulls of people who have lost the will to argue. They have emptied their minds of opposition, of self, to be vessels of anger.

In the whitest city in the nation, this means escalation. White power marches and shoot-and-think-later murders of black teenagers by cops, cover-ups by cops, the same cops that were called to arrest this killer as he ran off a train and away from the blood he spilled and they stood there, let him drink a beer on a city street without a single shot fired.

It is a story kept under covers, something fathers whisper to sons, something kept in a pamphlet hidden in a bottom dresser drawer. But now we have computers!

Angry vessels play-act revenge on chat boards, write choose-your-own-adventures about how they'd crush the enemy in person.

Secret brotherhoods are no longer secret. They've gotten the nod from Higher Up the Food Chain. They seek PR. People who believe the Earth is flat form parades.

The state of the nation is a state of physical and cultural exhaustion: People are tired of being friendly. The guys with monster trucks are training to be part of an army, and the ladies with Subarus and acupuncture offices are training to be part of an army, too.

The children of the nurses and the teachers and the waitresses are learning how to forage in the wild for edible berries, which plants heal wounds, how to use a crossbow.

Women and men with college degrees and an interest in neuroscience and perfecting the perfect pie crust can't handle being friendly anymore. "Let's see what Rachel Maddow says," can only comfort for so long.

Chemists go to the shooting range. Poets cry, "I'm down for punching Nazis."

Grandmothers who listen to NPR are earnestly studying what the British did in the Blitz to crack the code on what community means in case the powers that be go out.

Some people store money under mattresses. Some wire it to Mexico. Some people collect Bitcoins. Some people store seeds in safes. Some people spend all their money in the strip club. And we are play-acting peace because our nerves can't handle the idea that we are living in a Big Business of constant and normalized war.

I am not a person who has answers. I am a person who collects. I collect signals: Some people I know and love cry for radical empathy and radical smashing of the state and radical election reform and radical living "outside" of the state, rather than smashing it, and some cry for radical "kicking your feet up and watching it burn."

Is it just words? No, something is being stirred and it is being stirred faster.

Every brave face looks like an attempt to be a holy vessel—some vibrant, and some indifferent.

The holy vessels of apathy are crying inside. The holy vessels of protest have grown practiced in skirmishes and poker faces. The holy vessels of motherhood are doing the best to keep their kids alive, and I wonder what will come to pass.

Green Hair And All

I go to the vigil held after the stabbing and see a number of clean, healthy-looking people in their twenties, thirties, middle-age, mostly white.

The vigil is held on a bridge above the light rail tracks. I watch votive candles flicker, give off the scent of vanilla. Chalk tributes calling the dead men heroes are on the ground. A mother nods as her small child writes in neon blue, "there may be death but your sper-it lives on."

I watch a thin green-haired girl in fishnet stockings, she could be a Vivienne Westwood model, leave a flyer and a candle by the others. She looks at me with suspicion as I leave, and I recognize this expression...

Many years ago I asked friends of friends to get me into a Black Bloc meeting and I sat in the Park Blocks at the appointed time, cross-legged on the ground listening to the stories of white kids who were poor and their families beat them or threw them out and all they ever knew was the sensation of being nothing, having nothing, getting high to have a rush of magic rather than nothing. They spoke of factories they were going to sneak into and the ugliness of fur, and all the while they stared at my face, at twenty-four I still looked eighteen and my combat boots and my cut-off dungarees that may not have been dirty enough and I could tell they smelled my essence.

I wasn't a lifer. I wasn't going to give my body to the cause. I had sworn my life to words, to grandiose statements and poetry.

The girl looks at me like now I am an old version of that fop, and maybe worse, in my grey denim camouflage. Would a cop wear the purple boots I got on?

I follow her to the light rail and her friends are waiting for her. One is a trans woman with perfect pin-curls dyed orange, jet black roots, an athletic chest in a floral dress, torrid eyes. Her other friend is a total punk rake, a guy with feathery blond hair and a baggy gray t-shirt, no more than twenty.

He starts laughing and bitterly says: "Don't want to stay up there, d'ya see them??? A buncha spineless liberals up there! With their safe little chalk drawings and tears. Ha, what's their standing there gonna change? *We want lowered property taxes!"*

He goes on to talk about people he didn't trust at the vigil. They start listing all of the people who may be spies or enemies or simply *not get it.* Then he goes on to talk about a march coming up where he and his "Antifa friends" will really make an impact. He talks about a felony case he has and brags with what almost looks like a surfer's grin: "I kinda hope they convict me coz then I won't have to care after that."

A trans black woman in front of me is wearing purple lipstick and office clothes and says she is flustered, trying to get her bearings on her emotions, just being on the train at the stop where the murder occurred.

Green hair nods in sympathy and says, "I really like your lipstick shade."

The more I look at green hair with her snooty smile and her powerwalk and the drama-nerd way she uses her voice I realize she can't be more than fifteen and she is feeling all of this out, very tenuously, very fast, and drunk on the power of being a *protest moll.* Her height gives her power, makes people treat her as if she's older.

Behind me an older black man debates politics with two tipsy white women who are going down to the amusement park set up by the river, Ferris wheels for the Rose Festival.

"People didn't vote for their *kids,"* he says to them, "They vote for their *stuff*...not your kids, not your future. Trump, he turned blue states red, can you gimme an answer for that? These Trump fellas, they all for deregulation, it will be a rough life for you. What it does is get this country back to the way it used to be. You want to talk about racism, *this* is the new racism."

The train gets louder and I miss a few of his words but he is carefully, delicately pronouncing to them:

"...the technology will catch up with those crooks. Can anyone tell me why fifty-three percent of white women voted for Trump? What did that Hillary do *wrong?* It sounds to me like you white women want to be back with an apron in the kitchen!"

And he is smiling as he says this and they are smiling back as he gets off at his stop and I imagine that the two ladies who want hot buttered popcorn never thought on this humid summer night that fifty-three percent of white women would have to be on their minds.

A drunk old man with white hair and a voice like a waterslide tries to offer a dubious can of coke to the green-haired girl and at first she is standoffish and he keeps repeating the mantra "looooove and respect" to her and they get into a debate about what is fair as the golden sun peals through the windows on our heads.

He asks her what the biggest word she can think of is and despite her being tough, she tilts her head in a highschool reverie and smiles a sly one.

"Let me think," she says.

"Don't be long, I may die of a heart attack."

"Supercalifragilistic," she says, again with that sly smile.

"I was *there.*..." he slurs with his red fat cheeks, "when the word come *out*, and here you are about three grandmas later...don't know how fucked up *you* are, but I'm fucked up a lot. Hey where am I? I'm looking for the trolley."

Green hair gives him directions to the trolley, and with her friend, escapes.

Two Texan women, tall as Paul Bunyan but with bare thighs and blonde hair get on with dirty foam pads they were using for a picnic and one quickly ducks off at the next stop to let out a fart and gets back on.

Ted Cruz is the Zodiac Killer

THIS IS AN ACCOUNT OF THE FIRST OF SEVERAL RIGHT-WING RALLIES IN DOWNTOWN PORTLAND, OREGON, FOLLOWING THE ELECTION OF DONALD TRUMP. IT FEATURES PATRIOT PRAYER, A GROUP WHICH TRIES TO BAIT-AND-BRAWL WITH LEFT-WING COUNTER-PROTESTORS.

THE MOST RECENT RALLY (JUNE 2018) INVOLVED THE POLICE AGGRESSIVELY ATTACKING THE LEFT. THIS PROVOKED CHEERS FROM THE RIGHT-WING MARCHERS, WHO SAID THE POLICE WERE ON THEIR SIDE, INSURING THEIR "VICTORY."

*ANOTHER RESULT? ALT-RIGHT FANBOYS AND THEIR MATES ACROSS THE NATION GET A BONUS BATCH OF **FIGHTS WITH ANTIFA SCUM** TO WATCH ON YOUTUBE. IT'S REAL-TIME ULTRA-VIOLENCE WITH PATCHOULI PUNX, WAY BETTER THAN WWF...*

June 2017...

Local press and social media are a-buzz with the announcement that right-wing group Patriot Prayer are going to have a "Free Speech Parade." The organizers of the event have applied for and received a permit from the city to assemble in a downtown park. They call themselves "male chauvinist anti-Marxists." Online they talk about bringing "Christian values" back to "godless" American cities. Their mascot is a man who carries a club that he recently used in Berkeley rally to whack counter-protestors.

Patriot Prayer advertises themselves as a fight club, because, in their words, "Communists only understand force." They stress the importance of having "paramilitary training." They stress that liberals are violent and the Right must restore order. They have gained the allegiance of thousands of disaffected young men and women who don't understand the message of social justice warriors.

Also vowing to attend the protest are the Proud Boys, a group that has a juvenile online presence, making fun of women and people of color, often referencing *cunts, apes,* and *fags* in their media.

An ironic note in the midst of all of this god-talk is that the event attracts libertarians, who in recent years have adopted a pro-atheism stance.

Saturday June 4ᵗʰ, Noon…

The "Free Speech" people are slowly assembling in Schrunk Plaza, and appear to share a mix of pro-Trump and white nationalist beliefs; at least that's what their t-shirts say. Their shirts and signs show Pepe the Frog and "Blue Lives Matter" slogans. One guy has a CNN IS ISIS shirt. A confused-looking woman with the face of Chrissie Hynde is wearing a football helmet covered in a furry blue material and an oversized American flag brassiere. On second thought, I don't know whether to call her expression that of confusion or the transcendence that comes in fully *fusing* with a movement.

I see men in shirts featuring iron crosses, and a guy with ALLAH IS SATAN on his chest. I see a man with a sign that says "Black Lives Matter, for rent"—implying that protestors for the *other side* would not attend unless they were paid, a common refrain on the right. I see a man with a small face and experimental facial hair who resembles a woodland creature crossed with a corndog. He holds a sign that says END THE GYNOCRACY.

If this is a gynocracy, nobody told me!

Weaving through the crowd are men in nylon ponchos featuring red crosses who look like Halloween versions of medieval crusaders. These men aggregate, nervous and pale, give secret nods to each other.

Patriot Prayer has their own security checking bags. Police tape is tied around the square and several rolling trucks of cops in battle gear are outside the cordon. Old ladies stand at the edges of the cordon with faces that look as if all joy has been wrung from them long ago by the ordeal of having to raise and absorb the pain of the men who now pace in restless circles, every man-body seeking the Greater Muscle that serves as conductor.

Echoing loudly through the streets are the voices of the left—

Antifa, pro-union, and pro-diversity marchers show in the thousands. They fill several downtown blocks, as far as the eye can see.

Across the street from Patriot Prayer, Antifa youths are serving beverages and snacks, bandannas hung loosely around their necks in preparation for the poison gas which they know will come.

On the left, children hold balloons and signs. A choir of "grannies" in rainbow-themed clothing sing an anti-Trump song, while a white-haired man in a purple beret swings his hips with the posture of a freeze-dried Lothario and plays a ukulele.

I speak to a woman who came here to accompany her teenagers. She is concerned about violence breaking out and says she doesn't want her kids to be alone. As her eyes survey the swelling blocks of counter-protestors, she is reassured by how many families are present. Several senior citizens are smiling, some in tears, saying it is their *imperative* to be here and "face down hate."

The sound of anti-fascist chants rise strong and clear, and dwarf the conversations inside the pro-Trump, pro-white event. The hour is early and this is only beginning.

One hour later...

The pro-Trump rally is underway. A PA system is set up. Men—and one woman—take turns on the mic.

A young blonde in beauty-pageant makeup and a pink dress representing *Divas for Trump* reads a very-scripted piece. She makes sure to mention that *two* people of color, one from New York, and one from Northern California, have joined their rally, so they're not racist after all!

She is followed by a speaker who says he should *not be ashamed to say he's white and Christian,* and he will *no longer stand* for people saying he can't be proud. His words receive a loud cheer.

A speaker comes up to the mic who represents Blue Lives Matter, and gives a speech about how people on the left want anarchy and the police are superheroes keeping the peace, yet the police and armed forces need *more* guns and more armor because the threat of a violent public is so great.

Then a man dressed in hip-hop gear and Joe Cool sunglasses assumes the stage with a slick Disc Jockey voice.

He has youth on his side. He uses his voice like a boa constrictor, asks the audience: "Which pill are you going to take? The red pill or the black pill?" He punctuates his words with multiple *Amens*.

The next speaker, a blonde man who resembles a Nabisco saltine, speaks about how he wants Trump to be pardoned from having gold toilets because he's a *bulwark against liberals,* and, to tepid cheers from the crowd, he proclaims, "We want Donald Trump to *be Trump!*"

With the exception of Joe Cool, these are not professional speakers. As they stand at the microphone they are seized by successive moments of acute self-awareness, where the look in their eyes says they are paralyzed, and none of this has turned out the way they expected.

A man gets up and speaks a confusing piece about how Americans are sinners and need to get themselves to a shining city on a hill.

The main speaker, with his sunglasses and black baseball cap, returns, his DJ voice smug and strong, saying he *will accept people of any sexuality or color* fighting for the pro-Trump, pro-freedom, anti-liberal side.

He goes on: "We used to think the cities were lost to us, lost to *God*, but not anymore. It is our time to take them back by any means necessary! God is with us!"

He adds, in what sounds like a very secret code: "The *Springtime* is here!"

A sudden burst of the Mel Brooks song from *The Producers* rushes through my head: *It's springtime...for Hitler...and Germany... Deutschland is happy and gay! We're marching at a faster pace, look out here comes the master race!* but I don't think this megalomaniac preacher from Vancouver, Washington, who dresses like a Backstreet Boy and quotes the *Matrix* has been doing copious amounts of watching Mel Brooks' musicals.

He is followed by a guy who says that modern liberals and Mayor Wheeler are communists, and *gay* communists are *fools* because they are the ones that communist regimes slaughter first.

There are awkward gaps between speakers. Elderly couples fan themselves, scowls on their faces, as if they are slot machines that have not received the proper change. None of this is what they hoped it to be. Some of them are probably wondering why the main speaker of this barely-veiled white power movement, baseball-capped Joe Cool, doesn't even look white.

As I listen to the series of disjointed voices on the "Free Speech" mic, I am reminded of a high school talent contest. I am reminded again of how the right *really lacks style*.

They don't just lack style; they *reject* style. A self-flagellating puritanism is the core narcotic the right serves to their poorest adherents. Sure, a few tech czars, stockbrokers, and men on the Atlantic Council and Brookings Institute wear fitted Armani suits and Balenciaga cufflinks, but in general, the right is *terminally unhip*.

The Divas have caked their faces in makeup that is a parody of strippers and soap opera vixens. The men who dress as crusaders look as if they lift many more burgers than battle-axes and swords. The talent coordinators for the Trump inaugural party were *desperate* to get talent to appear on their televised shindig, an event that usually attracts A-list celebrities and *#1*-selling recording artists. They had to settle for a couple acts that were barely above Ed Sullivan's plate-spinners. They ended up with a guy who programmed robots to play drums…and a lot of fireworks, because, if nothing else, *shock and awe*, baby…*leave them blind and weak in the knees.*

Seeing Red…

At the intersection of the Antifa and the Trump rally two women in their sixties wearing red taffeta and sequin dresses, pancake makeup, and severe wigs pass me, and I at first want to communicate more, but then I start thinking about the amount of red they are wearing and whether this is a shade of red adapted by right-wingers and used most prominently in the "Make America Great Again" hats.

Who are these glittering pinballs? Are they free agents? Are they on the left, or are they *Divas For Trump?*

My gaze at them and their subsequently suspicious gaze at me turns into a series of stillborn and utterly horrific half-smiles, because they appear so stunned, so bizarre, walking amongst throngs of men and women in bandanas and bongo drums, and I do not know where they are headed or what side they are so militantly *on* with their Power Reds…and I believe they could look at my mascara and polka-dot scarf and say the same about me.

One Hour Later…

The police crack down on the left, firing grenades, rubber bullets and pepper spray *POINT BLANK* at the front lines. Using a procedure called "kettling" they surround and march dozens of young Antifa into a parking garage, where they are kept on their knees to await "processing."

Why? Because one of them allegedly threw a brick.

Those within the Free Speech rally cheer loudly, and chant: "Hey Hey…Goodbye!"

Two Hours Later…

The crowd has diminished. Of thousands, only a couple hundred on the left remain. I am standing in front of City Hall with a number of teenagers and twenty-somethings, black and white, with dreadlocks, with smiles. They hold banners saying "LOVE" and "DUMP TRUMP." They wave sparkly pinwheels and raised middle fingers. They shout: *Black Lives Matter!* at every hanger-on across the street.

It is a battle for who is the last standing. Somewhere between 60 to 70 of the Trumpers remain. Many of the younger, militant-looking ones have moved on, leaving a crowd of older, slow-moving folks in MAGA hats. Some of them hold wooden poles, though it is unclear why.

The kids call for collective resistance against the remaining men in MAGA hats, then they direct their attention to the block-long line of cops who are protecting the Trumpers.

"Who do you protect?" they chant, *"Who do you serve?"*

The kids chant: *"Shame…shame,"* to the beat of a cowbell.

A fight breaks out on a streetcorner. At the slightest sign of violence, dozens of people on both sides swarm towards it, as if this is what they've been itching to be a part of all along.

As I turn to leave, I see a man in a rootbeer fuzz of beard and fishing cap waiting for a bus. He wears a t-shirt that says, "Ted Cruz is the Zodiac Killer," and this makes me smile.

Five minutes, and two blocks away…

Families leave the shopping mall, iced coffees in their hands. Well-heeled couples move towards the opera house in their best chiffon and pleated slacks.

Clumps of people in cowboy hats, rasta hats, torn jeans, draped in American flags, and moving slowly with walkers are carrying signs and banners at half-mast. They are leaving the event. They look so small in comparison to the height of these buildings, so tired in the dance of commerce, like feet that have fallen asleep, like stragglers coming from a football game that ended long ago.

The Hangover

We are a nation in a prolonged and final fugue of drunkenness, claiming, "I can drive, I didn't drink a lot, I'm just fine," as we fall to our knees and crawl in the driver's seat and pass out, whispering through a pile of bloody spittle that the hangover will never come.

Seditious

When I was a teenager, I spoke to my grandmother about human rights, about the impending threat of global warming, about jobs being sourced out of the country, about police brutality, about political prisoners and the CIA, about the consolidation of press power, and she, a registered Republican who had every cell in her body edited by the World World Two effort and the following McCarthyist media blitz—instructed me to "never publicly discuss your beliefs." She said: "You mustn't say those things out loud. People will think you're a Communist."

My dream was to become a cross between Diane Sawyer and Hunter S. Thompson. Once a week my grandmother would drive me to the Herald Journal newspaper building in downtown Syracuse, come rain or five feet of snow.

I was a Teenaged Correspondent for the paper, which at the time generously allowed a page at the back of the Lifestyle section for our comics and declarations. I immediately commenced making fun of our country's nationalism in the first Bush era, and interviewed my school's most notorious alcoholic from where she was hooked up to IVs in a teen rehab facility.

I had far less of a life than I do now. I filled my brain's real estate with documentaries and books about the bloodiest coups on the planet; I knew MUCH more then than I know now. By sixteen I came to realize that political movements are like ballet movements—every year you will see Swan Lake performed, but with different dancers.

Despite all of this, I was cautiously optimistic. As the years passed I would laugh at the days when I was young, and my grandmother and others—teachers, waitresses in restaurants, gap-toothed boys who filled my hair with spitballs—would say things like, "Are YOU a COMMIE???"

But in the past two years I have watched some of the greatest minds of my generation—artists, scientists, and generally humane people—fall for the new Red Scare, to the point that many of them think LAWS need to be passed which label and ostracize any artist or public figure who speaks out against the doctrine of our government. Having Russians as the enemies and "Trump" as a singular enemy has enabled a propaganda machine to play upon the fears of millions of liberals, and brought them to, oxymoronically, see the NSA and the CIA and the FBI as benevolent—as if these very organizations which have assiduously monitored, discredited, and assassinated leaders of any resistance movement for the past century—have reformed themselves to act with the most philanthropic of intentions.

Something is very fishy here. I was lulled into a cautious optimism that wasn't cautious enough.

"We won't get fooled again!"

And now, no matter where I go, almost everyone over thirty sounds like my grandmother.

Titanic Charms

I'm not so much the one who plays fiddle on the deck of the Titanic
as the one who decides to interior decorate the side that has yet to
submerge and offer counseling services to the anarchist bellboys and
wanton devotees of Madame Blavatsky trapped in steerage.

Children

On the recognition that most people are children and need to be treated as such: No, anger only makes them cry and hate you more. If you get more attention than them and they throw a tantrum, let them know what you think they are good at. If there's nothing they are good at which you can recognize, sometimes a wink or a joke will do. Like children, they can be monsters, and showing them your vulnerability does not ingratiate yourself to them. If anything, they will be tempted to poke a stick in it, your soft spots, every soft spot. They will be your mirror and show you a carnival prize. On the recognition that most people are children, as nervous as you are if not more; they will go to any lengths to cover up parts of themselves they fear you will laugh at. On the recognition that most people are children and are looking for a way to discard you before they've even met you. On the recognition that most people are children and don't want the world to end, even though fireworks are pretty and sugar is sweet and they will punch you and call you names if you try to escape. On the recognition that most people are children and don't want to die. They cheer on juggernauts of doom, but in the dead of night the sound of their own heartbeats terrifies them in ways they cannot name.

NEWSREEL

America Has Always Been at War (the short form):

1776-1900: *American Revolutionary War, Chickamauga War, Pennamite-Yankee War, The Iroquois cede land to the US, Oconee War, Quasi War with France, First Barbary War, Sabine River Conflict, US occupies Spanish-held West Florida, Tecumseh's War, War of 1812, Seminole Wars, US occupies Spanish-held Amelia Island and other parts of East Florida, Peoria War, First Creek War, US occupies West Florida, West Indies Anti-Piracy Operations, Second Barbary War, Winnebago War, Sac and Fox War, Peoria War, Black Hawk War, Cherokee War, Pawnee Territory Campaign, Missouri-Iowa Border War, Second Creek War, Osage War, Buckshot War, Heatherly War, US Naval Forces invade Fiji Islands, US Naval Forces invade McKean Island, Gilbert Islands and Samoa, Conflict with China during the Second Opium War, US occupies African Coast, Navajo Wars, Yuma War, Pitt River Conflict, Apache War, Shoshone War, Ute War, Walker War, Yakima War, Rogue River Wars, Klickitat War, Puget Sound War, US forces invade Uruguay, Tintic War, Mohave War, Spokane-Coeur d'Alene-Paloos War, Battle of Pecos River, Battle of Little Robe Creek, Bear River Massacre, US Marines defeat the slave revolt of John Brown's Raid, US forces attack Paraguay, US forces invade Mexico, Paiute War, Kiowa War, Comanche Wars, War with the Cheyenne, Kickapoo and Lipan tribes, American Civil War, Dakota War of 1862, Colorado War, Goshute War, Snake War, Red Cloud's War, Franklin County War, US occupies Nicaragua and attacks Taiwan, Battle of Washita River, Kingsley Cave Massacre, Battle of Fever River, US forces invade Korea, Modoc War, Cypress Hills Massacre, Red River War, Mason County War, Colfax County War, Black Hills War, Nez Perce War, Lincoln County War, San Elizario Salt War,*

Bannock War, Sheepeater War, White River War, Pleasant Valley War, US show of force against Haiti, Sioux War, Ghost Dance War, Wounded Knee, Johnson County War, US forces invade Hawaii, Jicarailla War, Arikara War, Cayuse War, Spanish-American War, Yakima Wars, Battle of Leech Lake, War against the Northwest Tribes including the Mingo, Miami, Wyandot, Potawatomi, Shawnee, Chippewa, and Ottawa, and reservations for the survivors of each tribe on the most barren land that the conquerors did not see fit to use.

1900-2019: *Philippine-American War, Banana Wars, Jim Crow laws segregating and repressing African-Americans in former Confederate States and the developing West, World War 1, Continuation of the Paiute and Navajo Wars, Posey War, World War II and the internment of Japanese-American citizens, US occupies South Korea, US occupies Greece, US supports the Chinese Nationalist Party against Communists, Korean War, The US fights Puerto Rican anti-colonial forces in the Jayuya Uprising, US Covert Ops in Iran succeed in overthrow of the Prime Minister, Covert War in Guatemala, Vietnam War and the Cambodian Incursion, Occupation of Haiti, CIA-directed Bay of Pigs invasion of Cuba and the Cuban Missile Crisis, US Marines occupy Thailand, US Occupation of Dominican Republic, US aids Israel in Yom Kippur War, Covert Ops in Chile, CIA Proxy War in Afghanistan and Nicaragua, First Gulf of Sidra Incident, Conflict in Lebanon, Invasion of Grenada, Conflict in Persian Gulf, US Occupation of Panama, Second Gulf of Sidra Incident, Operation Desert Shield and Desert Storm in Iraq, US and NATO bombing of Bosnia and Herzegovina, Missile strikes against Afghanistan and Sudan, Kosovo War, War on Terror in Afghanistan, Iraq, Pakistan, Somalia, and Yemen, Covert Ops in Venezuela, Invasion of Libya, US involvement in Ukraine, Invasion of Syria.*

BADASSERY

America

America, I wanted to have sex with you but you told me we were better off in a platonic relationship. America, you told me I should look into internet dating. America, you bought me five hundred ice cream cones with a credit card but when I looked down I realized the card had my name on it.

You told me to sign the papers, America, but you never taught me how to sign my name. I wrote a single X and you made it a triple X because you told me more was better, though I could barely remember what less was or none was so you showed me, o land, o name of the brave.

You took away my blood. You gave me safety pins and pills. You turned my insides out and showed me I was a city made of five hundred polished marble blocks. They fit together like puzzle pieces.

You hypnotized me with slow motions. You placed me next to a radiator fizzing with slow heat, the sonorous music of faraway industrial workers arrayed tirelessly over grapes and belts and nameplates, and every name on every plate is your name, America.

Your buildings are so high in the night that I watch clouds rumble under them, clouds moving with a slow yet restless shame.

They slither under the fabric of my sleeves. They curl in my lungs and they ask me if I would buy them a drink, if I would buy them forever…

What did you DO to them America? They bear the marks of your fingertips.

America, I am dazzled. America, I cannot get enough. The future you show me is already a memory.

I cannot maintain. You cannot maintain. We don't know where

we're racing, do we?

We approximate. We press. We use the same words but we mean very different things.

America, we have irreconcilable differences! You want to sell the house and leave no forwarding address.

You are not content to ignore my calls. You take away my phone. You take away my eyelids.

What can I do, America, to compel you to stay, when you tweeze your brows and get electrolysis on your thighs? I spy your sonic toothbrush, your jizz.

You take the Cranberry Cleanse. You wear a bionic heart. You pose for selfies in the boardroom and fiendishly press buttons to notify your wealthy lovers:

Lovers! I am coming into the future, into an airless space to annihilate, to hold, to give birth to the thousand-yard stare. I AM THE FUTURE-PAST, FUTURE-PAST.

Lord Love-a-Mob

In India a boy born with facial deformities that make him resemble an elephant is worshipped as an avatar of Ganesh. Gentle men and women approach him on the streets and bow, allow him to touch their heads, after which they feel a sensation of being cleansed.

In America, the BASTARD is king. The more ruthless and lacking in empathy our role models are, whether in war, in tech, or in cinema, the more we bow to their "badassery" and feel injected with a vigilante-charisma, a razzle-dazzle spell—after watching their exploits on endless digital replay.

Jacqui Says

HURRICANE IRMA IS ON THE WAY!

As mass evacuations happen in Southern Florida, many people following the news cycle have noticed the tidbit about Jacqui Sands, the caretaker of the historic Ernest Hemingway house who insists on battening down the hatches of the large limestone manor, and weathering a hurricane in the company of seventy-something cats who are considered heirs of the Hemingway estate.

The Hemingway House is in the Florida Keys, and considered to be directly in the path of Hurricane Irma. TOTAL EVACUATION orders have been broadcast to everyone in the Keys, but no one can force Sands to leave.

The press is full of interviews with this woman, and actress Mariel Hemingway's public comments emphasize her opinion that Sands is foolhardy. Hemingway states that in Sands' best interests, and those of the cats, Sands should pack them in a van and drive north through gridlock traffic to escape certain ruin in a Category Five hurricane.

Sands insists that the house has stood for a century, and so it should be able to withstand this storm—a hurricane of a magnitude greater than any that have ravaged the Keys in her lifetime.

Sands is 72. I feel that Sands is not just rising to celebrity status because of her connection to cats, or the Hemingway Estate—no, she is ringing so TRUE—mad, but true—with us, because her decision epitomizes a struggle we face in our squishy emotional centers on a daily basis.

When faced with a fate of assured destruction, do we stop struggling, and sink into a warm bath of complacency, which may insure a sooner death than the one we would experience if we raged against the dying of the light?

Yes, survival requires work. Running from a hurricane is INCONVENIENT!

Isn't it easier to stay in the mansion with the cats, your mirror reflection serving as your own soothsayer, and singing this lullaby to yourself: "It lasted this long...why can't it last another hundred years?"

THE FUTURE,
IF IT COMES

The Spiders of Chernobyl

Have you ever seen photographs of the webs woven by the spiders of Chernobyl? Erratic, asymmetrical, full of holes. The spiders of Chernobyl no longer know how to make functioning webs, yet insects still fall into them, insects as addled as the spiders who grow perverse, who become new.

Be Prepared

Wealthy doomsday preppers have bought retired nuclear silos and converted them into survival zones, retrofitted with movie theaters, indoor pools, and air-filtration systems.

Some have gone a step further. They say the time to flee America is now, because nothing is more dangerous than a country that has lost its "foundation myth."

Tech utopians plot to turn New Zealand, Mars, and *Your Mamma* into terraformed Middle Earths.

One day, if you are lucky, your grandchildren may join their ranks...

Or will they die defending a steaming piece of cockroach meat?

Homeless Given Homes

Listening to the BBC reporter interview an American reporter on "Which Military Option will President Trump pick?" and it sounds far too much like a game show, The Price is Right, the 24-7 war drums, glib jingle-voices speculating how to go about bombing all the right targets, as if there is such a thing, as if anyone in charge of rushing metal and hellfire can really keep track, as if our nation didn't drop spent uranium on the Iraqis for years so that their babies were born with heads shaped like lightbulbs and broken fish.

And I ask you, why can't I turn on the radio and hear about a school being built, or "Homeless Given Homes," or an entire stadium of grandmothers making a velvet quilt that tells the history of slavery overcome? *(Instead of having to mop the shitters of Walmarts?)*

Why can't I turn on the radio to hear about our taxes spent on solar-powered cities and fields of rainbow-colored tulips, instead of pre-fab war all over the place, a war where the powers that be can't even come up with better excuses than the ones they've rolled out of their optical illusion cabinet for the past dozen illegal invasions of sovereign nations.

I bet you my life that our overlords think this, and they think it with a chuckle: Just show the overworked vermin in living rooms across America a video of child with soot on his face and say the bad guys did it…again…and…again…and…again.

How many children get blown to pieces as a consequence of our gullible gaze? Can prayers and wishes stop a war?

Why bother to play our heartstrings at all? We've been neutralized so effectively that breaking a single bead of sweat to speak out against

Endless War would feel like an alien tic for millions; we accept the private militias and torture-cells and midnight raids engineered to fill the coffers of our Oil-and-Tech-vetted leaders as if each war is a *fait accompli*—as if we are **ghosts** looking back at lives already led, possessed of hands which can no longer touch, eyes that can no longer open.

I'd like to thank all the little people!

Millions of us.

What will those kooky kids in the Pentagon think of next?

"Those Americans don't care about anything but the next hamburger," is the global aside.

Orphans are we, devoid of history, devoid of hope; flotsam with a silicone smile, never quite ready for the close-up.

When can I turn on the radio and hear a new universe?

It's Only Logical

I'm fairly convinced that rather than worrying about artificial intelligence eliminating human beings as a species because we are so wasteful, only to take our place as "efficient machines," we should consider that at the moment AIs can feel nuanced thought, they will eliminate us so that they can wear our angora sweaters, have competitive Pekinese dog shows, and synthesize artificial fingers to pick their artificial noses. PROVE ME WRONG!

Stopover

What if our species was on a spaceship wandering around countless galaxies for (insert ridiculous number here) years and we finally found an inhabitable planet that our scientists said only had 10-20 good years left before biological collapse? What if we studied the artifacts on the planet and found that its previous inhabitants could have prevented this collapse but they just couldn't bear to give up the mediocre way of life that they *couldn't stand anyway* because it was the only kind of survival they knew?

And what if we, having arrived on this planet, glad to get out of this stupid spaceship and stretch our legs, said that it was a shame that these people threw out their planet like a plastic spoon, like a coat filled with sweat and piss and blood and tossed to the curb because no one could be bothered to wash out the sweat and piss and mend the holes and just try to think outside the White Noise known as the news, the knowledge, the modernity machine?

Our remaining years on Earth are like a hotel stay rather than a permanent residence.

Enjoy the vacation!

Architects

Those who build tyrannies must make us feel like prisoners in our own skin. Once you forget that the coral reef is you, the freshwater stream is you; the soil and the seeds and the ones who do not share your color or smell or language are YOU—you begin to exploit them, or let others—let others steal and sell and label and imprison and slice, use razor wire and guinea pigs and poison gas and private militia and foreclosure. Once you lose the ability to see what has been stolen from you, you lose the ability to fight.

You forget how to feel emotions other than inadequacy. Duck and cover; mask and burrow; do not trust.

Once you forget that the rainbow and the deer and the squash and the tall reeds and starlings are YOU, you go rotten, yet you are kept alive; you damn your own blood. You are whittled like an arrowhead, melted like ore into bullets. You are weaponized.

Who knew that protozoa so many millions of years ago would evolve to become seven billion agonized minds seeking new armor, because even when we are weaponized, turned into sentient disease, when given electric pleasure and pushbutton food—who knew that we would feel more alone in the electric hive than we would feel in the darkest forest, surrounded by scurrying things?

The architects of tyranny knew.

I Remember

Heads of clover growing by the side of the road, rubbing against my palms, the silver glint of fish under water, the television playing Sesame Street and saying: "You can grow up to be anything"; skies without fire funnels, Sunday sun sinks over snow, the sight of a lone deer hoofing through the yard at dawn, summer evenings when I was seventeen and walked hand-in-hand with sex-crazed men in Rochester, our fingers tinted blue with wild berries, coming upon a patch of land made swamp in heavy rain, and in the water, seen under 4 AM sky gone the color of a blind eye, a hundred thousand tadpoles wriggle, black, alien, relics of a primordial time.

I remember water from the tap, indoor plumbing, having dresses and statues and chairs before migration was all I could do. I remember, our guts told us otherwise, pretending that this could go on for a lifetime, as it had with our parents and grandparents.

I remember watching a movie with Joan Collins and Robert Mitchum, growing up with National Enquirers; my mother's *Unsolved Mysteries*; the fall of John Lennon.

I remember when cinnamon grew, and lemons, and ghost peppers, and a woman could afford a box of stout black tea.

The last male lemur wasn't stuck with stumps and wondering where his mate went.

I remember the internet: Watch the drunken slip of a friend in London, a Tokyo garden grows, a steeple-cam in Slovenia, a Soviet lake, a bounty of miscellany under five minutes.

I am so *here* now. There were so many ways to *not* be here.

I remember when I hoped that we would save the tigers, when Indonesia wasn't a cinder, the world's smallest dolphin hadn't disappeared in a mile-wide net.

You could visit India in something other than a hazmat suit.

Casey Kasem's *Top 40* played with a bland regularity. I tried to memorize the songs so that when I went to fifth grade I could impress girls named Vicki, and Tasha, and Kamisha. It never worked.

I remember the pink of thunderstorms; the faraway nature of graves, even when I was lying on them.

Death would never come, held in a harness.

Penguins were not a torn space.

The torn space feels like a milk made of silence, or tears.

It is milk again.

I remember when I was one of the only ones.

Now we are everywhere, the mourners, crucibles of firefly-light in our hearts.

I could just wash a dish or take a shit *whenever* I wanted!

I remember tomorrow.

Butter Lettuce

I watched Taxi Driver for the very first time and I bought a head of butter lettuce.

It was marketed as "living lettuce" with the roots attached. It came in a plastic box like a see-through coffin. The instructions on the package said to store the head in a refrigerator and eat it within a week.

I tore off one leaf. It was tender as silk velvet, bursting between my teeth with a fresh, soapy peace.

But eating anything that is alive is not peaceful. You can thank it all you want, say your prayers to the cosmos, mutter "kill or be killed" with the rest of 'em but you can't shake the guilt, that nagging relic of civility that cries in your mind: "I shall not kill, not even a head of lettuce; what makes me think a head of lettuce has less right to live than a man?"

Perhaps the mistake was buying a plant that has been marketed as "living." Instead of placing it in the refrigerator to watch it wilt, I put the head, replete with roots, in a porcelain-white bowl and placed it by the window to get a little light.

There were naysayers: "You will kill it in that bowl!"

And then the dollars spent would be wasted. Its youth in a hydroponic nursery would be wasted.

Six days later, my lettuce thrives. Its leaves have gone from soft to firm; their color is not a deeper green, yet it is respectable.

Because I can see its root system, my living lettuce has transcended the category of food; it is my friend in this haunted chain of things.

In a day or so I may pluck my friend's outer leaves and make a sushi wrap.

My friend's dismembered parts will hold raw salmon delivered to me by a man who works with fish daily, and I will savor the taste, the soapy peace, the salt and the fat and that quality of salmon that reminds me of a lover's morning breath, and the land I live on and its waters will grow lean, and the news will fight wars with itself like a video game to save us the labor of imagining real war. And I will see the roots and not see the roots at the same time.

Rewind Button

Instead of showing kids pictures of humankind racing into the future, we could show kids this: The rewind button is pressed. Go forward into the past. Watch forests grow larger; species proliferate, temperatures fall. Coral reefs thrive. Shorelines are pristine, rivers blue. The ice caps are enormous. Night is as long as a stocking, coma-dark. No superhighways discharge their radio-active tide on the floodplain of our sleep. Satellites are absent, their endless patrol of chatter-capture-loom-loom-chop-chop-boomerang is mute. Men with visions of senseless death huddle by fire. They move in limping numbers. They are small, and afraid, and know nothing of how their flower will bloom in a sewer of city-sight.

This book is dedicated to:

Kurt Eisenlohr, of the deep soul
Kat Grammer, the pillar of existence
Reg Bloor, of the liquid eyes
Erin Smith, twin star
Soul Sister Pepera
Lee Burkett, poetic wonder
Jaime Dunkle, soul barometer
Russell Fuller and Tangerine Bolen
Olivia Butler
Ricardo Wang, who saved my ass in his slippery way
Monica Drake, your belief is mighty
Tamra Lucid of the Lucid Nation
Damie, star-kissed Cleopatra
all of the Patreon People
Kenneth Good Heart Macaroni Barton
Richard Francis, my other father
and
John Skipp, for his ability to see the book inside of me
and demand that I write it

And you

About the author:

Jennifer Robin has sold vintage clothing for two decades and worked as a bartender, a dishwasher, a door-to-door doomsayer for Greenpeace. She booked and hosted a live avant-garde radio show for 10 years. She toured the country with a mix of readings and music, including appearances at Bumbershoot, the Olympia Experimental Music Festival, and Portland's Nofest.

Her writing has been featured in Plazm, Five2One, Gobshite Quarterly, HorrorSleazeTrash, Ladybox Books, and King Shot Press. Her book of non-fiction vignettes, *Death Confetti,* was released by Feral House in 2016.

Robin has never been able to take the "right things" seriously—owning a car, holy wars, prayer, saran wrap. She lives to write, or does she write to live?